THE MESSENGER

THE
MESSENGER

A novel by

KYLEN GARTLAND

ISBN: 1512195847
ISBN 13: 9781512195842
Library of Congress Control Number: 2015907973
Createspace Independent Publishing Platform
NorthCharleston, SC

To my mother, Shannon, for all her love and support.

ONE

A wolf pack lay slumbering in a sparse clearing. Amongst the pack, a young female known as Ameliora twitched. Her head was tucked down, neatly huddled within her thick fur. Her eyelids were tightly shut, though one could see her eyes rolling in the back of her head as she dreamed. Every so often she would shudder as the disquiet of her dreams revealed itself in soft vocalizations. The young female was engulfed in a hauntingly familiar dream. She was running through a forest of pine trees so fast her feet seemed to fly as they skimmed the earthen floor. It should have been exhilarating, but her heart hammered with fear. Paws pounded behind her, but each glance she threw over her shoulder revealed only the absolute emptiness of the dark woods. She ran with the desperation of an inkling of hope, pursuing in turn an unknown entity she instinctively knew would save her from whatever hounded her steps. The greater part of the fear came from the knowledge that whatever was following her knew her while she had no idea what she was seeking.

Each time that she found herself trapped within the nightmare, the light would fade and she would panic as whatever was behind gained on her. She would hear its light paw steps, then she would feel its breath on the back of her legs and, finally it would disappear. She would run blindly while looking and scenting all around her until it leapt out at her, fangs bared. She would howl in horror and try and turn away, but she could never elude the killing vise of its teeth sinking into the soft flesh of her neck. The worst part, worse than the dying and the attack and the look in her captor's eyes was that just as she breathed her last, another's voice would make its way to her–sweet whispered words floating into her mind and carrying a message she was desperate to receive. Try as she might she could never make out the message within. Those sweet whispered words. She only knew that the message was what she had been chasing and searching for her so desperately, and now what she had died for. As she again tried to cling to the fading words and hold on to conscious life, the world faded to black and she awoke to a sky brightening with the early sunrise.

She stood, shaking her pelt and trying to rid her mind of the remnants of the persistent nightmare that had plagued her these last months. She stretched quietly and tip-toed on light paws around her pack-mates. As soon as she was far enough away, she relaxed her muscles and began to pad towards the stream. She could hear its trickling constant rhythm and it comforted her. She walked slowly, letting her paws sink into the ground still soft from the light shower in the night and smelling of pine and sap from the many trees surrounding her. As the sun gained height in the sky, light rays filtered through the thick canopy above her and lit up the awakening world around her. Her ears twitched as they picked up sounds of the start of daily forest life. A mouse scurried across the protruding roots of a tree and a branch cracked as a careless raccoon tramped over it. The quiet crackling of the once distant stream grew steadily louder. She gained speed as she neared the water and emerged from the dense bushes and onto the soft grass along the flowing current.

The stream always calmed her. There was something about the frigid sensation of dipping a paw lightly in the carefree current that gave every troubling thought a quieted peaceful nature, but she didn't submerge her paws today. Somehow she knew that even the tranquility of the water would do nothing for her nightmarish thoughts and the inner turmoil accosting her.

She padded, with a sense of care and respect that seemed appropriate for such a place of peace, to the very edge of the stream. She just watched the water, watched how it flowed always away. No obstacle could block the force of water, even a stream as small as this one. Pebbles lined the clear streambed and swift flashes of silver fish darted in and out of the caverns and holes created by hours of constant movement. A stray maple leaf that had been caught in an unseasonably strong wind floated gently down from its wayward branch to land in that stream and be swept slowly away. She watched it and a pained expression came over her usually calm features as she wished fervently that all her nightmares and problems could be swept away as easily as the maple leaf in her stream.

She shook her broad gray head once more and stood, even her special place nestled in a sometimes overcrowded world could not settle her on a morning like this. She turned away from the stream and its quiet wisdom and began to trot back down the path she had taken close to an hour before and returned to a pack that was just waking to what would be to them a perfect early spring morning.

The pack was up and active by the time She arrived back at the den area. Her thoughts were scattered and her mind preoccupied. She didn't even notice when she tread lightly on Romaus' jet black tail. He yelped in surprise and turned quickly to face her. She whined her soft apologies and kept low to the ground in front of the now somewhat annoyed dominant male of her small streamside pack. She made herself as small as possible, looking up at him with her placid amber eyes. His stormy brown eyes smoldered down at her from his scarred and faded black muzzle. He swung his head sharply away signaling his rapid disinterest, but she saw his hard eyes soften just a bit as he did so and she tried to keep a grin from spreading across her beautiful features. She stood tall once more and padded by Romaus, gently nudging his shoulder as she passed. Romaus glanced back at her once more and shook his head before padding off to check on the rest of the pack. Ameliora watched from the edge of her sight as his muscled pure black form traveled slowly around the clearing, stopping at each individual for a quick check in.

A quick movement caught her sight from the left and whirled around just in time to avoid being tackled head on by Haska. His sandy brown coat flashed past her as she sidestepped his clumsy attack and he shot past her with a surprised look on his face and a quiet yelp as he tumbled to the ground, tripping over his own oversized paws. He picked himself up and shook the clumps of dirt and dust off his pelt before grinning ruefully at Ameliora who, although she was rolling her eyes and had an exasperated expression upon her face, had eyes dancing with laughter. Haska padded up to her, still dropping dust from his tumble. He had his head tilted to one side and a puzzled expression came over him.

"What's troubling you Ameliora?" Despite his youth and inexperience, Haska knew her better than any other member of the pack and he always seemed to be able to hear her very thoughts. She shook her troubles from her mind; Haska was not one to carry her burdens. She smiled genuinely,

"Just a foolish nightmare Haska, one that will disappear from my mind faster than a healthy hare down your throat." She said this with amusement in her voice and a friendly smirk in the upward twitch of her mouth. Haska laughed good-naturedly and swung his head away from her,

"Speaking of food…when do you think Romaus will take us on a hunt again? I'm starving." She rolled her eyes for real this time, Haska could think of many things at one time and it was guaranteed that one of those trains of thought would lead to food.

"Why don't you go ask him Haska?" He nodded absentmindedly and trotted away to where Romaus was now conversing animatedly with his mate.

His mate in question, a wolf by the name of Levada, was nodding and smiling while adding in a comment here and there to keep him talking. Her tail was curled around her paws as she sat and the sun shone upon her, lighting up her shining silver fur against the darker pelt of Romaus. At a glance, Levada appeared a soft silvery gray, but upon closer inspection it could be seen that she had light cream highlights throughout her fur. The two of them were perfect opposites in everything from appearance to personality, but somehow the perfect dominant pair.

An irritated growl sounded behind her and she turned, already knowing whose anger she had provoked now. Her older brother was standing behind her with his perpetually aggravated expression on his face. The same old hard glint was in his eyes as he looked her up and down. Derment finally stopped his soft growling and spat out harsh words at her,

"Sneak off again this morning? Sulking again down by your precious stream where you think you can go to escape all your pack duties? Everyone knows your upset about something, and whatever it is I don't care but try and come out of your I'm-the-center-of-the-pack world for once." He stalked away past her after finishing his short outburst, no doubt looking for the next unfortunate member of their small family to harass. She sighed. Derment had been cold since his sister Tharamena had been killed when he was still just a pup.

The pack didn't talk much about Tharamena. Common thought was that she had been killed quite suddenly by an unknown predator. The pack assumed it was a bear because the body had disappeared. She had wandered off on a walk and no one had bothered to follow her because at ten-moons old, the pack was sure she could take care of herself. And she wouldn't stray too far to be in any real trouble. When Tharamena didn't return, the pack went searching. The small pool of blood and the fur caught in thick brambles followed by a rough path along which something had obviously been dragged had told the tale of her demise. The pack had given up the search and trudged away mournfully. They didn't even return to their old den but moved to a new one. It was their way of surviving. The adults had taken turns guarding Derment and pushing him onward and away so he wouldn't run back searching for what was not to be found. He had convinced himself that if he had accompanied Tharamena on her ill-fated walk, that he could have protected her. He was sure that if he went back, he would find her hiding behind a fallen tree and waiting to jump and play with him once more. The pack tried to convince him otherwise. Tharamena was gone and she took with her Derment's joy far away in the realm of the lost, gone and irretrievable.

She cast a glance back towards Derment where he was now accosting poor happy Haska. She stretched and settled into a sitting position as she looked around her. She was slightly puzzled, something from the normal atmosphere was missing, one of the wolves that made up her small pack wasn't present. She counted again, Romaus was still talking to Levada, Derment was sitting alone on the far side of the small clearing obviously having finished scolding Haska over some perceived fault. He was waiting impatiently to talk to Romaus even though he steadily ignored him. At last count there were six pack members, including herself.

She scented curiously for Versitha, the only unrelated wolf in the pack. Versitha's usual quiet aurora of sensibility made others comfortable. The lack of her calming presence made her slightly uneasy. She walked slowly around the clearing with her muzzle to the ground searching for her scent path, but everything she encountered was stale. A light zephyr from behind ruffled her fur and Versitha's lavender scent drifted to her. She turned round. She saw Versitha emerge from a darkened pathway rarely used by the pack because it passed so close to the edge of their territory and their neighbors were often hostile.

She barked a greeting and prepared to head over to talk to Versitha about where she had been, but she was stopped by Romaus' commanding howl. She turned instead, as she knew she must, to Romaus. She padded over to sit around him as the rest of the pack was. She threw Versitha another glance and was shocked by the swirling rush of uncharacteristic emotions that her eyes revealed. Versitha caught her glance and she twitched her ears in question but Versitha's eyes darted quickly away as her body grew slightly rigid and she focused on Romaus' words.

Her thoughts were so centered on Versitha that she missed Romaus' call to hunt. The pack rose as one and set off at a loping run away from the clearing. She stood and sprinted to catch up as Derment snarled a demeaning comment on her unwillingness to make herself useful in the pack hunt. The pack ran as one through their forested surroundings which were bright and welcoming in the morning light from a clear sky and a shining sun. Trees flashed by her in shades of green and brown as she followed Romaus and Levada down a well-worn path to the lush valley where a herd of elk were known to spend their spring and summer days. As she ran and terrain passed by in a blur under her light paws; she could not help but think of the emotions shown in Versitha's eyes. She had seen the piercing look of raw guilt.

TWO

The dense forest of pine and cedar gave way to an open meadow of swaying slender grasses. Sparse bushes dotted the open expanse of peaceful green, and spread out on the far side seemingly unaware of the world living and changing around them, were the elk.

The occasional bellow sounded from within the herd as a mother called a calf or a male asserted what dominance he had. Ameliora breathed in the sharp tang of prey, now that the hunt was so close and her next meal before her eyes. She longed to sprint headlong across the quiet meadow and run between the legs of frightened prey, nipping at legs and dodging well aimed kicks, but she withheld the instinct and waited patiently for Romaus' command.

Romaus stood silent and strong, the rest of the pack slightly behind him. He turned his dark head slightly, nodding to Versitha. Her eyes still showed traces of the inner battle she had glimpsed earlier, but she hid it well and took off veering to the right of the not so distant herd. Versitha was the fastest runner of the pack and it was always her job to round up the herd and find the weakest link and separate it from the group.

Versitha neared the herd and slowed to a quick trot. With a slight pause and muzzle low, she disappeared into the mass of shifting hooves and flat munching teeth. With no further warning, Romaus moved forward, padding nonchalantly towards the prey and somewhere the flashing russet brown coat of Versitha. The pack followed him, spreading out slowly as they did as to prepare for the chase but not frighten the weak-minded prey before they actually had cause for terror. They all stood, waiting for Versitha.

The wolves sensed a disturbance in the herd and watched as the herd scattered. Different groups of elk were sprinting in all directions as males and females alike bellowed their confusion. She grinned to herself, watching the dim-witted prey run from Versitha's snapping jaws as she singled out the weakest member. Romaus watched intently for a few more precious seconds and the pack began to grow restless, Haska almost leapt to his paws a couple of times and his ears were twitching impatiently.

Romaus turned his head to gaze at his pack, assembled and standing in formation behind him. With the slightest of nods, he took off at a sprint down the diminutive hill. The pack fell in as one, fluidly moving to surround the elderly elk as it bellowed for help and lashed out feeble kicks at the swift wolves nipping his heels and clawing his flanks. Versitha barked her welcome and started to slow, her part of the hunt was now accomplished and she stood panting as she watched the pack continue for the kill.

An elk was tiring and now too far separated from his herd to have any hope. The elk stopped running and turned to face his pursuers, head lowered and branching antlers pointed outward. Romaus growled loudly and the almost teasing nipping ceased, the most serious part of the hunt had come. Romaus took a step forward and the pack closed in, with heads and tails low and snarls in their throats. The elk's wild eyes darted from one dark form to the other, his breath was coming in shallow huffs as the toll from the long fight and his multiple small wounds began to take effect. Romaus came threateningly forward looking the elk in the eye as Haska, Levada, and she copied his movements.

Meanwhile, Derment slunk around the back side of the elk as it was distracted by his pack. A sudden dart forward from Romaus and the elk reared and as it reared, its hooves flailing and kicking at the air as its bellows shook the ground, Derment sprung onto its backside. He dug his claws in ripping and biting as the elk bucked and kicked trying to dislodge him. Derment lost his grip and twisted mid fall, landing on his paws and preparing to launch himself once more before he noticed the elk staggering to its side. The elk was weighed down heavily by a now ferocious Haska on his back and Ameliora holding and tearing at his neck with her strong jaws. The elk gave a final, muted, bellow of defeat as his legs buckled and he fell to the ground. His eyes began to close and his body was shaking with exhaustion, but he took one last glance at Romaus as the giant black wolf stood over his defeated adversary. Romaus bent his head towards the elk's extended neck, preparing to break the tough bones of the elk in his powerful jaws. A gasp and the elk breathed its last breath. Romaus lifted his head sharply; surprised this final part of the kill had been taken from him.

She and her brothers quickly stepped back from the carcass and the sweet smell of fresh meat as Romaus and Levada approached the meal. Versitha appeared beside her, quietly. Whatever had been on Versitha's mind was no longer present. Romaus and Levada bent their heads and tore into the meat, as was the right of the dominant pair. Haska shifted his paws and whined softly with impatience and frustration; as the lowest ranking member of the pack, he would eat last.

Romaus and Levada finally stepped back, their muzzles dripping and stained. The bright red of the fresh blood was especially vivid against the pale white of Levada's mouth. Romaus dipped his head to the rest of the pack and they jumped forward, eager to bury their mouths in the fresh meat and tear at it with sharp glinting teeth. Versitha took the best place at the carcass, being the next highest ranking. She was followed by Derment beside her, Ameliora at Derment's side and finally Haska trying to squeeze in to the best meat while the older wolves growled sharply at him. Haska settled for a back haunch, gnawing at the thick bones and marrow, pleased with the pack's successful hunt and a full belly.

The pack continued eating while Romaus and Levada stood back, washing to meat off their muzzles and whispering to each other. The pack was too concentrated on their meal to notice much and so ignored the whispered conversation and each other. Derment snarled occasionally when anyone got too close to where he was eating, but besides that the pack was quiet. She felt better than she had in a long time and her worry for Versitha had gradually faded as Versitha seemed to return to her normal motherly character. Whatever had been bothering her earlier seemed to have been banished from her mind.

She finally stepped away from the carcass, washing the blood off her fur and muzzle. Her tail was wagging happily as she stood watching Versitha, Derment and Haska finish. A short time after she finished cleaning herself; she was joined by Versitha. Derment sat himself off to one side, staring silently at the now abandoned meadows. They sat in a small group talking amiably among themselves. Haska continued eating, he was like a bottomless pit and she had no doubt that he would work on that carcass until the bitter end. She laughed quietly to herself before turning to Versitha.

"Do you remember the stories you used to tell?" She smiled fondly at the surfacing memories. "You used to tell them to us before we were old enough to join the hunt.

They kept us entertained until the adults would return." Versitha laughed a genuine laugh and her eyes glittered.

"I'm surprised you even remember, considering you usually fell asleep before I was even halfway through." She chuckled, heat rising to her cheeks. Versitha's soft voice had lulled her to sleep on more than one stormy night.

"There was one you used to tell though, one about a great battle." Her brows knitted together as she attempted to remember the story. "I always fell asleep before the ending."

"A great battle?" Versitha raised a brow, her eyes pensive as she tried to recall the story she was referencing. Her ears twitched. The two females were quite oblivious to Haska who had crept in to join the conversation.

"I think I know which one you're talking about." Haska piped up, startling the two older females. "Isn't that the one about the spirits of good and evil?"

"Yes!" She barked triumphantly, beaming at Haska. She turned her gaze back to Versitha. She grinned, "I've always wanted to know the ending."

"Well I have no qualms about telling it." Versitha settled herself down, passing her tongue quickly over her fur. She and Haska moved in closer. Unnoticed by the young wolves, Romaus and Levada had finished their meal. The elder wolves join in the outskirts of the group. Romaus made a small noise of approval in the back of his throat. Even Derment seemed to angle his ears towards the group, though her refused to budge from his place.

Romaus and Levada smiled happily as the small family gathered around Versitha and settled in for the tale. She pressed against Haska, leaning in as Versitha began.

"Many moons ago, before even Romaus was born," A joking growl came from Romaus' direction at this comment. "A young male wolf by the name of Sararo roamed the land. He had a pack of his own and a beautiful mate and pups, but he was unhappy. He was dominant male of his pack, but he longed for more power. He knew a time would come when a new stronger male would take his place and he dreaded this unavoidable future. Sararo began to spend more and more time alone, plotting and scheming a way to keep his power and possibly gain more. He became obsessed." Versitha's tale began and the pack was spellbound as she wove the tale around them.

She told of Sararo's decent into madness as he imagined enemies where there were none. He watched his own pups grow. His two sons and daughter developed into young wolves although they were still pups. He watched his sons especially carefully, noting the strength they gained and the energy their youth gave them. Sararo's heart grew heavy with jealousy and suspicion as he watched his sons, certain that one day one of them would overthrow him. He descended further and further into a violent madness that none could bring him from. Yet in his madness, he developed a cunning and twisted malignant mind. His envy and lust for power brought him to the final brink. He snuck out on a black moonless night and summoned the one the wolves called Nithil. Nithil was the dark spirit or the entity of corruption and chaos. He was found lurking dark corners surrounded by murder, deceit and torture.

Sararo called on Nithil, having heard rumors of the power the dark spirit controlled. Sararo begged Nithil to reveal to him the source of the Great Spirit's powers and how he could obtain some of his own. Nithil listened to the wolf, reaching into Sararo's mind and reading his heart. Nithil saw a potential for darkness and hate in Sararo and seized the opportunity. Nithil whispered in Sararo's ear,

"A power like mine cannot be gained from simple giving or granting. A power like mine is found in the life of others." Sararo was confused by this answer and pleaded with Nithil to explain his words. Nithil answered, "You must be willing to sacrifice much to be one as me." Nithil weaved his dark words around Sararo. Nithil, being a spirit and thus not mortal, had become frustrated with his inability to rise or affect the living world. Nithil could only become tangible again through the joining with a willing mortal host. Nithil had chosen Sararo for his potential host, but needed consent and action from the young male. Sararo spoke up,

"Just tell me what it is, great one, so that I may do this and be as you. Your words are my command." Nithil wished to test Sararo's true nature and so told him,

"To become like me, you must be able to take a life. Not a life of prey, nor a life of stranger. Your two sons, Sararo, you worry they plot against you. How much harm would it really be to exterminate a future threat to you and your pack?" Nithil's words of poison pierced Sararo's heart that night and Sararo vowed to become like Nithil so he too could be all powerful.

A warm summer day, he took his two sons out into the woods. He told them he was going to teach them how to fight like real wolves. The rest of the pack watched unsuspecting at Sararo led his two young pups away from them. He took them quickly and quietly away, leading them further and further from the den site. In a clearing far enough away that any sound would be a mere echo to the pack, Sararo turned on them. He rounded on his two sons, swatting them with his great paws and stunning them before quickly dispatching them with swift bites to their necks.

The pups couldn't even struggle, they knew nothing of combat and the shock of the sudden attack had left them unable to respond before their short demise. Sararo licked the blood from his paws and muzzle before dragging the bodies away to be hidden. He smiled a cold smile before turning away from the bloody clearing and racing back to the den site, already preparing the tragic story of the bear that had killed his pups. Of course he had valiantly defended them, but been unable to stop their cruel slaughter at the hands of the predator. He reached his pack and relayed the story, fake sorrow spread across his countenance. He joined in the mournful howls that echoed through their valley, not on member suspected the truth behind the murders and slowly but surely pack life went on.

Sararo went out again to contact Nithil on a black moonless night. He called to the dark one and the dark one answered. Sararo told Nithil he had done what he was instructed, that the threat was eliminated. Nithil barely contained his morbid joy as he congratulated Sararo, seeing that the hate that he had glimpsed in Sararo's heart had grown and spread to a deep blackness within him. Nithil once more whispered his poisoned words in Sararo's ears.

"You have proved yourself worthy of power, but power I cannot give you. I am but spirit and no longer mortal. If, however, I were to become mortal once more, I could give you all the power you would ever need. Bond with me Sararo." Sararo listened to the words, growing excited and missing the deceitful malicious glint in Nithil's black eyes. Sararo growled his agreement, imploring Nithil to bond with him so he too could wheel the power of the darkness Nithil controlled. Nithil howled in cold joy as his spirit entered and bonded with Sararo.

Sararo howled, shrieking in pain as the spirit moved and settled in him. Nithil seized control of Sararo, bonding them together. They became Rangatha. Rangatha was an almost black gray and in all aspects appeared to be a wolf, but where amber eyes should have been there were only black pits. Rangatha returned to his pack to begin his reign of fear and murder, his mind forever the combination of Sararo and Nithil who had ceased to be individuals.

Packs far and wide began to fear this powerful menace, certain that the spread of his dominion would encompass them too. Tales were told of the deep gray wolf, some said his coat was so dark because it matched the growing blackness of his heart. Others said the black pits that served as his eyes could see into the very soul of any wolf foolish enough to make eye contact.

"The wolves cried out for someone to rise against Rangatha, someone who could set them free from his tyrannical ways." Versitha paused to survey her captivated audience, no one stirred as she smiled watching her pack. Before she could continue Haska interrupted, speaking quickly and excitedly.

"Rangatha was defeated Versitha! Morenia sacrificed herself to become the mortal form of all that is good! She was able to defeat him!" The pack groaned in unison, annoyed at Haska's interruption and consequence ruining of the ending. Versitha opened her mouth to chastise him, but was stopped. All hope of the end of the story was lost as a distant howl had broken the silence of the peaceful afternoon and the raw pain and anguish in the voice of the unfamiliar wolf struck the hearts of the pack and they winced as one. She felt the pain like a physical blow and longed to howl comfort to the unknown sufferer. She cast a glance at each of the other members, looking at their reactions. All of them matched hers, full of pity and partially shared pain for the member of the pack in the neighboring member. All of them matched, excepting Versitha. Her eyes shown with the same immeasurable grief from hours earlier and a pain unlike that of the pack, where the pack's eyes shown with pain of another wolf grieving, Her eyes shown with the pain as if it were her own, as if she was the one who had lost. She stared at her, but she seemed not to see her and with a shake of her head and a quick mournful howl sprinted away from the pack. She watched her run, too surprised to follow or call out as if her voice and strength had escaped her like Versitha's vanishing form.

❦

THREE

"Where is Versitha?" No one wanted to answer Romaus' query, though all were wondering the same question. Where was Versitha? Why had she run so suddenly? Levada braved her mate's wrath,

"She's gone Romaus. She took off running seconds after the howl started." Romaus swung his head towards Levada, growling under his breath.

"Does anyone know *why* she is gone?" His low amount of patience was already running out because, although he would never admit it, the raw emotions had affected him too and he was at a loss for the right action to take. She thought back to that morning and what she had seen. She contemplated speaking up and opened her mouth, but no words came out and she closed it once more. The wolves all looked at each other from the corners of their eyes, all silently. Even Derment had no snide comment now. For once the flint-like hardness in his eyes had softened to sorrow and she guessed he was remembering his own grief for Tharamena. Levada spoke up again,

"Calm down Romaus, we will send someone after her. She will have left a clear scent trail. The rest of us should go back to the den, there is nothing more to be gained here." Romaus' growls quieted and died off in his throat as he thought about his mate's words. He eventually nodded his head. There was rarely a time that Romaus didn't follow the wise words of Levada, in fact she was the one the whole pack looked to for sensibility and reason. He twitched his ears toward her in question, but before he could open his mouth to ask, Levada spoke again.

"Ameliora, find Versitha and talk to her. She will listen to you, as I expect you will to her." Levada's eyes were directly on her daughter. She wondered if Levada had guessed she knew more than had been said, but without another word she scented the air and padded off after Versitha. She didn't bother to sprint full speed in the direction her slightly fading scent trail took, she knew her speed could never match Versitha's. She followed the scent trail, her mind whirling. She thought mostly about Versitha, about how she had looked that morning and her sudden flight and most of all how it all related to that mournful howl. The whole pack had been struck by it, but Versitha had reacted so abnormally strongly. Worry traced deep lines in the young she-wolf's face.

Time passed as did land under her quick paced trot as she followed Versitha's seemingly endless path. The meadow faded behind her, disappearing along with the valley, as she entered the dense woodlands once more.

She twisted and turned, winding through the thick trunks. The light began to fade from the sky and she watched the moon come out with apprehension at how far Versitha had gone.

The trees began to thin and the distant sound of trickling water floated to her ears as Versitha's scent grew steadily stronger. She broke into a run, sprinting over the now familiar ground and crashed through the last feeble bushes. She stood before her stream. Her special place all her own where she went to do all her thinking, the place that made her calm. It was here that she found Versitha, sitting on the water's edge looking into the flowing current but eyes seeing nothing. Her face was covered in agony and guilt and all of the raw emotions she had but glimpsed in Versitha's disturbed eyes that morning. Versitha spoke, in little more than a whisper,

"They sent you to find me, didn't they? They want you to bring me back. They want to know how it happened. They want to see me suffer for what I couldn't do, while they don't know that I am already suffering. I am dying inside, Ameliora and they want to finish it. I want to let them." Versitha trailed off, and if she hadn't heard the whispered speech coming from her dear friend's mouth, she would have sworn Versitha hadn't said a word. Versitha was still as stone and spoke no more. She was puzzled, wondering who the "they" Versitha had mentioned could be. It was impossible she was referring to their pack. She took a breath intending to say comforting words to the wolf who had been like a second mother to her, but let the breath escape through her parted jaw when no words came.

She padded softly to sit beside Versitha. The water flowed by the two of them, swiftly and unchanging as it always had been and always would be. She sighed heavily and finally spoke in a steady voice that masked the shaking uncertainty of her thoughts,

"I'm not going to ask you to explain to me, Versitha. I know that isn't something you can do. I am going to ask that you come back with me, that you let us take care of you. We are wolves and we are pack, your suffering shall be our suffering. Whoever this "they" is that you speak of, we fight them for you. No one shall make you hurt more than the world can see you already do." She finished her short speech, sure that the words she had spoken were true. Neither of them moved, nor made a sound. The quiet trickling and bubbling of the stream continued on as the night descending around them grew blacker and stars began to light the spaces alongside the moon. Versitha dropped her head low, and a calmer expression crossed her face before defeat took over her features.

"I have to go back, don't I?" she said in a louder voice than before. She sounded less like the gentle young caretaker she had always known, and more like the whimpering pup from years long past. She only nodded her head slowly in answer as Versitha pushed herself into a standing position and turned to look at her for the first time that night. "Just promise me, when what couldn't be has become what must be, that you remain true to the understanding I have always seen in you." She looked her deep in the eye and said to her,

"I will." Together they walked, side by side, away into the night. They walked towards a worried pack, an unsure future, and possibly most powerful of all, a grieving mother.

Light was beginning to touch the tops of the cedars as Versitha and Ameliora padded the last few feet along the dimly lit pathway and into the pack clearing. It was obvious by the thick tension in the air that none of the pack had slept that night. Levada and Romaus were lying next to each other silently, but communicating with eyes that held nothing but worry. Haska was pacing the small clearing and whining softly to himself, unable to sit still. Derment snapped at Haska every few minutes, but even his harsh words didn't hold the same sharpness they usually did. All heads and eyes turned their way when she and Versitha stepped haltingly into the clearing. The courage Versitha had displayed by the river, and the quiet determination to return, seemed to vanish as she took that step. Her ears drooped and her tail curled between her shaking legs. Her eyes held a pleading look and betrayed once again every conflicting emotion that had run across her features down by the stream.

There was a moment of quiet relief that could be felt as much as the tension had only minutes before. The pack jumped up and was soon assembled in a barking frenzy of welcome and expression of concern. Versitha looked startled for a minute before returning the affection of her family. Although some of the fear had gone from Versitha's eyes, the pain was still present. A small smile tugged at the corners of her mouth as her family crowded around her. Tails wagged and eyes shone. Haska was beside himself, barking and yapping like a young pup. Versitha returned the affection whole heartedly, thinking to herself that maybe her pack didn't care what had happened, that somehow they had understood. She yapped and wagged her tail, surrounding herself in the love and support of her pack. Versitha's guilt and pain started to ebb away just a bit as she thought about dealing with what had happened with a pack around to support her. The sun had risen and the brightness it gave the forest below seemed to mirror the brightness of the hope Versitha was feeling. The guilt of what she had done would forever be with her, but she wouldn't be punished anymore than she already was by living every day to remember it. Versitha shook the thought momentarily from her mind and looked gratefully around her. Her eyes were soft and full of care. Even Derment didn't have a mean word to say now. She looked at her and spoke softly,

"See Versitha, didn't I tell you we would care for you?" Versitha blinked gratefully back at her and looked to where Romaus and Levada were sitting close together. One thing was still puzzling Versitha, she turned her head towards the dominant pair and twitched her ears quizzically.

"Romaus, Levada, weren't the other wolves angry? Didn't they come for me? Didn't they want to punish me for...?" She trailed off as what was going on began to dawn on her.

Versitha took a step back, her smile fading once more. The pack didn't understand what had happened. It wasn't that they didn't care. They didn't simply love her in spite of what had transpired. They didn't know. The other wolves, they hadn't come for her. The other pack hadn't told her pack. Versitha's paws shook as she took stumbling paw steps backwards away from the confused faces of her loved ones.

Some part of the mixed jumbled of questions that had poured from Versitha had been partially understood by Romaus and a look of understanding took over his stern features.

"Versitha," he said softly, taking a small step forward, "I think you need to tell us what happened." Versitha's eyes went wide, but she didn't step away from him. Her shoulders slumped and she sighed deeply with defeat and resignation in her every move. She padded back towards them. She sat down heavily taking a last look around at the intent eyes of her pack mates before starting her story.

"I woke up early," she began, "the pack, and the world it seemed to me, was still slumbering and the sky was still wrapped in darkness." Her ears twitched, Versitha had been awake much earlier than she had thought. How had she missed the absence of Versitha that morning as she had slunk away to her stream? Versitha continued her tale,

"The early morning darkness seemed so enticing to me, and since sleep was determined to evade me, I crept around Haska, who was still sleeping beside me as he did every night. I was careful not to wake anyone." This was how Versitha's tale began. She told of that dark sleepless morning. Versitha had stretched stiffly and blinked the symptoms of a sleep she hadn't attained out of her eyes. The sleeping pack dotted the clearing with dark lumps. The only movement was the subtle rise and fall of the pack's chests. She had slunk on light paws around Romaus and Levada, curled around each other, and Derment sleeping on his own as always under a tree on a far side of the clearing. Ameliora she passed last, the younger she wolf was twitching and whining in her sleep and Versitha stopped by her for a second before walking on and escaping the slumbering clearing.

There were three obvious paths away from the clearing. Off to one side was the pathway down to the stream, covered in the stale smell of Ameliora's pine tree scent. In the middle was a wider path that the pack often took down to the meadows and deeper into the woods. It split often into many paths and a wolf unfamiliar with the territory could get lost easily. This was the major trail used by the pack. Being as distracted as Versitha was, she had chosen to stay off the twisting pathway. That had left the third and final pathway, one that was used even less than the stream trail.

The third darkened pathway beckoned to her. The grass and sponge like moss grew over the dirt path, making it only partially visible and in obvious disuse. The idea of a late night adventure down the old trail was irresistible to Versitha's rest-deprived mind. She set off at a leisurely trot down the trail, skirting boulders and hopping fallen branches that often barred her way. She had begun to pant with the effort of actively dodging so many obstacles down the dark trail. She almost didn't notice the light paw steps and the whispered beating of heavy wings.

She stopped, muzzle high, and looked around her. A light spring breeze ruffled her fur and an unfamiliar scent accosted her nostrils. She swung her head to her left and peered through the tight trunks and foliage around her. She was frozen, listening intently. Twigs cracked and snapped as careless paws trod over them. She took a silent step forward and looked closer through the leaves and darkness.

A small clearing was just on the other side of the trees that made up one side of her midnight pathway. The clearing was roughly oval in shape and so cramped that its insignificance was obvious to any who cast a glance its way. Tonight, however, it was not insignificant nor would it ever be again. For playing and jumping around the clearing, tail high in the air and wagging furiously, was a young pup. Versitha was surprised to see it there, and all alone. She belatedly remembered that the path she had chosen went along the outskirts of her pack's territory and bordered the territory of their unknown neighboring pack.

The pup gallivanting before her must have belonged to that pack. How had it gotten out of their den so late at night? Did its mother know it was out here alone? Versitha worried, but felt hesitant about crossing the borders. There was no chance the pack this pup belonged to would appreciate her trespassing. As she pondered her course of action, all thought of continuing her lone nighttime adventure out of her mind, the earlier whoosh of beating wings came faintly from above her.

She lifted her eyes and muzzle to the sky, looking for the owner of the wing beats. A shadow passed across the waning moon above her, and her keen eyes were able to distinguish its characteristics. The following low hooting confirmed Versitha's theory and she watched the owl circle above her, momentarily forgetting the pup and her moral dilemma. She watched the owl circle once, twice and a third time before it gave a sudden plunge, talons extended. Versitha had always enjoyed watching fellow predators hunt. She lost sight of the owl and wondered briefly what sad animal had become its next meal. The sudden yelping and whimpering from the clearing beside her gave the horrible answer to the question she wished she had never asked.

Without a second thought Versitha leapt across the boundary line, seeing the owl was struggling to fly away with the young pup that was a great deal heavier than the owl had predicted. The owl's beak was plunging and pecking over and over as its talons scraped and tore into the young pup's once soft fur. Now the fur was quickly becoming matted and stained dark crimson with blood. Versitha launched herself headlong at the owl, snarling ferociously and clawing at its tossing and swaying form.

The pup had gone limp and the owl began to lift slowly into the air, bringing the pup with it. Versitha jumped again, sinking her teeth into the owl's scaly leg. The owl screeched its fury and dropped the pup. The pup crashed unmoving to the ground. The much disgruntled and meal-deprived owl flew off looking quite a bit more bedraggled than it had when it was circling quietly above Versitha moments ago.

Versitha's snarls died in her throat as she turned her nose from the sky and back down to her feet where a bloody pile of fur lay. She bent her nose and nudged its face gently, whining her distress. No response came from the small wolf, and the total silence of its un-beating heart gave away the truth of the stillness of the small form lying before Versitha. Light was beginning to show through the blackness of the night as Versitha whined and pushed the small body, desperate to make it live again. Finally, when dawn had touched the tree tops, Versitha turned away in horror and forced herself to flee from the dead pup of the pack she had never known. She padded away, leaving her lavender scent covering the cold body.

"If I had acted sooner, if I had been faster, if I had seen it coming…" Her narrative trailed off. She swung her head away from the blank eyes of her pack mates as they took in her tale. Not a breeze blew, and birds ceased to sing as understanding began to glow in the eyes of the wolves. Versitha spoke again, in less than a whisper, "It was an accident." The last line was where her steadiness broke and the quiet courage that had always defined Versitha shattered and surprisingly it was Derment who stood up slowly and padded the few feet to where she sat. Every trace of the characteristic coldness and anger that had been Derment after Tharamena's death was gone, and it was replaced by a caring instinct so deep that none of the other pack members moved to disturb the moment Derment and Versitha were sharing.

"It's not your fault; it was never your fault." Derment said to her softly and evenly, repeating the comforting words to her. The whole pack got the sense that Derment wasn't speaking just to Versitha, but maybe to himself too. The hushed words were the only sound in the clearing aside from Versitha's shallow desperate breathing.

It was just then, as hope's fragile wings began to flutter once more in Versitha's heart, that the silent malevolent presence that had arrived unnoticed some time earlier made itself known. A deep rumbling growl echoed through the clearing and the pack turned as one to see the creature in question. Standing stock still, as if he had just emerged from the forever black trail Versitha had taken the morning before, was a massive ash gray male wolf. His hackles were raised and the wild furious look in his chocolate brown eyes had an undercurrent of pain. His growls grew louder as he took a threatening step forward and

Romaus darted in front of the pack to meet him, snarling with unbridled aggression.

"Who are you? Why do you disturb us in our own territory in which you are trespassing?" The words spat from Romaus' snarling muzzle had no effect on the great gray wolf before him. The stranger had eyes only for Versitha, at whom he was glaring ferociously. His speech was jumbled. Little by little, the phrase he was essentially throwing at her became distinguishable.

"How dare you call it an accident? How *dare* you call it an accident!"

FOUR

A silence descended upon the pack as the vicious words echoed in the quiet clearing. Romaus' snarls started anew and grew louder as he advanced another step towards the ash gray wolf whose whole body was shaking with barely controlled fury. Romaus' already deep voice grew deeper and it shook with the effort of keeping control as he questioned the ashen aggressor once more,

"I asked you a question! Who are you? Why do you come threatening a member of my pack?" Romaus' head was lowered and in the midmorning sunshine his charcoal pelt stood out and rippled with an almost shining quality over his heavily muscled body. The stranger tore his eyes away from Versitha and stared deep into Romaus' brown gaze. The stranger spoke in words sharper than adder fangs,

"I don't come threatening a member of your pack. I see no wolves here worth threatening. What I see is five wolves defending what is rightfully theirs to defend. I come only for the pup-killer." With these last snarled words, his eyes gained a cold hardness that she suspected was only a shield to his pain. The stranger took another step in Versitha's direction. Derment's previously flint like eyes turned to fire as he moved furiously in front of Versitha.

Derment's tail was stiff and straight out behind him and his hackles raised as his lips curled back in a rumbling snarl that showed his brilliantly pointed teeth. The stranger momentarily lost his hateful expression, so surprised was he by the show of ferocity and protectiveness from Derment towards Versitha. Derment's thunderous voice came from within the snarling lips.

"You take one more step towards her," he said with difficulty, momentarily oblivious to the position of the dominant male as protector of the pack, "and I will tear every scrap of fur from your body to feed to that owl that missed out on the meal of your pup." Romaus didn't move to Derment, didn't reprimand him for stepping out of his place in the pack. The stranger took a full step back from Versitha, eyes slowly regaining the coldness they had lost in reaction to Derment. The stranger's hackles lowered and the persistent snarling that had filled the air faded away as a look of stony determination crossed his features.

"I am not so foolish," he said calmly for the first time, "as to take on your pack at full strength alone. In fact, I am quite surprised you didn't simply hand her over. She could be a future danger to you, now that she has a taste for pups. I can't imagine harboring a murderer in my own family." He finished this last sentence staring into

Romaus' eyes without his previous coldness or anger, just the unchanging stony determination. He had a sureness that came with certainty in one's own words. This stranger, whoever he was, had no intention of letting the crime he believed to have taken place go unpunished. She listened to the words of the stranger and she suddenly partially understood him. The stranger really did believe Versitha had killed his pup. He truly believed he was protecting the neighboring wolves and himself by taking her. In a twisted way, he was being wise and strong in order to protect his family. He was taking the necessary steps to rid his pack of a future danger to his pups. Something in Romaus' still burning chocolate eyes flashed, and she wondered if he had realized the same thing. She gazed intently at the stranger. Had she met him under different circumstances, she might have respected him for those two predominant characteristics.

Without another word the stranger turned on his heel and trotted back down the shadowy pathway towards his own territory. He left no name and asked for none in return. He left only a threat, and certainty of meeting again.

The pack stood silently in the wake of the passionate speech, with the exception of Derment who was still snarling with his hackles fully raised. They were all watching the stranger pad away and fade into the darkness that shielded the overgrown pathway. The day's events and plethora of information that had crashed upon the pack was being dissected and mulled over in the pack's thoughts. She found that she was suddenly very tired, both mentally and physically, and remembered she hadn't slept at all the night before. She smiled a weak smile to herself; at least a night without sleep was a night without her haunting nightmare. The smile disappeared once more when she heard another much fainter hopeless howl in the distance. She let herself sink to the ground from her upright sitting position and rested her head on her paws, whining softly in distress. Ever happy Haska was still as stone, a blank shocked look still spread across his wide face as he sat at her side. Romaus' eyes were downcast and a heavy frown had plastered itself to his muzzle. He paced in slow short lines. Levada was the only one who seemed remotely calm. Her golden yellow eyes were closed and her face expressed a sense of peacefulness that she doubted Levada really felt. Her bushy gray tail was curled daintily around her paws and she sat perfectly straight, giving off an air of regality that shone from within her silver form. She felt her paws lighten just a bit when she looked at Levada, who gave her the sense that somehow everything would be worked out.

She dragged her eyes away from Levada and stole a glance at Versitha, who hadn't spoken since she had finished her story and who now looked worse than death itself. Her eyes were wide, but unseeing. Her tail twitched without feeling. She breathed without taking in any air and every ounce of her being gave off waves of uncertainty, doubt, pain, sorrow and guilt. The only thing that seemed to have any effect on her was Derment, who finally managed to calm himself down and turned to gently prod her with his nose.

Versitha jolted out of whatever oblivion her mind had taken her to and shook her head slowly as her eyes refocused. She swung her face to look at Derment. She was still silent. She appeared numb, as if she had been robbed of all emotion. Yet somehow, she saw him and she felt him near and air began to enter her lungs once more. He pressed himself close to her, giving a sense of a comforting presence that Versitha needed. She looked up at him, seeming smaller than she ever had before, and whispered a question.

"How long?" The rest of the pack strained their ears to hear the quiet question but it had been meant for Derment and only Derment. He leaned down, catching her faint words and he knew what she was asking without needing to hear. How long until the pack came back for her. He shook his head and whispered back,

"Soon." Derment wasn't going to lie and say they would leave her be, or tell her she had plenty of time. He knew that wouldn't help her, so he told the truth. Versitha simply nodded in return, as if he had told her what she already knew. Her eyes regained the vacant look and even though most eyes were on her, it was as if Versitha didn't notice them. She probably didn't.

Every member of their small pack was either preoccupied by Versitha or thoughts of Versitha. All eyes were on her, either in a long gaze or quick stolen glances. No one noticed her stand up and slip quietly down the far path and trot on heavy paws to a peacefully trickling stream.

FIVE

She reached the stream, collapsed on its bank, and buried her head in her paws. In so little time everything had changed, well almost everything. She raised her head and watched the stream. The stream never changed. It always flowed and trickled down through the grassy hill. A small smile played across her face as she drew comfort from the one constant in her life. She lowered her head back to her paws and sighed deeply. The sun warmed her back, and had she not been so worried about Versitha, she was sure she could have been quite content in this moment. Her heavy eyelids began to droop and she fought to stay awake as sleep washed over her like the stream over its bed of pebbles. She took one last look around her before sleep claimed her and her head rolled to the side. Her breathing became deep and even.

Almost immediately she found herself trapped once more in her nightmare realm. It was as if she had fallen asleep and awoken in a different world all together. She blinked open her eyes, but the gentle water and warm spring sun had disappeared. They were replaced by dead leaves on cold ground in a nighttime forest. Darkness seemed to seep from the air around her and she leapt to her paws when she heard the distinct crackle of paws upon dead leaves. Her ears twitched and she strained trying to catch some sound in the silent forest. She breathed in deeply, every sense was on edge and her instincts told her danger was near. She scanned the spindly trees of the forest and watched them sway in the sharp wind. The forest seemed naked without the green covering the towering branches. The overwhelming amount of broken brown only added to the darkness.

She shivered, partially from cold and partially from the creeping feeling of fear she felt deep inside her. An echoing howl sounded far away, and somehow - although no command or knowledge was spoken - she knew the chase had begun again. She sprinted away, crashing through piles of dead leaves while branches that seemed to be reaching for her caught and tore at her fur. She ran and leapt over roots and the cold earth beneath her, heedless of the noise she was making or the trail she left behind. There was no pathway here, so she made her own. Stealth was not needed; she knew instinctively that no amount of care she took could keep her ghostly pursuer from finding her.

The familiarity of it all sank in, but something was different. She ran desperately from the snapping jaws and hot breath on her heels while frantically searching for what she didn't know was lost. Her eyes darted everywhere and scanned her surroundings, trying to spot or get some faint clue as to what she was looking for. Her attacker was gaining on her and time was running out as she pelted through the thick black woodlands. Her heart was beating faster than a hummingbird's wings and her breath was coming in quick shallow gasps as she ran. The snapping jaws were suddenly absent as was the pounding of heavy paws and she feared for where the creature had gone.

She hadn't long to fear or ponder. A crashing weight descended on her back. She realized her attacker had leapt onto her from behind. Her legs buckled under the sudden pressure and she fell to the ground, crushed under her darkly chuckling captor. Hard paws pressing down on her kept her from moving. She squirmed and bucked vainly trying to dislodge her pursuer. As her muscles weakened and she began to envision a slow death at ripping jaws, the weight was flung off of her.

She squinted against a bright shining white light. Her attacker had been cast off her. Stunned, she turned her head to where it was laying. It got up and for the first time, Ameliora got a good look at it. It was a wolf, although she couldn't tell whether it was male or female. It had huge slavering jaws and its pelt was dark gray. Where eyes colored amber, brown, or yellow should have been; all was black. She couldn't see the pupil because it blended in with the deep black pits that were the eyes of the fearful wolf. She began to shake with the horror of it all.

The bright light moved forward towards her and the wolf backed away. It was growling at the light, but something kept it from attacking or coming any closer. It suddenly howled, loud and long, a bone chilling angry howl that echoed through the cold woodlands. The wolf turned away, throwing her a last black gaze and dark chuckle, as it ran away back into the surrounding trees. She just stared in shock, for the first time she was alive. She realized with a start, she could hear the faint words trickling into her mind, the words she had been searching for.

"*Wait for me.*" They echoed once through her clamoring thoughts and faded away. She began to growl angrily, she had died again and again each night to hear these words that meant nothing to her. As she was struggling to her feet, an annoyed scowl spread across her muzzle, the bright white light began to take form. She was too distracted to take notice and it wasn't until she turned with the intention of padding off in the opposite direction that she came face to face with her unlikely savior.

The bright white light had slowly taken shape and now a shimmering iridescent ivory wolf was standing silently before her. Although no words were spoken, she knew that this wolf was a female and powerful in some way. Ameliora watched the shining wolf that was still solidifying and taking shape before her. The wolf gave off so much light, that the deep blackness of the dead woods seemed to lighten and some of the fear eating away at her heart faded. Finally, the wolf seemed solid and she slowly blinked open her eyes.

She gasped slightly, like the eyes of her attacker, the eyes of her savior contained no pupil. They were bright white and shone with a radiance that dwarfed the moon. The eyes focused and became clear as the she wolf swung her head in her direction. She took a faltering step backward, wondering if she had been saved only to suffer a fate worse than the death at the hands of her previous attacker. The wolf's gaze softened and she took a step away from her before sitting down and wrapping her glowing tail around her dainty paws. Her jaws stayed closed, but she once more heard whispered words.

"Do not fear me, Ameliora. Have I not just saved you from the one who hunts you?" Her eyes went wide with shock. Although what this unfamiliar wolf had said was true, she was still skeptical of the glowing form before her. She spoke out loud, even though the sound of her own voice in the silent dark woods seemed the echo to all ends of the earth.

"You say I should not fear you, yet you know my name and appear in my nightmares. I have never met you, but you save me from my pursuer. The attacker who follows me cannot be defeated by any amount of strength I have. You manage to throw him bodily from me with no movement. Why should I not fear a power such as this?" Her words came out steady and clear which gave her a small confidence boost. The shimmering apparition seemed to smile and the words came again, still without any sound from the white wolf.

"What you say is true. Your earthly body cannot defeat him who hunts you, but I am no such earthly bound being as you. Neither, for that matter, is your hunter. It is for this reason that my strength may rival his, as it always has. As for your name, well Ameliora I know you better than you could imagine." She felt a wave of calm wash over her and she wondered briefly if it was the doing of the white wolf before her. She also realized the white wolf had given her an important piece of information, her attacker was male. She rolled this over in her thoughts for a few brief moments. She questioned the being again, although without some of the former distrust in her voice.

"You say you know me, but I have never met you. If I am to trust you, to believe you, I must know you as you say you know me." She waited, watching to see what effect her words would have on the white wolf. The corners of the white wolf's mouth twitched as the smile lengthened and she responded once more.

"Ameliora, you know me as you know yourself. However, I cannot expect you to understand and I have not the time to explain it to you. We have very little time today, but there is one thing you must know." She perked her ears, listening intently as her suspicion and doubt was ebbing away. The white wolf continued, "First, the one who hunts you. He is Rangatha." She snorted to herself. How appropriately named was her tormentor Rangatha;

a character from an old legend who caused mayhem and destruction. She stared long and hard into the white beings eyes.

"You expect me to believe that Rangatha murders me every night in my dreams?" She snorted a laugh again before continuing. "Rangatha is a pup's tale, or a name given to killers. Rangatha isn't a true being." The white wolf's eyes looked sad as she listened to her.

"Have you ever heard, Ameliora, that all stories are based on fact? Rangatha is as real as I am, and as you are. He is as real as the pain he makes you feel every night." Her smug smile fell from her face at the sadness in the white wolf's eyes and the seriousness of her voice. She thought over all the stories she had heard as a pup of Rangatha. Not many had been told in the den, Levada was usually too busy for such nonsense as legends. She scoured her memories for what she remembered from the few fragmented moments of the spellbinding tales. She sighed, she couldn't recollect much. The two things she remembered were that Rangatha was said to be evil in its purest form, and he forever did battle with another spirit who was the embodiment of good. The name of the spirit battling Rangatha escaped her and she scowled angrily.

The white wolf cleared her throat quietly and she looked up into the bright eyes again. "Time has run out on us. Someone comes for you now, so wake young Ameliora. Wake and return to the living world as you left it." The white wolf's form was dimming, as were her words that faded into the darkness that was closing in around her. She stood quickly, calling out to the fading light. Her fears of the nighttime realm had diminished, but a burning question had been rolling through her mind and now it exploded from her parted jaws.

"Who are you?" The question echoed around the dead forest as the last of the light blinked out. A faint voice floated back and wrapped around her mind like a snake to a small rodent.

"I am Morenia." She didn't have time to mull over this new information as she was jolted from sleep. A soft nose had prodded her back gently and she awoke to see Haska staring worriedly down at her. The light was different than it had been when she had drifted to sleep and she realized that night had past and morning was upon her. She shook her head slightly, the sleep had done her good. She stretched and yawned wearily before swinging her head towards an anxious Haska. Haska was pacing back and forth waiting for her, whining softly. She looked quizzically at him and asked,

"What's wrong Haska? Settle down, you act as if we're going to be attacked." She said it with a smile in her eyes but he answered in so hopeless a tone that it was soon gone.

"We won't be, Ameliora, but the rest of the pack may. It's why I was sent to get you. The other pack has returned." She whirled around to face Haska and barked angrily at him.

"Then why do we waste time here? Run Haska!" Haska swung around and took off at a full out sprint with Ameliora on his heels. As she sprinted towards the clearing and the furious argument taking place, she couldn't help her mind wander to her dream. She had finally recalled the name of the spirit that forever battled Rangatha. She was named Morenia.

SIX

Ameliora and Haska raced back up the narrow path-way, running faster than she could remember ever having run before. Her paws seemed to barely touch the earth passing beneath her. Wind whistled lightly in her ears. Her eyes were wide and worry was creeping slowly back across her spine as the calm that Morenia gave her faded.

They burst through the small pathway and hurtled into the clearing, skidding to a stop. Both were still pant-ing as many pairs of eyes turned their way. Gathered in separate groups before them were the two packs. Levada, Romaus, Derment and Versitha sat in a close semicircle to one side. Directly across from them was the other pack, with the ash gray stranger from the previous morning sit-ting in the center of a loose circle of four other wolves.

She surveyed the other pack from her peripheral vision as she padded to Romaus. She dipped her head in greeting and joined Haska, sitting next to Derment and Versitha. Romaus turned upon seeing her join in the ranks of his pack and padded a few feet forward. He spoke in a loud voice that was steady despite his growing anger.

"Here, we have all gathered. Now say what it is you need to say so that we may settle this before anything gets violent." The other male's clear eyes surveyed Romaus through the short speech. Romaus sat after finished, hard eyes resting coldly on the obvious dominant male of the rival pack. The ash gray stranger stepped slowly forward from his pack, coming to stand a short distance from Romaus. They locked gazes and both pairs of eyes held a hard determination that sent tendrils of worry through her heart. The stranger spoke, in a quiet voice that none the less held a great deal of authority.

"I have no intention of engaging in any act of violent hostility with your pack unless absolutely necessary. My pack has already lost *one* member," he snarled out the last two words with a harsh glare fired at Versitha before continuing. "No need for more lives to be lost don't you think? You know whom, or rather what, we have come for. I have simply brought my pack to insure we do not leave until retribution is distributed either by you or by us." The ash gray speaker's face was devoid of emotion, but the clearing had taken on a quality of grimness that hung thickly in the air.

"May I at least know the names of those who accuse me?" Versitha's quiet voice floated through the clearing and both Romaus and the stranger turned startled gazes towards her. Her head was down and shoulders slightly hunched. Her tail was curled around her paws. Her eyes were raised to look imploringly at the stranger and suddenly she looked smaller than she ever had before. The stranger recovered and growled curtly.

"Armourn, Armourn is my name." He flicked his tale and a small tan female with darker brown highlights padded up to sit next to him. He continued, "This is my mate Clea, the mother of the pup *you* killed." She felt a growl rumble in her throat, Versitha's request had been a reasonable one. Yet this stranger, Armourn, still saw fit to torture her. She sent a piercing glare in Armourn's direction, either he didn't see it or ignored her because he flicked his tail once more. This time a larger heavy set male wolf stepped forward. His muscled form towered above most the other wolves and he had the look of a fighter from the numerous scars across his muzzle. He was a deep chocolate brown color and his deep amber eyes were set off against the dark brown coat. His height and size seemed large enough to block the light coming from behind him and she surveyed him warily. Armourn spoke again without turning to look at the chocolate brown male.

"This is Ontris." He let out a small genuine chuckle and a miniscule twinkle of mirth entered his eyes as he continued. "You can see why our pack would want him standing behind us if this meeting were to turn violent." Ontris gave a slight smile at this and bowed his head before stepping back to his place once more. Armourn again twitched his ashy tail and this time a pair of females stepped forward. She was momentarily stunned. These two wolves were exactly identical. They were more than simply sisters with the same coloring, they were exact replicas of one another. The two females seemed to be younger than Ontris, but older than Haska which meant they were somewhere around her age. They were both a medium gray shade with streaks of darker gray throughout their coats. They had brighter golden eyes. She even swore they blinked in sync. Identical twins were an oddity among wolves and she gazed at them long and hard, envying their uniqueness.

"And these two beauties," Armourn began fondly, "Are my daughters Elera and Forella." Elera and Forella dipped their heads, sad smiles playing across their muzzles as they stepped back to sit beside Ontris. They even seemed to move in unison and she wondered if they practiced it or were just hyper-aware of each other. Armourn swung his head as the fond expression melted from his features. He glared coldly at Versitha before speaking to her.

"Are you happy now that you know who has come for you? Can we not begin without more useless interruptions?" She sighed quietly, another rare glimpse of who Armourn really was had passed by in a second blink of an eye. The cold harsh personality that masked the grieving and caring father fell once more into place. Armourn took a threatening step forward, but an angry growl from Romaus stopped him. Armourn sat down, keeping his head held high proudly. Romaus spoke clearly in a strong voice.

"You must know by now that there is no way that Versitha shall be given up by us willingly. However, I implore you to let us as two packs discuss the issue at hand. May we not hear both sides of the story before we get to decision making? We may yet still avoid needless violence." Armourn growled quietly but nodded his head before returning an answer.

"You ask for both sides of the story, yet you know our positions. My pup was murdered and lays dead at the paws of one of your pack members. There is no more to discuss." Armourn's clear eyes flashed pain as he spoke, but for once a glance was not aimed hatefully at Versitha. Romaus spoke again.

"Is it at all possible that our Versitha is not responsible for this act? You have heard her story, as you were present for the ending but a day since. Did you take time to inspect the wounds on your pup and confirm it was killed by a wolf?" Romaus spoke calmly and rationally. She was surprised at the lack of aggression in his voice. The stony resolve in Armourn's eyes flickered hesitantly. He shook his head, speaking loudly again.

"Don't try and shift the blame. You're well aware of what your precious *Versitha*," he spat the name "has done." Romaus looked him in the eye and replied.

"So you have inspected the wounds?" Armourn shifted his paws.

"Well, no, but dead is dead! My pup is dead and your wolf's scent covered his body!"

Romaus stood, speaking firmly in a booming voice that held deserved authority. "I have this to say Armourn. You send two of your wolves, along with one of mine, to the body of your pup. They shall inspect the body carefully and report back. If the wolves are able to find evidence that your pup was killed by a wolf, Versitha is yours." There was a furious gasp and following snarl from Derment and Versitha's eyes flashed pain and then resignation. Romaus continued. "But if no such evidence is found, you and your pack leave us. You shall never threaten my family again." The deal was a fair one, more than favorable towards Armourn and his pack. Armourn flicked his ears, looking thoughtful. She almost sighed to herself. She had never met a wolf who expressed so many emotions as Armourn did. Finally Armourn reached a conclusion.

"Elera. Forella. You shall go to your brother and inspect him." The twins rose and padded to the side of the clearing, sitting and waiting patiently. Romaus nodded and turned to his pack, his eyes met hers.

"Ameliora, you shall accompany Elera and Forella." Her eyes widened and she stood up to join the twins. She was sure she looked as startled as she felt. Romaus had entrusted her with an important duty. Her observations would save Versitha – or doom her. Her paws shook nervously as the twins rose and the three of them crossed the clearing to the far path. They trotted quickly through the dark tunnel and disappeared, leaving the silent clearing behind them.

The twins padded quietly ahead of her. The silence began to feel uncomfortable and she longed for conversation. She spoke suddenly, and although she hadn't really thought about what she would say, she knew it was true.

"I'm sorry for your loss." The five words escaped through her parted jaws and the twins halted suddenly. One of them, she couldn't tell which one, turned around to face her. Puzzlement clouded her gaze as she questioned her.

"Your voice sounds genuine and I can see in your eyes that your words are meant well. Why do you give us your condolences? Our pack is here to take away one you love. There has never been a kind word exchanged between our packs." At this point the one twin left off and the other continued.

"Yet you reach out to us in our time of need." The she wolf finished quietly. Both wolves had turned and were now standing facing her on the narrow pathway. She looked down at her paws and then back up into the gentle eyes of the twins. She whispered her answer, as the silence of the dark woods seemed to demand.

"I believe you see beyond your own pain and loss. I believe you can see into reality, which is something Armourn cannot." She raised her head higher as she finished, "And I believe that you can help me stop the black thunderstorm of violence looming in our futures." The twins' eyes stayed clear as they turned their heads to look at each other. She watched them. She wondered briefly if they were speaking telepathically to each other, as twins were rumored to be able to do. They looked back at her and she saw a new tenderness in their gaze as well as determination.

"We shall always grieve the loss of our little brother, but you need not grieve a loss as well. Our only intention is to find the truth of what happened that morning, and if you can help us do that then we want you with us all the way." She blinked gratefully and the twins turned again, once more trotting down the pathway. As they ran the other twin called over her shoulder.

"By the way, I'm Forella and she's Elera. I know you can't tell us apart." There was laughter in Forella's voice as she called out to her. She felt a sheepish grin spread across her face as she took off down the trail with a renewed vigor.

After only a few more minutes of fast paced trotting down the dark trail, Elera and Forella slowed to a stop. She padded up behind them. Forella turned her head toward a small clearing that Ameliora had just noticed off to the side of the path. Elera was whining quietly and nuzzled her head into Forella's shoulder. She took a closer look in the clearing and she saw a small bundled shape. She gasped slightly, realizing that the pup was still there in the clearing. Suddenly the full weight of what had happened came down on her. Before seeing the body, the whole issue and events of the past days had seemed more of a bad dream than a reality. She felt a whine build in her throat, but she swallowed it back. This was not her place to grieve, but only to prevent future grief.

Elera and Forella seemed to take deep breathes before stepping lightly off the path and walking slowly and solemnly into the clearing. She followed them, hanging behind slightly. The two sisters approached the little bundle of fur. She watched Elera nudge the tiny body with her muzzle sadly, still whining. Forella pushed Elera gently away from the pup, leading her a little ways away. They sat close together and whispered quietly for a few minutes. She sat at a respectful distance, giving them their privacy.

Elera and Forella stood finally and she could see them pressing against each other for comfort. They padded back across the clearing to join her. She looked at them calmly, although pity darkened her gaze. Forella cleared her throat quietly and spoke to her.

"We're ready to start now if you would like." She simply nodded her head in reply, at a loss for words. The trio padded over to the pup. The stench coming from him made her want to crinkle her nose or turn away, but she ignored it for the twins' sake. She scanned the pitiful bundle of fur, searching for the fatal injuries.

Dried blood was encrusted in the pup's matted fur, making it hard for her to tell where the actual wounds had been. Small flies and other bugs were beginning to settle on the body to help with decomposing, which was only natural but was still of no comfort to Elera and Forella. Elera called out quietly. They looked up at Elera and then to where Elera's eyes were glued. She had found one of the wounds. Four puncture wounds in a small row and on the pup's opposite side, there was only one. Forella gasped slightly and said the word both Elera and Ameliora were thinking.

"Talons." They nodded and after a few minutes when they found an identical row of puncture wounds farther down the pup's side, the image of the owl began to appear in their minds. With the wounds laid out before them, it was easy to see how an owl would have plunged down, sinking it's talons deep into the pup's side to pick him up, leaving deep punctures. She took a deep breath before turning to Elera and Forella,

"If Versitha's story is true, we should be able to find scratches and peck marks from the pup struggling against the owl." Elera and Forella nodded slowly before going back to their search. She noticed that neither of them had looked at the pup's head and she stood quietly and padded around the body towards the small muzzle and ears sticking out from the rancid body. She nudged the head carefully, rolling it to the side so she could check it for peck marks and scrapes. Upon seeing the face of the pup, She recoiled in surprise. Elera and Forella lifted their heads to flash identical puzzled gazes at her. Her face expressed a horror unfit for words and the worried sisters quickly circled around to stand by her. Her gaze were glued on the pup's face. Elera and Forella slowly dropped their gazes to where hers was aimed.

The clearing fell silent as Elera and Forella saw what had made her so disturbed. The pup's face was undistinguishable. Long jagged cuts and scratches covered almost every inch of the matted fur. The rotting flesh was clearly visible in the obviously mortal wounds. Worst of all were the smaller holes near the pup's skull. They were a different shape than the talon puncture wounds from before and Elera blanched upon realizing what they were. The wolves could clearly see where the sharp cruel beak of the winged predator had dove in again and again with deadly force. Elera and Forella backed away from the carcass, eyes still wide with terror and agony at seeing their brother as such. She tore her eyes away from the destruction before her and turned to Elera and Forella. The two sisters were standing close together, no words passed between them. Somehow she knew words would never comfort them after what they had seen. She looked quickly back at the mutilated face of the pup and saw something that she hadn't before. Lying half hidden under the pup's muzzle was a single tawny spotted feather. She bent her head hesitantly down and grabbed the feather gently in her teeth. She was careful not to bite down or harm the perfect feather in her strong jaws. Forella looked up briefly, her eyes meeting Ameliora's for a quick second before darting back to the ground and her paws. Forella spoke in barely a whisper, although in the silence of the clearing it echoed like thunder.

"We have our proof. Let us leave this place and go back to our packs. There is nothing more to be gained here." They nodded their heads in agreement and the three set off across the clearing. None of them took a last glance at the small body, not wishing to look upon it and further encase it in their memories. They walked three abreast down the narrow trail, pressing against each other for a physical steadiness that could do nothing to calm their ravaged nerves. She reflected on how close she suddenly felt to the twins, despite having known them for so short a time. Elera was padding in between Ameliora and Forella. She suddenly found a difference in the identical twins. Forella was the stronger one; Elera would always be emotionally weaker than her sister. This was why Forella did most of the talking that day. She glanced sideways at the silent Elera, feeling somehow that she knew her much more intimately than she had minutes ago.

The three padded silently together back up the dark trail and finally emerged into the clearing once more. The packs were as they had left them. The two small family circles stood apart from each other, whispered conversations disturbed the almost complete silence. Levada had been watching the dark doorway and upon seeing Ameliora and the twins emerge, she nodded toward Romaus. Romaus turned his head slightly, nodding towards her. She gave no reply and simply waited with Elera and Forella. The feather was still held carefully in her jaws, although it seemed as though none had noticed it quite yet. Romaus stood slowly, seeming older than he had days earlier. She could see silvery hairs starting to sprout around his muzzle, although his eyes retained the same discipline as always.

Romaus called softly to Armourn. Armourn's ears perked at hearing his name and turned to face Romaus, noticing the returned wolves for the first time. A sad smile crossed his lips as he looked at Elera and Forella.

"We shall have your word then. Elera and Forella, what is your testimony?" A mingled look of hope and apprehension danced in his eyes as he spoke. He was both hopeful for the justice to be done, yet afraid of what the twins had found. Elera and Forella had walked slowly, although with a definite purpose, back to Armourn. They began to whisper to him and she could see Ontris and Clea straining to hear their words. Armourn shook his head at them, signaling them to be quiet. He spoke out.

"You need not tell only me, this is between both packs. Please, if you would, tell us all what you have seen." Elera began to shake slightly and Forella said something to her that she couldn't hear. Elera sat quietly, head down and still shaking. Forella walked to the middle ground between where the two packs were gathered. Her head was held high despite the events transpired that day. She felt a sudden rush of pride and admiration for the brave she-wolf. Forella sat between the two, glancing at both Romaus and Armourn before beginning.

"Elera, Ameliora and I have been to see my fallen brother. We inspected his," Forella paused here, taking a breath and glancing towards Armourn with something like an apology in her eyes. "Body, and we have drawn our conclusion. He was killed by an owl." She said that last words loudly and with a clarity that expressed her strength of character. She stepped back, walking to sit once more beside her still distraught sister. Armourn was silent; his face expressing shock. His eyes betrayed the wavering of his convictions. She realized Armourn would need physical proof before he would ever concede. She remembered the feather in her mouth and padded respectfully over to Armourn with her head and tail low. She approached him cautiously, not looking at him as she laid the feather carefully at his paws. She backed away, turning to trot quickly back to her own pack and to sit beside Haska and Versitha. She chanced a rapid analysis of Armourn's eyes and she saw what she knew they all needed. His conviction was broken. Armourn was looking down at the tawny killer's feather with some mixture of grief and disbelief. Ontris and Clea had caught sight of the feather as well. Ontris' unchanging stony face showed no signs of reaction. Clea's face was a swirl of the same grief as Armourn, but her face also showed her acceptance of what was.

Her pack was silent. Derment had a look not unlike triumph on his face, a small smile on his muzzle. Haska's ears were twitching and a confused look was plastered on his young face. She sighed, understanding how much the young wolf still had to understand about pack life. Versitha was sitting placidly beside Derment and although some of the sorrow had faded slightly from her features and she was visibly more relaxed, her eyes were still glued nervously on Armourn. Romaus was sitting stone still, back straight and head high. The flash of weakness or age that she had seen earlier seemed to have melted away as she gazed at her pack leader and father. He might just have saved both packs from the surely vicious confrontation. Levada sat next to him, her face as expressionless as ever and radiating the same calmness and control she always did. Her silvery pelt was ruffled as a light breeze blew through the clearing. She couldn't help but think of her mother as majestic. Even if Levada had never given Ameliora the same motherly love that Versitha had, she loved her all the same. In a way, she understood Levada's character and why the love her children sought had never been hers to outwardly give. Her thoughts were interrupted by Armourn.

"I'm sorry." He began as he took a small step forward. His face expressed his genuine regrets as well as a new sense of relief. It was much like the look of relief Clea had. The two parents were relieved to finally understand the consequences and events that had taken their son from them. They no longer felt they needed retribution. Armourn continued, "I'm sorry for the sadness we have brought to your family. I'm sorry for the accusations I made against you, Versitha. Most of all, I am sorry I let my own sorrow cloud the good judgment I have always prided myself on." Clea stepped forward, nuzzling her mate as he finished his short speech. Romaus dipped his head in acknowledgement of Armourn's words before he answered.

"I too know what it is like to lose a pup." The sadness in Romaus' voice startled her briefly and she realized he was talking about Tharamena. She had never thought of Romaus as grieving over Tharamena, but it made sense. Romaus was very private with his emotions and thoughts. She snapped her attention back as Romaus continued. "Our condolences are with you in this hard time. May you know that our forgiveness returns with you and your pack beyond these borders. You shall find no grudges held by us." Armourn smiled gratefully at Romaus' words and he looked up to respond once more.

"Our time in your territories has long since come to an end. My pack and I shall be on our way, but just because boundary lines end doesn't mean our gratitude towards you does. You have helped us gain acceptance to what has happened." Armourn turned then, flicking his tail lightly. The rest of his pack gathered around him as they set off at a brisk trot towards the dark pathway. Her whole pack watched them vanish down the trail. Romaus' words suddenly couldn't have been truer, for the wolves found that no hardness was held in their hearts. She found herself hoping to meet up with Elera and Forella again, already missing the company of the twins.

After the last bushy tail was gone and paw steps had faded into silence, it was as if the spell holding the clearing to solemnity was broken. The pack gathered as one into a licking, nuzzling and yipping mass of relief and joy. Haska seemed to have given up understanding and was simply expressing his joy over the safety of Versitha. Versitha was surrounded on all sides and for the first time in many days, she saw a small smile play across her russet brown muzzle. The individual wolves began to disperse throughout the clearing, curling up in various positions. She belatedly looked at the darkening sky, dusk had come and the pack was settling down for a well deserved sleep. She only wished she had the certainty of an undisturbed slumber.

SEVEN

As darkness descended and the faint light of faraway stars began to light up the sky, Ameliora began to feel restless. Her eyelids were drooping and her paws ached, yet her fear of what she might find within her own dreams kept her from drifting into slumber's sweet embrace. She shifted slightly, being careful not to disturb Haska whose flank was rising and falling as he slept next to her. She raised her head, surveying the midnight clearing. Although the moon shone bright in the sunless sky, the clearing was still pitch black. The lack of light, however, made no difference to her. Her amber eyes glinted as she surveyed the clearing, her night vision illuminating the blackness.

On the far side of the clearing lying under one of the pine trees on the edge of the forest, she could see the silent forms of Levada and Romaus. They were nestled together in the soft grass, their pelts stirred infrequently when a cool night breeze blew by. They were lying side by side and Levada's gray muzzle resting on Romaus' deep charcoal back shone like the stars in the night sky above her. Both wolves looked peaceful in their sleep and for all Romaus and Levada's privacy concerning their feelings; nothing could hide the obvious love between them.

She smiled to herself as she turned her gaze away from her slumbering parents. She instead looked down at Haska beside her. She longed to lean her head down and nuzzle him gently like a pup, but would hate to awaken him. His youth was evident in his face, as his eyes had yet to develop the aged look of having seen much of the world. His muzzle and brows lacked the tell-tale worry lines of an older wolf. Most of all, even in his sleep Haska seemed to have an almost carefree smile plastered on his features. She longed to wake him and ask to know what he dreamed of that kept him smiling through the long night. Instead she settled herself with a quick lick to the top of his head before shifting her gaze elsewhere.

Her eyes widened slightly in surprise when she was finally able to find Derment. She had checked his usual secluded sleeping spot, which was uncharacteristically empty. She had scanned the small clearing, almost missing his dark form curled protectively around Versitha. She looked swiftly around her, she hadn't noticed that Versitha wasn't sleeping in her usual spot on Haska's other side. She turned back to look at Versitha and Derment, feeling her puzzlement melt away and small trickles of joy seep into her heart. For so long Derment had been alone, by choice separating himself from the love of his pack mates. It seemed to her as if Derment had finally found a connection with Versitha, since she had been through much the same ordeal he had undergone as a pup. A grin spread across her light gray muzzle as she felt a sense of calm enter her.

Her heavy eyelids began to droop once more and the weight she felt in her paws was growing, but instead of feeling the need to pace or the fear that accompanied thoughts of sleep, she found she was able to lay her head gently on her paws. She wrapped her tail around her paws and muzzle, burying her head in the warmth of her own fur. She blinked sleepily once before drifting peacefully into slumber's waiting arms.

She was unsurprised to find herself blinking her eyes open and feel the coldness of Haska's absence beside her. Somehow, although she knew she had entered her persistent nightmare once more, the memory of her glowing savior calmed her. She raised her head cautiously, peering around the familiar nightmarishly black woods. The silence that once sent chills down her spine and her heart racing now seemed almost welcome. The whole environment still had the overall feeling of terror and of a dark lurking presence. The fear still dug sharp claws into her heart, but instead of reacting and taking flight from the dark forest, she was able to control her fear. She stood, stretching her heavy paws that felt as if they still needed a good night's sleep. She smiled to herself, they probably did since she hadn't had a good rest in weeks.

She swung her head to survey her black surroundings. She scanned the woods searching for any sign of her bright savior from the night before, and at the same time praying the dark shadow of Rangatha wouldn't leap out at her. The forest was silent, she could see no trace of either entity. She smiled to herself, feeling braver. If Morenia hadn't come, that meant Rangatha wasn't near. She held her head higher and lifted a paw to take a step forward. However, she froze in place upon hearing a bone chilling voice directly behind her.

"Good evening, fair Ameliora." She turned slowly to see who had addressed her, although she already knew who the voice belonged to. Sitting half in the shadows and half out of them, hidden by an overhanging branch, was the shape of a wolf. The horrifyingly familiar almost black coat sent shivers down her spine. She lifted her eyes to its face, looking directly in the black pits that functioned as eyes. All her bravery and courage melted away as she looked into the pupil-less eyes. It was as if every good feeling she had ever had had been sucked out of her and hidden within those black pools. The wolf, who she recognized as Rangatha, said nothing more. He sat still and expressionless, his eyes locked with hers. She found she couldn't look away; she was being drawn in and drowned in the depths black despair and hopelessness of Rangatha's eyes.

A chuckle came from the shadowed shape. No breath stirred the fallen leaves in the dead forest and it was as if Rangatha didn't breathe at all. The quiet laughter felt like ice slowly freezing over her heart. Whereas most laughter expressed a sense of joy; she heard only malice. The voice spoke again, coming from the unmoving form of Rangatha.

"Where might your bright protector be on a night such as this? You never know what malignant shadows are lurking under drooping forest branches." Rangatha's muzzle twitched as he spoke and she realized a sort of twisted smile was spreading across his face. She took a deep breath, trying to gather up what little courage she had left in her quaking body.

"I need no protector Rangatha." Saying his name out loud seemed almost taboo and the moment of surprise from Rangatha himself gave her strength as she continued. "You cannot truly hurt me. No matter what destruction you rain upon me in this world, you are not mortal and I am. I am stronger than you." The shaking in her paws seemed to lessen as she spoke, standing up against the shadowed wolf. If she had expected to win a battle through her short speech, she was disastrously disappointed. Rangatha chuckled again and a morbid merriment glowed in the black pools of his eyes.

"You *genuinely* think I can't hurt you!" A terrible grin had spread across his muzzle and his pelt was quivering with excitement. "You think I send you back to wakefulness unscathed because I am unable to change anything outside this world, don't you? Sorry to disappoint you, fair Ameliora, but I am just as deadly outside your thoughts as inside them." The strength melted from her bones once more and every ounce of bravado she had once had was gone. Rangatha's poisoned words stung and wrapped around her mind, planting seeds of doubt deep within her.

Rangatha stood silently and she was stunned at his size. The shadowy gray-black wolf was massive. His broad shoulders and heavily muscled body radiated strength and power. He padded quietly towards her; even the leaves his large paws crushed made no sound. She looked up at him, realizing for the first time how he towered over her. She unconsciously shrank away from the grinning wolf, her ears back and her body low to the ground. He only continued smiling as he walked in slow tight circles around her. She could feel his fur brushing against her and his tail flicking her lightly. She was paralyzed, completely under Rangatha's control. Rangatha's voice lowered to a whisper, the horrible merriment in his voice tinged with malice.

"Do you fear me now Ameliora? I bet you wish your bright protector was here now to keep me at bay, don't you? Go on, call for her. See if she comes to save you now. Although truth be told, I would much prefer she left you here with me for a while." Rangatha stopped circling, standing directly in front of her once more. He was looking down on her. He suddenly seemed to grow tired of the little game he was playing with her as his grin faded and his tail began to lash from side to side impatiently. His paw lashed out at her before she could react and struck her muzzle. She cried out, yelping in pain as she felt the sharp claws slash deep cuts in her muzzle. She stumbled back, falling to her side from the power behind the sudden blow. Rangatha was shouting at her, his words like thunder against her ears.

"Call for her, Ameliora! Call for her! See if she comes for you!" Rangatha's fury came from nowhere, but took complete control of him. She struggled to her paws, feeling the warm sticky feeling of blood running down her muzzle from where Rangatha had struck her. Her eyes held defiance as she steadied herself and lifted her gaze to Rangatha's boiling black pits. She clamped her jaws firmly shut, refusing to cry out for Morenia. This infuriated Rangatha further and he lunged at her. She steeled herself for the blow, tensing her muscles and squeezing her eyes tightly shut.

A whoosh of air hit her, but not the searing pain she was expecting. A startled bark echoed in the clearing and she blinked open her eyes, just as a familiar bright white light flashed passed her and slammed into the lunging form of Rangatha. The startled bark had come from Rangatha as the materializing shape of Morenia had knocked him away from her mid-lunge. Rangatha's body made a loud thumping sound as he crashed to the ground, but after moments he was standing again. Furious growls rumbled deep in his throat and his lips were pulled out in a vicious growl. His fur was standing out completely on end and his ears were back as his pelt bristled. His already massive body seemed to double in size with his fur standing on end.

Morenia stood facing him, her pure white body radiating light. She was flooded with relief at seeing Morenia. Morenia was growling too, although not as loudly as Rangatha. Her calm words, although laced with a threat, dominated the silent forest.

"You dare attack her once more Rangatha? You think I would leave her alone with you. I warned you to stay away from her." She took a small step forward, her white eyes drilling into Rangatha. Rangatha stood facing her, not reacting to Morenia's challenge. His snarling had subsided partially and he replied with a laughing malice in his voice.

"You left her here alone, I was simply watching over her until you arrived." He threw a glance her way and lifted a paw, the same paw he had used to strike her, and licked the dark crimson liquid off of it. She shrank back, glancing at Morenia in terror. Morenia growled angrily before swiping a paw at Rangatha. Just as she had been thrown from Rangatha's blow, Rangatha stumbled and fell snarling in pain. Morenia's claws had left cuts identical to the still bleeding ones in her face. She watched with dread as Rangatha's injuries began to heal and dissolve away, leaving his face looking as if he had never been touched. Surprise shone in her eyes as she watched Rangatha's wounds disappear. Rangatha noticed her surprised and chuckled darkly.

"You said it yourself, fair Ameliora. I am not like you. I am not mortal." His face was now unmarked and not a trace of the vicious scratches from Morenia remained. She took a frightened step away from Rangatha, momentarily doubting Morenia's ability to protect her. Morenia, although her eyes were still glaring angrily at Rangatha, spoke without turning her head.

"Do not back away. What he has done to you cannot be repeated now. His wounds may heal quicker than yours will, but he has constraints. Even now his power is weakening due to my presence." An angry growl erupted from Rangatha upon hearing Morenia talk of weakness. her eyes flashed between Morenia's steadily glowing form and Rangatha's dark shadowy body. She noticed a change in Rangatha, and Morenia's words began to make sense. Rangatha's muscled outline was growing indistinct and the obvious lines of his body were becoming blurred. A small smile spread across Morenia's muzzle and her quiet growling subsided as triumph lit up in her eyes. Rangatha only seemed to get angrier and angrier, his whole body shaking with fury. He spun away from Morenia, turning his back on both females and began to pad away. His shoulders were hunched in frustration and as his near black body melted into the midnight forest, howled words reached her ears.

"You cannot be everywhere at once, Morenia, and it is in those places you are not that I shall be. I shall find you, Ameliora, when protection is not yours to be had. A time is coming when my power shall exceed yours, and then shall you quake in fear of me." His words faded and silence descended in the woods. She turned away from the wall of towering pine branches and faced Morenia apprehensively. All traces of irritation and anger in the glowing white wolf had disappeared and her usual placid calmness was radiating from her once more. She felt newly wary of her bright protector after having seen the fiercely aggressive side of Morenia. Confusion muddled her thoughts as she attempted to straighten out what had just transpired. Morenia turned away from the dark green brown wall the night forest and fixed her calm white gaze on her.

"He's right, you know. There are only so many places my spiritual form can be at one time." These were not the comforting words she had longed to hear and her hopes sank again. The blood was starting to dry on her face and the matted fur felt stiff on her face. She protested weakly,

"What about what you just did? What was it that was happening to him? He was so strong and muscular and then you came and it was as if he began to…dissolve." She spoke slowly, mentally trying to wrap her mind around the impossible concept. Morenia was nodding her head patiently, her eyes still steadily on her.

"Ameliora, what do you know of the old legends?" She was puzzled at the question and thought back to all the old stories that Versitha had told when she was a pup, and later again for Haska. She looked at Morenia quizzically as she replied,

"Versitha used to tell me the old legends when I was a pup. She must have told every one of them at least three times." Morenia only continued nodding as she probed further,

"What of the legend of Rangatha and," Morenia paused before continuing, "Morenia. When was the last time you heard it? How much of it do you recall?" She thought back to the legend and remembered Versitha telling the tale days earlier on the pack hunt.

"Versitha was telling that one to us a few days ago. She told about Sararo and how he bonded with Nithil… but she never finished it." Her face fell slightly remembering what had interrupted the story and the image of Versitha's vanishing form flashed across her thoughts. Morenia smiled grimly.

"Then you do not remember the rest I assume? I don't have the time to tell you the full story now, daylight is approaching quickly and you must return to wakefulness at some point. Here is what I can tell you. As you must have guessed, that legend in particular is truer than most. I am all that remains of the Morenia that once was, just as Rangatha is the spiritual remainder of the Rangatha in the legend. Unfortunately, that story is quite accurate."

Morenia began to tell of how generations ago, when Sararo and Nithil became Rangatha, terror reigned over the wolf world. No one could stop the killing and destruction Rangatha spread, his power was just too much. Packs fell and none withstood his rule. The wolves called to the sun and moon for a savior to come to them. Just as Nithil had been the entity of all evil in the mortal world, so was Karena the being of all purity. The wolves knew that only the bonding of a mortal wolf with Karena would create a being powerful enough to stop Rangatha, but they feared the bond. They realized that after seeing Rangatha, whoever bonded with Karena would cease to be themselves and instead become an entirely new entity. The wolves searched for the perfect host among themselves. The host had to be pure and willing to sacrifice themselves, or the bonding could go awry.

It was when the wolves had given up hope, that a young she-wolf named Joseliana stepped forward. The young wolf had not yet reached dispersing age, but had great love for her family. She feared Rangatha's harming them and so gave herself. On a full moon, she became one with Karena and it was similar to the birth of Rangatha in that Joseliana and Karena ceased to be separated individuals and together became Morenia. Morenia had a pure snowy coat that shone brightly and pupil-less glowing white eyes. When Rangatha heard of the newly formed Morenia he was furious, howling his anger nightly in a summons to Morenia. Dutifully, Morenia went to him. Packs far and wide gathered to watch the fight between the two of them; one that they all knew would be legendary.

The two fought in broad daylight, in a pine clearing seemingly devoid of life. The competitors were evenly matched and neither could gain the upper hand. The fight soon moved outside the clearing as the two obliviously moved through the woods; trampling delicate ferns and kicking up clods of dirt. They reached the edge of a steep precipice and Morenia danced along the edge, careful not to lose her balance. Morenia, as well as Rangatha, was tireless due to her only being half mortal and feared the battle going on indefinitely. She circled around Rangatha, slowly maneuvering his back to the precipice. As he stood snarling at her with his fur bristling and bunching his muscles to spring at her once more, Morenia lunged at him. She barreled her full strength and weight against him. Rangatha was caught off guard and they toppled in a tangled heap over the edge. Rangatha howled as he fell, while Morenia was silent already having accepted her fate. Rangatha continued his furious growling until a loud thump forever silenced him.

The wolves who had been present peered over the side, looking down at the two broken bodies lying at the rocky bottom below them. Purest white and darkest gray forever entangled in each other. They now rested silently. The wolves sent out their calls of mourning, calling packs far and wide to mourn the death of their selfless savior. Morenia was forever remembered and her name honored. Although over time, she grew from historical figure into spiritual legend and some forgot she had ever truly existed. The raging battle was believed to have ended with the deaths of Rangatha and Morenia, but it was not so.

Being that Rangatha and Morenia were not quite mortal, nor completely spirit, they only died in one aspect. Morenia killed Rangatha's mortal body and sacrificed her own in the process, but their spiritual forms were as alive as ever. Rangatha found that, like Nithil, he could no longer affect the living world being that he was not mortal. He realized that to be able to gain power over the living world once more, he would have to perform the same bonding ceremony that had created him. He needed a willing host. Morenia's battle was not over, for now she fought to keep him from returning.

"Thus we forever battle in the kingdom of the never dying, across generations and through dreams. We battle for your world, a balance must be kept." Morenia finished her story, her voice fading away as she looked at her. She sat, still processing what had been told to her and something clicked. She looked up at Morenia in bewilderment.

"If you are *the* Morenia and he is *the* Rangatha, why am I involved in this?" She was almost afraid to ask. If the centuries long battle between Rangatha and Morenia was still raging so long after their mortal deaths, what possible affect could she have on them? Morenia looked as if she might respond but her body turned stiff. She froze too as a reflection, frantically searching for whatever danger had set Morenia off. Morenia's eyes were wide open but unseeing and her rigid muscles unmoving. She opened her mouth, speaking in a voice that was somehow hers and not hers.

"When Rangatha breaks from his prison,
And no longer is kept bound.
Then shall one dead be risen
And then shall the lost again be found.
A loss that turned all gaity black
And drowned a brother in pain.
Returns to beckon the torturer back,
Enveloping all in sorrow's chain.
Hidden amongst the quiet obscure,
Are the four who will depart.
But oh the trials they will endure,
Only three return with a story to impart.
One shall be the Unspoken.
Known to none but Four.
Two was always the Broken,
Able to laugh no more.
Three will be the Unknown,
Bear neither truth nor reason.
At the last minute it will be shown,
Always destined to end a season.
And Four is but the Messenger,
A high purpose all its own.
To be only ever the Messenger,
And to her the pathway shown.
Hope lives on to breathe anew,
Life into those with hearts unbound.
One survives who always knew,
Revealer of secrets however found.

Good and Evil a battle shall rage,
And two shall die as to portend.
Remember this through the coming age,
The wolves who watched Rangatha's end."

The vacant expression melted slowly from Morenia's muzzle and eyes and her body relaxed once more. Ameliora was staring in astonishment at Morenia, unsure of what had happened but convinced it was important. Morenia appeared to be quietly returning to reality, or whatever reality was to be found in her dreams. Morenia's eyes completely cleared and she gazed once more at her.

"Once more it is time for me to bid you farewell. Travel in safety, Ameliora, morning comes to fetch you from me." Morenia turned and dissolves into a mist that blew lightly threw the dark woods to disappear in the surrounding blackness. She began to open her muzzle to call Morenia back to explain her strange words, but she was jerked out of her slumbering reality and back into a shining new day.

∾
EIGHT

The soft fur of Versitha's muzzle buried itself into Ameliora's side. Her eyes blinked open and she raised her head staring bleary-eyed around the clearing. Exhaustion settled in her paws once more and she rose stiffly, regretting her recurrent loss of sleep. She stretched, standing on sore paws and yawning as she glanced around the awakening clearing. She turned to face Versitha whose bright eyes and cheerful smile filled her with joy as always. It was a relief to see the light of hope in Versitha's eyes. Versitha's momentarily bright eyes turned dark with concern and a puzzled expression transformed her.

"Ameliora, what happened to your muzzle?" Versitha was staring in confusion at her. She tilted her head quizzically at Versitha.

"What do you mean Versitha?" Versitha looked concerned and flicked her tail towards her, beckoning her to follow. She padded hesitantly after Versitha across the clearing. Versitha glanced back at her over her shoulder, her eyes clouded with worry and puzzlement, before disappearing down the stream trail. She followed, walking cautiously along the familiar peaceful pathway. The two padded down the trail in silence, even as the forest around then began to murmur with the sounds of its smaller inhabitants awakening. Birds began their morning songs as springtime sunshine shone through the gaps in the overhanging branches. She twitched and perked her ears as carefree twitters and tweets echoed through the quiet forest. She was lost in thought and hardly noticed when Versitha came to a halt beside the river bank. Versitha turned her gaze on her again, flicking her tail to motion her over to the stream bank. She approached hesitantly, still unsure of the source of Versitha's confusion. Versitha motioned towards the water and she bent her head, staring at her own reflection in the glassy calm of the flowing creek.

Three parallel scratches stood out against her otherwise unblemished face. The cuts appeared to have been a day or two old, as new skin was already growing over them and the wounds had closed up. They were not so deep as to leave scars, but anyone who even glanced towards her could easily spot the injury. Ameliora gaped at herself in horror as realization dawned on her. Although the wounds may have looked old and wouldn't scar, she knew their source. Rangatha had done what he had only hinted at. He had hurt her in both dream and reality. She shook as she reviewed every aspect of the previous night's dream.

She clearly remembered standing tall against Rangatha and then his paw lashing out at her. She shook harder upon imagining the true force and brute strength Rangatha must have put behind his blow to hurt her as he did. Versitha was still peering anxiously at her and occasional worried whines slipped from her slightly parted jaws. She thought rapidly, attempting to come up with a reason why she had these scratches and where she had gotten them. She tore her eyes away from the river and her own rippling reflection to look Versitha in the eyes. She plastered a fake grin on her face and hoped a carefree twinkle lit her otherwise bleak gaze. She let her tongue hang foolishly out of her falsely grinning jaws.

"You were talking about that?" She chuckled in what she hoped was a sincere voice. "I thought something terrible had happened!" She continued chuckling with false mirth as Versitha's countenance slowly changed from worry to disbelief to reproach. She looked her hard in the eye and she gazed back while still maintaining her faltering smile.

"Well Ameliora, since you are evidently unsurprised by the injuries that just appeared on your muzzle, perhaps you could let me in on the joke?" Versitha's gaze was darkened by distrust and skepticism was written clearly in her facial lines.

"There is no joke Versitha. You made me think something terrible had happened, but nothing has. These scratches are nothing, I promise you that." She stumbled slightly as she said 'promise' and prayed that Versitha wouldn't notice. The look of skepticism on Versitha's face was faltering as she spoke again.

"Well where did you get them from? I don't remember seeing them yesterday. Even if you did get them yesterday, how are they healing so quickly?" Doubt still lingered in Versitha's eyes, but she was slowly convincing her.

"I went on a walk and scratched myself on a thorn bush trying to duck underneath it. Versitha, it's been a rough couple of days. It would make sense if you don't remember everything that's happened. It was so minor." She felt guilty for so blatantly lying to Versitha, but the need for secrecy pushed her to stray from the truth. Brief pain mingled with acceptance as Versitha drank in her faltering lie. Pain pierced her heart as Versitha believed her, but she kept her foolish grin on her muzzle. She pressed past Versitha and lightly flicked the older she-wolf with her tail as she started back up the path.

Versitha seemed to hesitate slightly but followed her back towards the pack clearing. Soon enough the packmates were talking about whatever it was that came to mind and the smile on her face became genuine. They walked side by side up the narrow trail until they stepped into the overcast clearing. Neither of them had noticed the threatening dark clouds hovering over the horizon earlier that morning and now the sky was covered in the bringers of future rain. She lifted her muzzle and glared at the clouds. The somewhat unseasonable spring warmth seemed to have come to an end.

Romaus stood upon seeing them enter the clearing. He had been sitting and quietly discussing something with

Levada, but evidently the conversation had ended. Romaus padded to the center of the clearing and gave a short bark. Haska bounded over from where he had been harassing a squirrel in one of the tall pines. Derment slowly stood from where he had been laying alone and shook his fur out before padding to join Romaus. They padded over from the entrance to the stream trail and stood around Romaus. The pack was assembled in a rough semicircle around Romaus. Her brow furrowed in confusion as she looked around and noticed Levada's absence.

Levada was still sitting serenely under the same pine with her eyes closed. She looked exhausted and her mind swirled in puzzlement. Romaus growled quietly in her direction and she reluctantly snapped her attention back to what he was saying. The pack was going on another hunt. She nodded her head; it had been days since the wolves had had a decent meal. Romaus padded away without another word and disappeared down the middle trail. Four heads simultaneously turned to glance questioningly at Levada's still unmoving form. They looked at each other, all asking the same question. Wasn't Levada coming on the hunt? None of them had moved to follow Romaus; they were still waiting for Levada to take the second lead position. Romaus' black pelt appeared once more out of the dense woodland trail and a rumbling growl distracted the four wolves from Levada.

"She isn't coming and unless you wish to go hungry tonight, you will follow me now." Romaus' irritation was obvious through his clenched jaw and deep growl. The four wolves threw one or two subtle questioning glances at each other before trotting quickly over to join Romaus. Romaus' tail was flicking back and forth with frustration and she wondered if it was a hint of worry she saw in his smoldering eyes. Romaus turned around, his shoulder stiff and padded once more down the trail. Derment reluctantly followed him and after him came Versitha, Ameliora and finally Haska. The young wolves' minds were consumed with questions about Levada. Was she alright? Was she hurt? What was she going to do while the pack was away? Why was Romaus so irritated? Did Romaus know what was wrong? These swirling thoughts distracted the young wolves as they followed Romaus. Silence descended among the pack-mates and even the busy life sounds of the smaller forest creatures seemed to ring on deaf ears.

The pack was still trotting silently down the trail to the meadow when a small sound came from the back of the line. Haska had quietly cleared his throat and now he was standing looking at Romaus nervously. Romaus had halt-ed and now the rest of the pack had stopped and turned to face Haska. Haska's voice shook slightly,

"Romaus, why isn't Levada with us?" Romaus' eyes were hard as he stared back at Haska. They looked at each other and then back and forth in between Haska and Romaus. The agitation was spreading and all of the wolves were jumpy. Romaus' eyes softened slightly and he took a deep breath before answering Haska's hesitant query.

"Levada isn't here because she can't be. She won't be assisting us today. She is not injured or ill." Romaus answered calmly and simply. Haska raised his eyes from his paws and watched Romaus. All four of the younger wolves knew there was something Romaus wasn't telling them, but knowing that Levada was unharmed was enough for the moment. The pack continued down the trail, eventually emerging into the meadow. Nothing much had changed in the placid grasses since the pack's last visit. The swaying green blades seemed a little less bright under the overcast sky. The wide valley between the two meadow covered hills was strangely empty and she stared down at the emptiness curiously.

Romaus' muzzle was lifted towards the clouds as he breathed in deeply and swung his head in an eastward direction.

"The herd has moved, so we're going to have more work than we bargained for." The younger wolves simply nodded their heads in agreement and followed Romaus as he set off eastward at a quick paced trot. Every so often, Romaus would lower his muzzle to the earth as he checked the trail the elk had taken. The pack followed a direct course; evidence of the herd's travels was all too obvious to stalking predators. Trampled grass and patches of bitten down blades marked where the herd had stopped to eat and replenish strength. There were patches where ferns and occasional bushes were beaten down and lay limp on the ground. She smiled to herself as she surveyed the damage and the clear trail the foolish prey had left for them to follow.

The sharp scent of elk grew steadily stronger as Romaus led the way to the meandering herd. The pace quickened as the excitement of the hunt began to mount. Pretty soon, bellows and various grunts could be heard from afar. Her heart raced happily as she listened to the careless prey shouting their existence to the world. The pack crested one of the many foothills and were greeted at last by the sight of the herd grazing obliviously below them. Romaus sat, looking down on the elk and panting as he caught his breath from the effort of tracking the elk so far. The pack settled down, the small group was content to rest and catch their breath while keeping a watchful eye on the fickle herd.

Romaus got to his feet eventually, stretching and yawning as he did so. She hauled herself up off the ground where she had been lying comfortably and looked down once more on the herd. They had moved a little farther away, but not so far as to be a hassle. Romaus' sharp bark brought her thoughts back to the hunt and her paws itched with the urge to run into the surging mass of moving prey. She turned her bright yellow eyes to Romaus and watched him intently, waiting for the signal. His tail flicked slightly and with a grin, Versitha ran off. Her lean russet body was clearly visible and she watched as Versitha disappeared into the herd. Versitha had slowed to a quick walk so as not to disturb the feeding elk. She only caught glimpses of her red brown fur as she flashed in between the thick legs and arching antlers.

A familiar disturbance came from within the herd as Versitha chose their target and she leaned forward in anticipation, her eyes glued to the shifting bodies. The end of Haska's tail twitched as he waited impatiently for the moment when he could take off after the elk. Derment was making an attempt to seem calm, glancing at Romaus from the sides of his eyes every few seconds. His stiffness gave him away, the rigidness was on obvious tell of the anticipation that raced through his veins. She smiled to herself as she looked at him and watched his attempts to display the serenity that Romaus had as he sat looking down on the prey. Self-control like Levada and Romaus possessed came with age, and no matter how mature Derment thought he was, his three years of age put him far from wisdom. A quiet chuckle escaped through her closed jaws as she attempted to stifle them. Derment flicked his ears, but no other response came.

She shifted her gaze back down to the elk; Versitha was taking longer than usual. Derment's fragile appearance of self control was cracking with the onslaught of impatience. Haska was pacing anxiously. A sudden stillness entered the herd and the pack leaned forward expectantly and out from the seething masses came a stream of russet brown. Versitha was in her prime, her paws flying over the soft meadow grasses and her tongue lolling gently from her mouth as she occasionally snapped at the fleeing elk's back legs. The rapid bark from Romaus was completely unneeded at the pack took off after Versitha, adrenaline giving them speed and ferociousness. Pure animal growls and snarls were coming from the pack as they lost their calm personalities in the thrill of the hunt. Instinct took over as they assembled behind her to chase the chosen prey.

Versitha was panting hard as she slowed to a stop, her job once more completed. She sat, panting heavily and heart pounding as she watched her pack take over the kill. She continued chasing the elk, her eyes darting around its body looking for the tell tale weakness Versitha had spotted which singled this elk out. She squinted in confusion as she scanned the prey's fleeing form. Versitha had chosen a young doe, in her prime health. The doe had no outstanding weaknesses, no crippled limbs or open wounds. Her heart began to sink as she looked the doe over and realized the truth. Versitha had made a mistake; she had chosen a perfectly healthy elk. She closed her eyes briefly, sending a hopeful prayer for success to the sun that was hidden in the overcast sky.

The rest of the pack, minus the panting Versitha, was still chasing the doe and nipping at her heels. The doe was not tiring and her strong legs carried her farther and farther across the small valley. The pack began to fall behind the doe and Haska was panting and obviously winded. Romaus gave a curt bark and the wolves slowed to a stop. All of them were breathing heavily and their tongues lolled from their parted jaws. Frustration clouded Romaus' eyes as he called the hunt to a halt. He looked at each of them and then at the strong fleeing doe that was getting further and further away from them.

"This hunt is not ours to be successful in." She glanced at her fleeing meal, knowing the pack couldn't have brought down such a healthy animal yet wishing with all her might to have been able to sink her teeth into such tender meat. With tails and muzzles low, the wolves began the slow walk back through the valley. Versitha, after having caught her breath, was padding toward them at a leisurely pace with a hopeful smile on her face. The hope turned to confusion and then concern when she saw her pack padding towards her and no freshly killed scent coming from their worn bodies. She reached them and asked in a puzzled voice,

"What happened?" She was almost begging Versitha to remain silent, knowing what was coming next. Romaus jerked his head up and growled his reply.

"What happened? What happened is that you decided to single out a perfectly healthy young elk. We had no chance Versitha! What were you thinking?" The anger in his voice was apparent as he asserted his dominance. Versitha cowered low, her tail between her legs and her ears back as she asked for forgiveness from her leader.

"I'm sorry, there were so many of them and they were so close together. I found the weakest one and thought I was chasing her. I must have gotten them confused." She looked up at Romaus, her eyes pleading for understanding.

"Your confusion has cost us a meal, so we return tonight with empty stomachs." His growling subsided and he looked away from her. His anger was dying down, but he was still angry enough for the other three wolves to stay silent. He turned away from Versitha, who was still low to the ground and whining, and began padding back towards where the wolves had come hours earlier. Versitha raised herself, although her tail was still low and flicked in and out from underneath her legs. She glanced at them; her eyes expressing her sincerest apologies. Ameliora gave her a small smile, conveying her pity and her forgiveness. Derment and Haska did likewise as the foursome set off after Romaus. The younger wolves kept their distance from their seething dominant male as they began the long trek home to LEVADA.

The day had spent itself, darkness was slowly spreading across the sky as day turned to night and light faded away. The pack was traveling along the wood's edge. She wandered near the forest and picked up a clear scent marker. Her ears perked and a small smile lit her face when she recognized the scent of Armourn's pack. She realized how close her pack was to home if they were traveling along the outside of Armourn's territory. She had stopped to sniff the scent marker, but now trotted quickly to Romaus and relayed the news. He simply nodded stiffly and continued walking. She was saddened by Romaus' lack of interest and cast quick glances into the woodlands, hoping to catch sight of Elera and Forella. She was out of luck as the forest stayed silent, dark and unmoving.

An unknown amount of time had passed of the pack walking silently through the darkening meadow edge when Romaus paused. His muzzle was close to the grass and his ears were pricked. He lifted his black face and swung his head to his right. He twitched his tail before leading the pack away from the home route. He gained speed as they drew near to whatever he had scented. She was curious but stayed silent, still fearing his anger from earlier. Soon a tantalizingly delicious scent began to reach her. Her mouth watered and she wanted to howl with ecstasy as she realized what Romaus had scented. Food was nearby and Romaus was leading them to it. The whole pack soon had the scent and all pretenses at patiently walking were abandoned. They were running full speed towards the nearing scent of freshly killed meat. They soon reached the carcass, obviously having been killed and eaten some time earlier by another predator. There were still generous amounts of meat left and the pack rejoiced as the dug into the leftover meat.

The elk carcass had been killed by Armourn's pack earlier that day and had she not been so concentrated on filling her starving stomach, she would have noticed their scent clinging to the meat. The wolves scavenged their fill and Romaus took the largest piece he could carry in his jaws to take back to Levada. The wolves licked their muzzles clean and turned from the carcass with renewed vigor. With full stomachs and previous problems forgotten for the moment, the pack mates continued on their way home.

Their paws dragged heavily as they trudged tiredly back up the pathway to the familiar clearing. Too exhausted to do anything further, the wolves entered the clearing and laid down, falling almost immediately into deep peaceful slumbers. Even she slept well that night; her stomach full, her family around her, and a dreamless sleep to give her a well-deserved night's rest.

When morning light began to creep over the trees, shining through the thin clouds that were the remainder of the previous day's overcast skies, she blinked her eyes open. The rest of the pack were also just beginning to awaken and muffled yawns came from the various stretching bodies. It was Haska who broke the peaceful silence of the morning. He padded up to Levada, his eyelids still heavy but a question glowing in his bright gaze.

"Levada, why didn't you go on the hunt yesterday?" A new silence descended on the clearing. Derment, Versitha and Ameliora looked at each other worriedly. Levada's absence the day before had been almost like a taboo subject as Romaus had made it clear it was not to be discussed. Indeed, a rumbling irritable growl was building in Romaus' throat as he began to reassert his silence on the topic. Levada, for one, did not seem at all bothered by the question. She had sat up and, characteristically, her bushy silver tail was wrapped around her immaculate paws. A small smile played across her muzzle as she looked down on her youngest son.

"Don't growl at him Romaus. He's only a yearling, of course he's curious." Romaus looked at his mate with slight annoyance but the growls died in his throat. Levada leaned forward and licked the top of Haska's head affectionately and Haska whined happily in return. Levada looked up from Haska and across the clearing at her, Derment and Versitha.

"If I'm going to go to the trouble of explaining this, you three better hear it too so I only have to say it once." Ameliora, Derment and Versitha looked at each other quickly before all rising to trot quickly to where Levada was sitting. They assembled in a sort of semicircle around her and leaned forward, listening intently to whatever it was she was going to tell them. Levada glanced at Romaus who nodded his approval, then looked down at her paws. The smile was still on her muzzle, but growing slowly as happiness spread through her heart. She raised her head slowly as she opened her jaws to tell them her news.

NINE

Levada took a deep breath before telling them in a joy filled voice,

"I'm expecting a new litter." There was a stunned silence that followed. Of all the possibilities, somehow none of the young wolves had thought to consider this. Haska was completely slack jawed and staring. This news was a completely new experience for him because he was of the most recent litter. Romaus beamed, his tail thumped contentedly on the ground as he gazed proudly at his mate. Levada was waiting patiently for the news to sink in, the smile still on her face and laughter in her eyes.

She was shocked, but soon recovered. This was great news! The pack needed nothing more than a joyful excuse for merriment, and here one was. Versitha was grinning and even Derment was trying to hide the growing excitement in his eyes. Romaus lifted his muzzle skyward and let out a long deep howl. The song filled her heart with the warmth of her family and she joined in the echoing music with her higher young voice. Versitha joined in and then Derment's, Haska followed and finally Levada lifted her muzzle and joined in the excited song of hope in a new generation. Levada's voice was the richest and momentarily drowned out the songs of her pack mates.

As the song continued to be raised to the morning sky, a single raindrop fell on her muzzle. She opened her eyes in surprise as more drops began to fall and a shower became a torrent. The dark clouds that had only threatened to bring rain the day before now poured cold water down on the waiting forested lands. Within moments, her fur was soaked through. She shook herself vigorously and her pelt stood on end, but within minutes it was plastered to her body once more. Every trace of the previously unseasonable spring warmth was gone and she shivered in the rain as a sharp wind blew icicles through her body. The song of the pack had quietly died away as the storm had begun, but despite the violent storm the joyful mood of the pack persisted.

In no time at all, the dry earthen floor beneath their paws had turned to slick mud that clung to their fur. Romaus looked up at the sky, a joking smile on his muzzle as he spoke to his pack.

"Due to the small storm we seem to be having," Romaus paused as some of the wolves chuckled in response. "We will leave for the Den Site tomorrow." The wolves nodded in agreement and padded their separate ways, the short meeting seemed to have ended. The pack gathered in smaller groups, huddled under whatever meager shelter they could find. They curled around each other, sharing their communal warmth as they waited out the storm. Ameliora was curled around Haska with her nose buried deep in her tail. Haska and Ameliora were under a thick canopy of pine branches that kept them mostly dry, at least as dry as was possible under the current conditions. Derment and Versitha were under some another close standing group of trees not far from Haska and Ameliora. Lastly, there were Romaus and Levada. They were together under the same thick green Douglas Fir tree that they had announced their news under. Levada was now lying down, her head resting on her paws. Romaus was lying next to her, his head over her back as it almost always was when they were asleep.

Ameliora closed her eyes and evened her breathing, trying to give the appearance of sleep. In truth, she was much too ecstatic to sleep and for once she had had a full night's rest the night before. Morenia had not come to explain more about the strange words she had said, but her mind was awhirl. Different phrases kept floating through her mind as she attempted to decipher their meaning. It was no use though, none of the cryptic words made any sense to her. She lifted one eyelid and looked out on the overcast clearing. She cast a glance around, her gaze alighting on Levada. She longed to tell her mother of her troubles, of the spirits that came to her in her sleep and the words they imparted. She wanted some wisdom, some comfort in her fear. But how could she disturb the joy of the pack with her morbid dreams and horror-filled thoughts? She lowered her head again, tearing her gaze hopelessly from Levada. Although it was midday, what little light filtered in from the clouds seemed tinged gray. It could have been night, but for the absence of absolute blackness. The rain was still pouring down strong, coming in sheets. The wind that had seemed icy earlier had only become more ferocious. She gulped heavily, realized the intense storm they were in for. The trees were swaying from side to side with the force of the wind and the creaking of their trunks grated on her ears.

Smaller weak branches were coming down here and there; the mud covered ground was littered with pine needles and fallen debris. She lifted her head and gazed up at the intertwining branches that were providing her whatever meager shelter they could. A drop leaked through the thick canopy now and then, one plopped right on her nose and she shook her head dislodging the cold bothersome droplet. In the distance, thunder crashed and she became worried as she wondered just how much of a storm her pack was in for. Glancing around, she saw that Romaus had heard the thunder too. His ears were perked and he had raised his head. Concern shone briefly in his eyes as he looked out at the raging torrent of water and debris falling down.

Ameliora felt frustrated by the storm, there was always a lull of inactivity due to no one's desire to move from under cover and get soaked. She laid her head back on her paws, her tail flicking back and forth with annoyance as she watched the rain fall. The woods behind her were silent except for the pattering of rain against the foliage and dripping as the drops slid off of the leaves that were bent under the miniscule weight. All the smaller forest creatures were hidden away in dens, holes, hollows and nests. The birds didn't sing this morning and she didn't blame them; she wouldn't have wanted to sing either. She let her eyelids drop closed and the tension seep from her muscles. In minutes, she had escaped into a dreamless and undisturbed sleep, her flanks rising and falling gently as she slumbered through the raging storm. Had she been awake, she would have marveled as the thunder grew louder and lightning flashed across the sky. Everything below was lit brightly up as the rain continued to fall and thunder crashed, all of this was missed by the small pack of sleeping wolves in a clearing not too far from a stream.

It was a surprise in itself that she slept at all; the sounds of the storm were a symphony to waiting listeners. The day was spent as such, for what else was there to be done or that needed to be done? With full stomachs and content hearts, the pack slipped in and out of sleep through the storm. They were content to wait until nature raged itself into peace once more. She blinked in and out of slumber, occasionally lifting her head to check on her pack mates. Most of them were as unmoving as she, preferring to stay in the safety and relative dryness of their branch protected beds. The consistent rain and movement of the trees had changed their surroundings. The usual dry scent of shifting pine and sap was gone. It was replaced by the rising odor of wet earth mixed with soggy fur and still, the faint scent of shifting pine. Pine was inescapable in the forest, from the rounded cones dropping from overhanging branches to the thin fluttering needles floated down on an invisible wind. The scents and sounds of the forest were changing along with the weather.

She spent her night as she spent her day, sleeping and checking on her pack mates. Eventually the rain began to let up and the whining of tree trunks accosted by howling winds began to fade. Booms of thunder became steadily more distant until vanishing altogether in one final clash. Lightning ceased to light the sky and the moon was once more dominant in its black realm. Lighter clouds still hung in the sky, covering the land for miles in all directions. The clouds had lost the foreboding blackness they had had before the storm and now were a lighter shade of gloomy gray. When the moon once more relinquished its nightly reign to the approaching sun, she blinked her eyes open. She raised her muzzle skyward, smiling at the now only light drizzle falling from the depleted remnants of the vicious storm.

She rose slowly, stretching her legs out appreciatively. Her paws ached to run and run, her energy much replenished from her sleep and her complete lack of movement the previous day. Her tail was wagging in anticipation, it was most likely the pack would leave that day for the Den Site. She looked around the clearing, no one else had yet awakened and impatience rose in her like a tidal wave of excitement. She lifted a hesitant paw to creep away from Haska's quiet snoring and set it down right into the mud. She recoiled, not having noticed the thick covering. What had dry dirt, dust and clumps of grass been the day before was now a lake of squelching deep brown mud. She wrinkled her nose in annoyance, not looking forward to an almost certain day of padding through trails covered in the storm's last little curse. She put her paw out now, resolving herself to the fact that there was no avoiding dirty paws this day.

Her paws sunk into the mud, the brown muck came up through her toes, giving her an unpleasant feeling and the urge to shake it off. She realized, however, that the moment she set her paws back down they would be once more covered in the antagonizing mire. She sighed and gave up all hope of cleanliness. She simply concentrated on putting one paw in front of the other as she walked as quietly as possible throughout the clearing stretching and waking herself up further. Soon the other wolves began to stir as they were roused from their extended slumber. Various mutterings, yawns and sighs could be heard as heavy eyelids blinked open and limbs were stretched.

Soon the whole pack had gathered around the center of the muddy clearing. Mutual excitement for the much anticipated move to the Den Site could be seen in the impatient shifting of paws and especially the glowing grin on Haska's face. The rain continued to drizzle down from the overcast skies as the small pack prepared for their journey. It was especially exciting to Haska, who didn't fully remember his trip from the Den Site to the Summer Clearing they occupied in the time not spent at the Den Site. It would be Haska's first time back to the Den Site, and his first experience with pups besides his siblings. Finally, after much meaningless chatter between Romaus and Levada that she suspected was just to tease the anxious young wolves, Romaus barked sharply. The nervous chatter died away instantly and all eyes were on Romaus as he made the formal announcement. He looked at them all, his eyes serious. A small, though serious, grin started to spread across his muzzle as he said,

"Tread carefully, the sweetness that lies at the end of our journey will be tainted by trial." She grinned back at Romaus, for as long as she could remember he had always used the same words to begin their journey. She didn't know why and she didn't particularly care, but the tradition always warmed her heart. Romaus turned on his heel, his strong black figure creating a clear path to follow for his pack through the drizzling rain and light fog. He padded across the mud, seeming not to notice the sticky mire squelching beneath his heavy paws, and soon disappeared down the pathway that led to her stream. She followed, briefly blinking in surprise at their direction before remembering that they always took this route. They would cross the stream and continue south and a bit east of the Summer Clearing.

The Den Site was much deeper in the woods than the Summer Clearing. It was further from Armourn's territory and there weren't any other neighboring packs close enough to be a threat. A herd of Red Deer also made its home in the denser woods, providing the pack with a necessary food source. Her memories of the Den Site were shaky at best, although all were warm memories both from her own pup hood with her litter mates and from her last summer there when Haska was born. She glanced over her shoulder at her young brother, he had grown so fast. They were walking single file down the pathway and had not yet reached the stream, but to look at Haska one would think they were traveling through the Milky Way and treading lightly on shining stars.

The woods ended and the pack emerged onto the banks of the stream. She stopped short, her ears going back and a startled bark escaping her lips as she looked at her stream. Instead of the gentle grass and marsh plants giving way to the sandy rock bank of the shallow stream she had always loved, rushing water was lapping barely two feet in front of her. Romaus was standing on the edge, looking into the water with frustration and worry in his eyes. He surveyed the depth, growling under his breath before turning back to give his assessment.

"The stream flooded," He said loudly, "It must have been the storm yesterday. The stream isn't too deep that we can't cross, but you must be cautious. It's deeper than it looks and the downward flow of so much additional water has washed some of the firmer stream bed away. You might not be able to get as good of a paw-hold." He finished and looked each of them in the eye, making sure they had heard his warning loud and clear. Romaus turned away and looked to Levada. She nodded slowly and stepped forward, placing a paw in the water. The river briefly turned a brackish brown as the mud and dirt was cleaned from her paw and floated away downstream. She placed her other front paw forward, this one sinking further into the rushing water. The force of the current gently tugged at her leg fur as it wrapped and flowed around her submerged paws. Levada gritted her teeth and her jaw tightened against the cold, but she stepped forward again, padding into the deeper part of the flooded stream.

The longer fur on Levada's back and stomach was soon plastered to her body and the rest of the pack watched anxiously as she slowly crossed the rushing flood waters. The stream was more like a river now and the turbulent waters were full of fallen debris and muddy confluence. Romaus paced on the extended shore of the water, growling under his breath nervously as he watched Levada's tremulous progress. Ameliora glanced away for a moment, trying to distract herself, she looked farther upstream. Her eyes narrowed as she saw a moving shape further away. She took a step closer and peered intently at the brown object making its way swiftly towards them. She barked in surprise when she could distinguish twigs branching off a fallen log that was progressing along with the rest of the debris downstream. Levada had still not made it to the other side and at the rate the log was moving, she would be hit and swept away. She ran into the shallows, crying out her warning.

"Romaus, the log!" Romaus' head swung to his side as he spotted the obstacle and Levada froze as she heard the words. Romaus looked between the branches and his mate, terror written in his eyes.

"Levada, move!" He was yelling at the top of his lungs and was almost halfway submerged in the water as he called out desperately to the frozen Levada. She seemed to snap out of her reverie and began struggling forward once more. She was fighting the current with all her strength and dragging herself across the deepest part of the river which she had now reached. Her progress was quicker than it had been, but still agonizingly slow. The pack could do nothing but watch from the opposite bank as Levada swam against the current to save both herself and her unborn pups. her eyes flickered at lightning speed between the advancing log and Levada's small silver form. She had almost reached the opposite bank now and the log was less than a hundred feet away. The pack could tell when Levada's paws found the steady riverbed as her movement became steadier and her pace quickened. She scrambled up on the bank, collapsing on the opposite shore panting. Her regal gray shape was astoundingly diminished under her fur which was plastered to her. Even from across the water, she could see that Levada was shaking. The log passed by moments after Levada's rushed escape from the water, She could have sworn she saw one of the extended branches brush Levada's tail as it passed.

Romaus still stood on the bank, relief now mingled with his worry. He called out to Levada anxiously, "Levada? Are you ok?" Levada's head raised weakly and she barked an affirmative before lowered her head to her paws again. It was evident she was exhausted and needed some time to recover from her ordeal. Romaus turned to the remainder of the pack,

"We'll be traveling across in pairs from now on while the remaining pack members keep watch from the shore. Please make your traversal as quick as possible." He spoke curtly, and flicked his tail motioning for the next two to cross. She looked around before stepping forward. Haska approached beside her, his smile had diminished as he realized the peril that came with traveling. He looked to her for comfort and she nodded encouragingly, stepping forward and placing her paws in the water. The icy water surprised her in contrast to the usual soothing cool temperature of her stream. She reminded herself that for now, this wasn't her stream, it was a raging dangerous river and needed to be treated as such. She padded forward, the water tugging on her fur and making her steps heavy and difficult. She kept herself upstream of Haska, struggling forward while keeping an eye for any more dangerous debris. Haska's lankier yearling legs pushed forward against the current, he was having much more difficulty. She slowed her pace, matching Haska's.

The two of them made their slow but thankfully uneventful way across the river, emerging on the opposite bank with their fur tight against them and shaking from the cold. She immediately walked over to Levada, whose head was now raised. Her fur was beginning to dry and fluff back out and the fear in her eyes was replaced by their usual placid calmness. She glanced over her shoulder, seeing Derment and Versitha making their way towards them. Romaus was still on the opposite bank, waiting to see all his pack members safe before he began his crossing. Levada's flanks were still rising and falling as she took deep breaths, calming both her racing pulse and tired heart. She laid down next to her mother, pressing her back against Levada, trying to transfer whatever small body heat she had left to her mother. Haska was shaking his fur wildly while water droplets splattered around. The rain was still drizzling, making true dryness or warmth completely unachievable. Haska approached Levada and Ameliora, a happy smile once more on his muzzle and his fur fluffed out like an irritated porcupine. He laid down on Levada's other side, licking his mother softly and watching Derment and Versitha. Romaus was waiting patiently on the other side, his attention divided between watching upstream and Derment and Versitha's progress.

Derment and Versitha climbed out on the bank uneventfully, quickly followed by Romaus. The small pack regrouped, panting and drying off from their watery excursion. She looked around at her family; she had almost forgotten the ever present dangers life had. She had grown so used to the relative safety of the Summer Clearing and the quietness of life of late that the concept of peril had almost left her mind completely. It was times like this, and in her dreams with Morenia and Rangatha, that reminded her of what was really out there. They reminded her what she was heading towards as well.

TEN

When breath was once again caught and hearts had ceased their racing, the pack continued on. Ameliora sent backward glances at her swollen stream, bidding it farewell until summer and the return trip hopefully accompanied by yipping pups. For the most part, the wolves' pelts had dried although they remained slightly damp due to the incessant drizzling rainfall. They traveled single file or occasionally in pairs, most often with her padding silently alone. Haska spent most of his time talking to whoever would listen, yapping excitedly about everything everyone had already heard at least four times before. She looked around at her small pack, coming to a curious realization.

No one in her pack had their littermates anymore. She looked around, Levada had begun the pack with Romaus and her brother Jandem, however Jandem had passed on the previous summer during an especially drawn out battle with an elk. A flash of black shining hoof and Jandem was down, never to nip at persistent heels again. She remembered much of her uncle, having been a yearling at the time. Levada had loved Jandem deeply, him being her last connection to her birth pack after they had dispersed together. She distinctly remembered the days after his death, Levada had been seemingly inconsolable. Her sorrow had only deepened her already quiet nature; in fact she was resolutely silent for days. The only other time she had even heard of Levada deviating from her usual calm and placid manner was after Tharamena's death. She cast a glance at her mother reaching a decision, even stones have their weaknesses.

Her gaze shifted from Levada as her reflections carried her to Romaus. He had never once spoken about his history and no one had ever asked him. Death, life, love, and history were all in the category of things Romaus kept personal. He didn't seem to need to discuss anything, almost like he preferred to pretend that normal life tragedies and joys didn't affect him. She shook her head; no, that wasn't true. She recalled Romaus' face whenever he mentioned Tharamena, the pain and loss had no equivalent. For all that he may appear invincible; his love had hurt him too. She thought back to the confrontation between Armourn and Romaus, and the way that Romaus had spoken. Although Romaus didn't lapse into silence as Levada had, if one looked close enough they could see the pained father inside of him. Occasionally she would wonder what his birth pack had been like, if he had any siblings or what his fondest memories were, but her aversion to angering Romaus always kept her from inquiring.

A quiet tinkling laugh came from behind her and her train of thought halted on Versitha. Versitha was the pack's precious mystery. She had been a pup when Versitha joined the pack, Derment was a yearling. The pack had been staying at the Den Site when they found Versitha. Found, they had found her. She smiled softly as she recalled the fading memory. The summer sun was warm on her soft puppy fur as she rolled in the small clearing, thoroughly entangled as she wrestled happily with her littermates. The whole fight was a mess of high pitched yapping and blunt paws swatting at each other weakly. She had stood on shaky paws, her tongue lolling from her mouth as she bunched her legs and prepared to leap again at her siblings.

Instead, her brother had charged into her suddenly and the two of them rolled across the clearing with the force of his attack. They had come to a stop when she felt herself bump up against something solid, furry and wreathed in a lavender scent. She had raised her head, tilting it almost upside down as she stared wide eyed into the unfamiliar face. She had yelped in fear and scooted away, her brother right behind her. Romaus had swung his head to look at the pups and leapt up in anger. In moments the pack was surrounding the lavender scented stranger. She and her littermates were hiding behind Derment, who was standing just behind Levada and Romaus. Every few seconds Derment would snap at them to be quiet while he listened to the adults, the pups of course would do no such thing. They avidly debated whether the stranger was a killer and what the chances were that Romaus would attack her. As soon as the adults were there, the pups had lost most of their initial fear of the unfamiliar she-wolf.

Romaus had stepped forward, a fierce growl rumbling in his throat as he glared at the young russet colored female. She still remembered his first words to her and the response that changed them all.

"Who are you? Why do you come into the heart of our territory? Get away from my pups." Romaus was quivering with anger; a threat to his pups was like a threat to his own life.'

"Please, I am no threat to you. I come only to beg assistance." The russet female, a younger Versitha, had tilted her head slightly as she answered. She shot a quick smile at Ameliora and her brother who were peeking their heads around Derment's bulky form. Romaus was taken aback by her answer, eventually deciding this much confused female wasn't a threat to his pups or his pack.

"Where is your pack?" Versitha had turned back to him a small sad smile on her face.

"I wish I knew." Her answer was simple, yet filled with sincere honesty. She looked up at Romaus, a hint of a plea entering her eyes. He had looked down at her and then quickly at Levada. Levada had simply nodded her consent. Romaus cleared his throat awkwardly for a moment before he made the offer.

"What would you ask of me?" He waited patiently, his voice was cautious and tentative. Versitha remained utterly calm, her head lowered submissively. Her words, when she finally spoke, were cautious and pleading.

"I would ask only a home of you." Ameliora and her brothers watched with interest, oblivious to the tensions in the muscles of the older wolves. They were too young to understand the complexities of life.

"You may remain, temporarily. I do not make a habit of giving second chances." Romaus' words were curt, a warning in his eyes. He turned away quickly, returning to his mate. The tension in the air slowly dissipated.

It was then that she had snuck away from Derment and padded in between Romaus and Levada. She looked up at Versitha with her big blue puppy eyes; a curious expression was in her eyes as she tilted her head up at Versitha. A grin spread across her muzzle and she nuzzled her head into Versitha's fur.

"I'm Ameliora." So began the relationship that couldn't be named. It wasn't mother to daughter, sister to sister, friend to friend; it was something of the three of them. It was something new. Eventually the rest of Versitha's story had leaked from her lips to be poured into the pack's waiting ears. She had awoken quite recently and entirely alone, but without memory of anything. She had known instinctively that she should have had a pack, but none was to be found. It was not something to be understood, only accepted. Accept it Versitha did, it was not long until she was on the look for a new life. Her new life found her in the form of wrestling pups, a stern father, a wise mother and one unfixable broken heart.

She smiled to herself as the memory faded again. Levada was the one who, upon learning Versitha had not even a name to call herself, had bestowed a name upon Versitha with her usual regal grace and elegance. Versitha had become a blessing to them all. She was the mystery, the puzzle, the unsolvable, and yet completely understood. She laughed quietly to herself; Versitha was a good effect on everyone. She glanced over her shoulder at where Versitha was padding alongside Derment who was laughing at something Versitha had said. Versitha mended the unfixable and pieced together the broken up. Her gaze rested on Derment for a quick second, her thoughts unnoticeably switched from Versitha to her darker older brother.

Darker, that was a good word for Derment. His whole personality was shaped around Tharamena, she wouldn't have been surprised if he lived and breathed her name. She didn't remember Derment before Tharamena's death. He was already a yearling when she was born, already changed. Tharamena had been Derment's only surviving litter mate and after her death he was alone. From her earliest days, she had learned not to pester Derment. She knew the answers to her questions by heart. A usual conversation from her pup hood went something along these lines,

"Will you play with us?" Sometimes she would stare at him hopefully, blinking her bright blue eyes.

"No." The answer was always the same, although because she was a pup he didn't add on the cutting remarks or growls. It was just a simple "No". She would try a new tactic.

"It isn't really playing, it's more like training." Her siblings would nod their heads in agreement, chiming in on how it was very serious and adult work. This never even cracked a smile on Derment's face. His answer would still be the same.

"No." He didn't mean it unkindly and he wasn't trying to be cruel to the pups, he just couldn't play with them. The youthful energy and joy in their small wriggling bodies had left his prematurely and no amount of play wrestling could bring it back. She learned quickly to stop asking her big brother and content herself with bowling over her siblings or leaping onto Romaus' swishing tail. The pack as a whole left Derment alone, until Versitha came. She never gave up trying to help him, even when he continually shoved her away. He didn't want help or love, but Versitha was determined to give it still. Nothing got to her, and nothing got through to him. Nothing until Armourn's pup, that got through to Derment. She smiled to herself, in a twisted sort of way, Versitha had done it. She had broken through Derment's shell. Ameliora chanced another glance back at them; they were avidly discussing the best places to hunt nearest the Den Site.

The two were inseparable, fast friends and closer than any blood siblings could be.

She was too busy craning her neck to discreetly watch Versitha and Derment; she completely missed Haska come to a slow stop in front of her. A small bump sent a surprised Haska stumbling forward in the mud. She yelped slightly, startled from her Derment related thoughts. Haska picked himself up from the mud; his tan coat now turned a much darker brown with dripping mire. Versitha and Derment had slowed to a stop behind Ameliora and Levada and Romaus had paused to view the disturbance. Levada and Romaus were grinning and attempting to hide laughter as they surveyed their much bedraggled younger son. Haska stood; a vaguely annoyed expression on his face as he attempted to shake the mud plastered to his fur. This was not successful and only made patches of his fur stick up in stiff spikes. She held back chuckles, as did the rest of the pack. She couldn't help herself and her laughter rang out clearly. Haska turned to her, mischief in his eyes. He spoke with a thick layer of sarcasm in his voice.

"I know, aren't I simply the most hilarious sight?" She nodded her head, overcome with mirth. Romaus, Levada, Derment and Versitha had joined in her laughter. Haska was shifting from paw to paw as he attempted to shake even a fraction of the mud from his darkening coat. He looked up at her again, trying to hide a smile.

"I bet you look good with mud too." Before she had a chance to even cast Haska a quizzical glance, he had tackled her. She rolled to her side through the mud, yelping indignantly. Haska was laughing now too as she picked herself up off the ground. She was covered from head to toe in sticky brown mire and it hid her silvery fur completely. She glared at Haska playfully.

"You'll get it for that one." That was all she needed to say, she shook her fur having as little success as Haska had. She craned her neck, licking her fur methodically as she cleaned her pelt. She paused every few seconds to spit out the mud and dirt from her mouth. Haska was doing the same as little by little his tan fur and her silvery pelt began to show again under the thick layer of mud. The other adults waited patiently for them to wash, none minding taking a short respite. The others would occasionally glance over at them, sometimes not bothering to hide their amusement watching the two youngest pack members attempt to clean themselves. Eventually, however, the wolves deemed themselves clean enough and they rose to continue their journey. There were still sparse patches of drying mire in her fur and she resolved to bathe in the river when they reached the Den Site.

Haska was trotting along in front of her, any traces of irritation quickly forgotten and replaced by his recurrent excitement to reach the Den Site. She was now the last one in the small line of wolves padding through the winding trail in the dense woods. She let her thoughts wander once more until they decided to settle on Haska. He was trotting happily in front of her, his tail swishing back and forth as he walked along. She looked at him closely; Haska was still a yearling and not fully developed. His legs were lanky and his paws still seemed slightly oversized. He was growing quickly, She had to admit to herself, he would reach adulthood soon and he already rivaled her in size. She smiled to herself and shook her head, time and youth passed quickly. A pensive expression crept across her face as her mind went back to Haska's pup hood.

Haska had been the only survivor of his litter, his two sisters and brother buried before they even opened their eyes. Levada had grieved over the still little bodies, whining over small hearts that had never beat and miniature lungs that had yet to breathe. Romaus had picked them gently up in his mouth, bending his head with sorrow in his eyes. The three small pups were swiftly buried and attention was returned to the one surviving pup, to Haska. For all the weakness that his siblings had, Haska was strong from the beginning. His eyes popped open to gaze with blue eyed innocence around the dark den and from then he was unstoppable. If a corner was shadowed, he would explore it. If a twig cracked or a bird called, he found it or followed it and usually grabbed something to eat along the way. She laughed to herself as she added on to her own though train. She had been a yearling herself when Haska was born; she clearly remembered her own curiosity as she waited impatiently for him to come out of the den.

He had come out tumbling over his giant puppy paws, landing in the dust with a soft thud in front of her. She still remembered him standing and sneezing as he wrinkled his nose. She had gazed down at him enraptured by the tiny ball of energetic fur. He had lifted his head to look up at her, his eyes widening in amazement. It didn't take long for Haska to decide that she was his favorite. He followed her everywhere, spending countless hours climbing over her back and stalking her tail. Ameliora herself never got tired of him, the two forming a bond that lasted through the ages. She had been both a sister and a mother to Haska, which was what had often troubled her. She craned her neck around Haska's shoulder to catch a glimpse of her mother. Levada may have been their biological mother, but it was rare that she was there as an emotional mother. She had no doubt that Levada loved them deeply, but she was the one to be looked up to more than the one to snuggle with and fall softly to sleep. She shrugged to herself, it was just how Levada was. It didn't matter all that much, obviously her, Derment and Haska had turned out all right. She backtracked slightly, her and Haska had turned out all right but Derment's coldness was in no way Levada's fault.

Her thoughts began to turn from Haska slowly as she reflected now on herself. Her own two brothers had dispersed earlier that spring, leaving her the only one of their litter to remain in their birth pack. A small frown was now on her muzzle and sadness in her eyes. She often missed her brothers and worried for their safety. She was the smallest of their litter, her brothers growing quickly and filling out more than she did. The two of them were inseparable, a true dynamic duo. When they had dispersed, they had left together. Sometimes she would wonder if they had stayed together. She smiled a sad smile as memories from her pup hood resurfaced.

"Zanlac! Wresh!" One didn't hear one name individually, they were always together. "Get off your sister!" That was another commonly heard phrase. If they weren't attacking Ameliora, then the three of them were attacking someone else. It was a common joke around the pack that the three of them were warriors in training, just waiting for the day a battle came around. Despite her small size, she occasionally managed to hold her own against her larger brothers. She had been in the middle of one such tussle with Wresh on the day they had all met Versitha. Versitha was a miracle to them as pups, she was the only member of the pack who seemed to never tire of them climbing over her. Her pup days were spent as such, racing around the Den Site and later the Summer Clearing yapping and wrestling happily with her brothers. She had been sad to see them leave, almost tempted to join them as well, but in the end she knew her place remained with her birth pack. She had always promised herself that she would see them again, maybe with packs and little warrior pups of their own.

She didn't realize how much time had passed when she was again brought out of her reverie. She glanced around, taking in the change of scenery. The sounds of their swollen stream had long since died away and the woods had only thickened as they traveled. The path had slowly changed from well-worn and traversed to disused. She was carefully picking her way through dense trunks pressed up against each other. Her memories of Zanlac and Wresh faded away and her thoughts became almost blank as she simply walked behind her pack members. She raised her head when Haska spoke.

"Romaus?" He ventured carefully. Romaus perked his ears in reply, which Haska took as encouragement. He continued haltingly. "So, how long until we get there?" She smiled and Versitha stifled a chuckle. Romaus actually groaned, his deep bass voice still a boom compared to the others. He didn't bother to turn around as he answered Haska. He swung his head slightly and called over his shoulder.

"Soon Haska, we'll be there soon." Haska had had his head lowered as he waited to be chastised, but it snapped up in excitement when he heard Romaus' reply. Haska sped up slightly and she could see his paws itching to sprint the rest of the way. She felt her own heart race and her eyes brightened in anticipation. The territory was beginning to look slightly familiar to her now as she walked. The sun was slowly moving towards the horizon, darkness descending lazily. Ameliora watched the sky, the clouds beginning to disperse. The drizzling had gradually gone from constant pattering drops to only damp remnants which clung to their fur. The ground still squelched from the drying mire underneath her paws. The trail began to slope upwards gently and Romaus' pace quickened almost unnoticeably. Haska was panting with both excitement and exertion as he trotted behind Levada. Anticipation was growing inside her as well and she was grinning so hard it almost hurt.

The pack burst through a final group of thick trees. The small grassy clearing that greeted them could have been the equivalent to heaven. The ground was even and soft with gently waving blades of light green. An ancient looking oak tree stood near the edge, its thick branches extending up and away. Below the gnarled roots, a dark hole was barely visible. The den was small, and from what she remembered, it was cramped as well. There was just enough room for Levada and her pups until they were old enough to exit the den. The sky was still slightly overcast, but patches of blue were appearing in between the dull grays. She looked up and smiled, taking advantage of the sun to push away the dark thoughts that were rising once more in her mind. Despite Haska's happy bounding and the impending arrival of the pups, she still felt dread fill her heart at the thought of the dreams that certainly still awaited her.

⌒
ELEVEN

Romaus was cautious as always. He scented around the den experimentally, searching for signs of other occupants. When he had decided that it was safe, Levada stepped forward. She poked her head carefully inside the hole. The rest of the pack waited behind her, nervously shifting their weight as they waited for Levada to judge the den. Each year the ritual was the same, Levada had to judge whether the den was serviceable and they would stay, or unusable and they would all be forced to search out another den. As long as Ameliora could remember, the Den Site had always been serviceable. Levada stepped forward and her silver fur disappeared into the darkness. Faint sounds of scuffling paws and a quiet sneeze came from the opening and then Levada's head reappeared. She squeezed herself out of the small opening again, shaking her fur to get the dirt and cobwebs off her pelt. She looked over at Romaus and nodded solemnly, although there was an excited glimmer in her eyes. He grinned at her and wagged his tail.

She let out a breath she hadn't realized she was holding and Haska jumped to his paws. Romaus looked over at the four younger wolves, glancing in between them and his mate. He was still grinning as he spoke to them,

"Welcome," He said proudly, "to the Den Site." Even Derment cracked a small smile as the younger wolves leapt to their paws to crowd around Romaus and Levada happily. The safe journey to the Den Site was something to be celebrated and the joyous atmosphere was a beautiful gift to the former boredom and slight stress of the day. None of them had yet forgotten Levada's close brush with death at the swollen stream. The image of the log rushing through the water flashed in her mind and she shook her head trying to rid herself of the frightful memory. The quick celebration had ended and it was time for the pack to get to work. Romaus was assigning tasks and she perked her ears to listen for her job. Romaus was businesslike but the happiness in his voice was still evident.

"Derment and Haska, go refresh all of the territory markers and scent borders. Versitha and Ameliora patrol the area for any signs of coyotes or other possible threats, when you have finished report here." He nodded his head briskly to signal that was all he had to say and turned back to Levada. Derment flicked Haska with his tail and began to pad towards the woods, calling over his shoulder only somewhat moodily.

"Come on Haska, we've got a lot of work to do." Haska bounded eagerly after Derment, chatting away about whatever came to mind. She stifled a grin, wondering how long Derment would last with Haska buzzing in his ear. Versitha tilted her head and smiled at her warmly as the two males disappeared.

"Ready to go Ameliora?" She nodded her head in reply and the two of them padded in the opposite direction, vanishing side by side into the forest. She kept her ears carefully perked and scented the ground cautiously for fresh scents of coyotes or foxes which could be dangerous to the pups. The woods were mostly quiet, occasional drip drops of water still falling from laden leaves. Birds were chirping again as they flitted from branch to branch. All the smaller woodland animals were emerging from dens and hiding places where they had waited out the storm. She smiled as the forest came alive around her, spring was a time for life both old and new.

She scanned the surrounding woodlands, committing the terrain and landmarks to memory for later. The year that had passed since her last visit to the Den Site had left her unsettlingly unfamiliar with the landscape and her surroundings. She drank in every sound, sight and scent. She relished the repeated newness of it all. In truth, the pine trees smelled the same as the Summer Clearing, the towering trees still creaked and moaned as they swayed gently in the breeze, and she was still surrounded by varying shades of green and brown. Even the soft damp earth beneath her paws and the crackling of fallen leaves and branches had the same feel. Everything was exactly the same, and undeniably different.

She stopped, her ears perked. Versitha turned to her, a worried look on her face and spoke quietly, her eyes darting around looking for the danger.

"Ameliora, what is it? What's wrong?" Versitha's eyes were wide and her muzzle high in the air searching for some scent of danger. she grinned and began chuckling.

"Calm down Versitha, and listen carefully." Versitha's eyes lost their wide fearing look and her ears perked as she strained to hear whatever it was that had excited her. Eventually, Versitha's eyes brightened with understanding when she picked up a very distant roar. She grinned at her, rolling her eyes in mock annoyance. She teased her,

"Oh Ameliora, what is it with you and running water? We are sent to patrol the territory and you find the river within ten minutes." She laughed and shook her head as she replied happily.

"Come on Versitha! Can't we please go to the river? I am absolutely covered in filth. I think the rest of this task would be more pleasant for both of us if I were clean." She smiled slyly and stepped closer to Versitha, her pungent scent wrapping around Versitha's nostrils. Versitha stepped away, shaking her head vigorously and wrinkling her nose. She scowled at her playfully,

"Well we don't have all day and you smell worse than a week old dead skunk. Let's get you clean before I actually choke on your scent." She barked and took off sprinting in the direction of the distant thunder of the river. Versitha followed her, easily keeping pace with her despite the fact that she was running at a full sprint. Her tongue lolled from her mouth and she panted heavily as she ran. Despite her exhaustion from their long journey and her recent lack of sleep, her exhilaration kept her going at a steady pace. The once distant thunder increased as it became a roar.

She burst through the last of the dense trees, hurtling out onto the grassy banks of the river. Her jaw dropped momentarily and her eyes widened as she stood panting, her chest heaving, on the banks of the river. A year had made her memories of the river diminutive; she hadn't recalled it being nearly as vast or powerful as it was. It truly dwarfed her small stream. The far side of the bank could not have been reached even at the river's calmest and shallowest point of the year. This river was wide and powerful, a beautiful danger. The farthest any of the wolves could enter was into the close shallows, any farther and its deadly current could pull you in. A body caught in the current was and would forever be consumed by the river. Many a careless creature had wandered too far and been swept away and drowned. She smiled to herself as she thought back to her swollen stream, that in itself had been a dangerous crossing due to the debris, but nothing compared to this river.

Ameliora's stream was one of the small tributaries of this greater river which wound down from the mountains and twisted briefly through her pack's territory. She padded closer to the bank, Versitha close behind her. She dipped a paw in the water, shivering at the coldness. She raised her eyes skyward, although the storm had passed; the overcast skies were still gloomy and blocked the warmth of the sun's rays. She steeled herself and stepped farther into the water. She padded into the deeper area of the shallows, being careful to stay well away from the dark churning water where the current was its strongest. The water gently tugged at her belly fur, washing away the mud and mire from her tussle with Haska. She crouched, attempting to let the water run over her back, and submerged her head. She came up moments later, her fur plastered to her but clean at last. Versitha was standing on the edge of the bank, a slightly worried look in her eyes. She paced back and forth, her eyes on the darker water.

"Be careful Ameliora, watch for the current."

She laughed and turned her head to rest her sparkling eyes on Versitha. "I'll be fine Versitha, trust me I know the water better than anyone." She grinned and gingerly splashed more water as she washed away the very last traces of her disgusting mud battle. She climbed out of the water, shaking and shivering as a sharp breeze blew through her dripping pelt. She stood next to Versitha and grinned slyly as an idea popped into her mind. Before Versitha could ask, or even back away, she shook her fur wildly sending droplets of water everywhere. Versitha yelped in surprise as the cold water hit her and jumped back. She glared playfully at Ameliora, whose fur was standing on end and fluffed out from her impromptu drying. She grinned back and spoke amiably,

"Should we continue our task then?" Versitha rolled her eyes, shaking her head and sighing dramatically as she stalked back into the woods. She followed her, still chuckling. Soon enough her fur had dried once more and her light silvery fur was sleek and smooth. They padded along in silence for a while, keeping their sense alert as they patrolled. The weariness was flowing back into her paws, her long days taking their toll. She was about to recommend they return to the Den Site, the territory seemed safe enough to her. She hadn't noticed that Versitha had frozen, her ears perked and muzzle against the ground. She tilted her head in puzzlement and opened her jaws to ask what had bothered Versitha, but stopped, her lips pulling back in a snarl and a light growl starting to rumble in her throat. Versitha tensed and pulled her own lips back as a reflex; she lowered her head and sniffed at the patch of earth Ameliora was paused over. The scents assaulted her nostrils as she sorted through which had set Versitha off. There was the earthy scent of dirt mixed with pine, faint lavender from Versitha, small traces of mouse and something else. She concentrated as she identified the scent, something canine. She concentrated harder, attempting to identify the scent. Suddenly she lifted her head and her eyes widened, a growl she had been withholding rumbled in her throat. The scent was coyote. Ameliora raised her head as well, her growls growing louder. She swung her head to the right,

"This way." She spoke quietly and stalked through the trees. She followed her, slinking through the trees silently as they followed the coyote's scent. It got stronger as they went, the faint traces soon becoming an odor that wreathed her nostrils and filled her mind. It wasn't hard to track down the source; the coyote hadn't bothered to hide its existence or the location of the place it called home. Its stench permeated a small grass clearing, about a quarter of the size of the Den Site. A grassy hillock sat in the center of the clearing, with a hole right in the middle. Ameliora's growls grew louder and her eyes narrowed as she stared at the den. Her ears perked and twitched as she listened intently, she did the same. From the direction of the dark den came quiet yelps and whines along with the sound of small bodies wriggling against the hard ground. Her lips pulled farther back in a snarl and her hackles raised. It didn't matter to her that the coyotes were only pups, soon enough they would be full grown and a danger to her pack and their new litter. Ameliora's growls, and the scent of the two wolves, must have been detected by the small family. Out of the hole poked a tan brown head, small glittering eyes blinked at them momentarily before turning feral. Lips pulled back to reveal pointed canines. The coyote mother hissed and spat at them threateningly, although it must have known it would stand no chance against two fully grown wolves.

Ameliora took a step forward, her head lowered aggressively and her fur bristling. Her jaws parted slightly and the muted growls from before thundered from her throat. Versitha mimicked her, her tail straight out behind her and her amber eyes narrowing. The coyote hissed again and backed into its den, its eyes still glowing. It emerged again moments later, a smaller tan head poking its way in between the coyote's front paws. She glared at the coyote pup, her growls growing louder. The pup's eyes widened in fright and it backed away. It huddled between its mother's paws. Versitha's growls faded slightly and she took a step back, nudging Ameliora gently. Ameliora's head snapped around to gaze questioningly at her. Versitha spoke quietly,

"We can give them a chance to flee and then just chase them out; we don't have to kill the whole family." Ameliora stared at her in mute surprise for a moment and then turned her head as she pondered her idea.

"I don't know Versitha; they could be a danger to our pack and Levada's pups." It was obvious from Ameliora's voice that she wasn't too keen on the idea of killing the whole family either, but worries for her family overtook her reluctance. She whined slightly,

"Just give it one shot; if it doesn't work we'll kill them all." She spoke quickly before Ameliora backed out of the idea all together. She paused and thought over her own words, it wasn't often that she killed anything that wasn't prey. Sometimes the more violent side of herself, unsettled her. She shook her head, pushing the thought away and turning her attention back to the coyotes. She took a few steps away from the coyote den, Versitha mimicking her. She let her hackles lie down a bit and her growls quieted. She kept her lips in a snarl and quiet thunder rumbling in her throat. The coyote looked at her with confusion for a moment, trying to figure out what the wolves were doing.

Versitha motioned with her head, pointing towards the woods. Realization dawned on the coyote mother, no matter how troublesome and disliked coyotes were; they were not as unintelligent as some would have liked to think. The coyote mother disappeared for a moment down the hole, reemerging with a small bundle in her jaws. She cast the wolves wary looks before gently setting the pup down on the ground. She came up twice more until she had her three pups sitting terrified outside the den. They were all looking at the growling wolves with wide eyes and letting out high pitched whines. The mother came out and barked at them, nudging them to their feet and hurrying them away from the den. Ameliora looked towards her questioningly and she nodded her decision. The two wolves began to follow the coyotes, growling and snarling. The coyotes sped up slowly, finally coming to a stumbling run as the wolves chased them out of the territory. Jaws snapped at the back legs of the fleeing animals, keeping just far enough away to not actually touch them.

Eventually the two wolves came to a stop, not even winded with the effort of chasing out the small family. Versitha looked towards her and she smiled back. They turned together and started padding back towards the center of their territory.

"I'm starting to think that possibly your plan of action was better in the long run than my own would have been." Versitha's ears perked and she turned to Ameliora with mild surprise. She blinked but grinned at Versitha.

"I'm glad you think so." They walked the rest of the way back to the Den Site in silence, both comfortable with only the quiet thud of their paws over the forest floor. They found no other coyotes or threats within the territory and soon they were able to report to Romaus. They entered the clearing to see Levada lying in the grass, her head resting on her paws and her flanks rising and falling evenly in sleep. She took a closer look at Levada, noting the weight she had gained and her swollen belly. She smiled happily and her eyes glowed, it wouldn't be long now, days perhaps, until the pups were born. Romaus was sitting beside Levada. Alert as ever, his ears were perked and his eyes sharp as he sat stiff at attention. He swung his head around to look at them as they entered the clearing, choosing to stand and walk to them instead of risk waking Levada. Derment and Haska had not yet returned.

She let her mind wander as Versitha reported their encounter with the small coyote family, her plan and the uneventful completion of their patrol. Romaus flashed her a glance when Versitha got to the part about the coyote plan, faint curiosity and possibly a smidgen of pride in his daughter was present in his gaze. He dismissed them with a nod of his head, and having nothing more to do; they padded to a soft patch of grass and laid down for a nap. Eventually Derment and Haska returned, having completed refreshing the boundaries. They had nothing of interest to report, other than scenting the coyotes which had been taken care of. They too settled down to sleep.

Days returned to what they had been before the interactions with Armourn's pack. The pack spent their days leisurely, sleeping and patrolling and hunting when necessary. Levada became more and more inactive, as well as irritable as her time grew nearer. She spent most of her time sleeping or resting, eating meat that was brought to her by the other pack members. Romaus grew irritable and tense as a reflex to Levada's discomfort. The younger wolves kept out of the way as much as possible. Not too long after their arrival at the Den Site, Levada's time came.

Ameliora woke one morning to Romaus' frustrated growls. She leapt to her paws, her senses alert for whatever danger Romaus had found. Romaus was pacing in front of the small dark den, occasionally stopping to whine. She looked over at Derment, Versitha and Haska who were all sitting together and watching Romaus with laughing eyes tinged with worry. Understanding dawned on her and she too smiled. Levada was nowhere to be seen, but her threatening snarls could be heard from the den whenever Romaus stopped to check on her. She stood, padding over to join her pack mates.

"When did this start?" Versitha looked over to her, her eyes glowing excitedly.

"Early this morning, around sunrise. I woke when I heard Levada whine and watched her go into the den." Her eyes widened, it always surprised her how long it took the pups to be born. Haska was watching the den intently, his tail thumping on the ground. Versitha saw her look at Haska and laughed quietly. "He's been like that since he woke up, same with Romaus actually." Derment stifled a laugh at this, a small smile on his lips as his eyes glanced between the den and his pack mates.

"How much longer until they're born?" Haska asked without taking his eyes off the den. They laughed out loud.

"Quite a while Haska, Levada has only just entered the den." Haska's ears went back impatiently and he shifted. It was easy to see his desire to run over and check on Levada himself, but fear of Romaus kept him in place. Derment cleared his voice, speaking quietly to all three of them.

"It would be best if we just left her alone and continued through the day normally, us standing around waiting won't make them come any faster." Versitha and Ameliora nodded their agreement, although Haska began to argue. Derment quieted him with a gruff growl and gentle cuff to the ears; it was less of a suggestion and more of an order. Haska quieted without any more argument, in the social standing of the pack he was on the bottom and he followed orders given to him. Derment stood and padded to the edge of the woods, his tail twitching. Ameliora, Versitha and Haska followed somewhat reluctantly. Derment was determined to keep them distracted while Levada had her litter, and so he kept them busy through the hours. They hunted small mammals and patrolled the border lines, checking for threats wherever possible. She reflected to herself that Romaus was probably more than grateful; he had enough to worry about without younger wolves under paw.

She almost managed to clear her mind of her worries over Levada, throwing herself into any activities Derment suggested. They had no need to check on Romaus, they were all perfectly aware of how he would spend his day. Males were not permitted in the den while the females gave birth, but they would make themselves as much of a nuisance as possible. Romaus would spend his day pacing outside the den, growling and irritated while Levada's vicious snarls kept him from entering. She couldn't really blame him. Though Levada had never been a mother in an emotional sense, her cries set her on edge.

The sun had started to set and the younger wolves were just beginning to head back to the den when they were stopped. A furious commanding howl had risen into the night, floating loud and clear to the younger wolves. Romaus' voice was unmistakable, as well as the message. They took off sprinting, their paws flashing over the forest floor as they raced back to the clearing. Although the trip took minutes, it still felt like hours too long. Her chest ached and her throat burned but she kept running.

Fear pulsed in her veins as every horrible scenario went through her mind. The four of them burst through the last trees and into the clearing, their lips pulling back in snarls and their eyes scanning the area for the threat. Romaus was standing in front of the den, his legs spread and his body blocking the entrance. His hackles were fully raised and his fur bristled furiously. His ears were pressed flat against his head and his lips pulled back in a full snarl as vicious growls thundered in his throat. His ivory fangs glinted in the setting sunlight and his eyes burned. He barely seemed to notice his pack burst into the clearing, his eyes locked onto something to their right.

She turned horrified eyes to the side of the clearing, already scenting something she never thought to scent. It was both wolf, and not wolf. Its scent communicated something out of the norm, something wrong. The issue was obvious upon first sight, a medium sized male wolf stood at the tree line. His eyes were focused on Romaus, and the den he was guarding, but it was as if he couldn't quite look at anything straight. His eyes were slightly vacant looking and crazed, and his breath whistled through his parted jaws. His chest heaved as if no matter how heavily he breathed, he just couldn't get enough air into his lungs. His mouth itself was the worst. It was ringed with whitish yellow bubbling foam. It frothed around his jaws, blowing out from his mouth with each of his too heavy breaths. She gulped, her eyes widening in fear. She had heard of creatures like this male. The disease he was plagued with was known by multiple names including frothing sickness or foaming death, however the most common name was the true name; rabies. A rabid animal was more dangerous than a grizzly bear, the death more immediate than a shot from human iron clad weapons. Her heart fell to her paws, cold icy fear creeping up her spine.

A rumbling deep growl came from behind her and she turned to see Derment. He looked much like Romaus, fury burning in his eyes. The rabid male turned his eyes from Romaus and the den, locking his gaze onto the four younger wolves. Romaus shouted towards them, his words barely understandable because of his growls.

"Derment, guard the den; protect Levada. The rest of us have to get it as far away from here as possible." The pack nodded their assent. They moved slowly, as to not startle the rabid male into attacking. His eyes flashed between the younger wolves and Romaus as he desperately tried to decide who to go after. Romaus began to pad slowly and cautiously towards the younger wolves. Derment was moving towards Romaus and the den, his eyes also on the rabid male. She watched the male nervously, noting his gaze beginning to settle on the den. He obviously had heard Levada's whines. The male suddenly lurched forward, taking stumbling but quick steps towards the den. Derment snarled and leapt forward, sprinting until he barred the den with his body. She shivered and watched in horror as the male drew closer to Derment. Romaus was active in seconds, he ran towards the male growling and lunging but darting away before he could be touched. Romaus drew the male's attention away from Derment and the den, leading it across the clearing. Versitha ran to join Romaus, followed by Haska and Ameliora. Her pack mates were almost unrecognizable, their features transformed from her soft family to ferocious and deadly killers.

They circled the male, taking turns lunging and darting away as they led him from the clearing. The male couldn't decide who he was going after and the multiple wolves coming at him from all angles confused him. He growled and spat in frustration, his eyes getting more and more crazed as his anxiety and fury grew. The wolves were panting with exertion, but their adrenaline gave them energy. She shouted across to Romaus,

"We can't keep this up forever and we can't touch him, what are we going to do Romaus?" Romaus looked towards her briefly, shouting back.

"Tire him out!" She shook her head, her mind whirling. Simply tiring out this wolf wouldn't work, she scanned her brain for ideas. She came to a halt as something hit her. Her brows furrowed with determination and her growls became reinforced.

"Romaus, I know what to do." He looked towards her and opened his jaws to argue, but something in her eyes dissuaded him. He nodded and barked to the others, relaying his orders to follow her. She turned towards Versitha and growled out the only word she would need.

"River!" Versitha looked puzzled for a moment, but understanding dawned on her and she nodded. The group shifted their direction, heading towards a distant roar that was muted by the rumbling growls and snarls coming from the small group of wolves. She felt her muscles screaming out and weariness dragging at her paws as they led the wolf towards the river. The roaring grew steadily louder and soon the grassy banks came into view. She smiled grimly and shouted out again. "Everyone get behind him, back him up towards the river!" The wolves moved slowly, forming a line between the woodlands and the river with the rabid male between them. They advanced cautiously, pushing the male farther back. Soon enough the water lapped at his paws and then the current tugged at his leg fur. She saw the crazed look in the male's eyes change slightly as he seemed to realize the danger he was in. He stopped retreating, standing his ground as the line of wolves pressed forward. She began to panic, her heart was beating wildly and the water was sapping her already diminished strength. She looked to her family, all seeming equally exhausted. She stepped forward, growling louder and baring her teeth. She maneuvered herself slightly, facing at a diagonal to the male. He was almost close enough to the deeper current to be swept away, but he stayed steady and firm on his paws.

She took a deep breath and lunged, bowling into the male's side with the top of her head. He was startled to say the least and stumbled backwards a few steps. It was only the element of surprise that gave her the power to move the male, being that he was much larger and stronger than she. His paws flailed momentarily as he stumbled backwards and fear shone through the crazed glaze on his eyes as the current took hold of him. None of this she could see, for in throwing herself at the male and him being moved, she had misjudged her own force and the distance it would take her. She struggled to regain her paw hold on the bank furiously, but to no avail. She was up to her neck in moments as the river took her to the deepest part. Her paws flashed through the water as she attempted to gain some sort of hold and keep her head above water. The rabid male was already long gone, swept down the river and to his death. She fought frantically to keep her head above water even as it washed over her muzzle and into her nose. She could hear her pack calling from the bank as they ran down to keep up with her. She was quickly being swept downstream. She struggled in vain against the current, her hope beginning to fade as the first boulder sticking out of the water signaled her entry into the rapids.

Fear coursed through her, it was the rapids that were the most deadly. If an animal reached the rapids without having already drowned, they were guaranteed to be repeatedly smashed against the heavy rocks. She could hear the faint voices of her pack mates as her struggles grew feebler. Versitha and Haska were crying out to her, telling her to just hold on. She wasn't sure if she even could hold on. Her eyes began to close and she started to let herself just be carried by the current. Romaus' deep voice pulled her out of her resignation.

"Ameliora! Swim to me, just to the edge of the current. You have to pull through." She opened her eyes, seeing Romaus at the edge of the tumbling current. He was struggling through the water to keep pace with her. Something in his voice, the undercurrent of desperation, gave her a last push of strength. She pushed her muscles, paddling in a diagonal line as close to the edge of the current as she could get. The first of the boulders were drawing near and she stared at them in horror before closing her eyes and preparing herself for death. She felt only contentment, if her death meant saving Levada and her unborn pups and the rest of her family, perhaps it was worth it. She braced herself for impact.

Tight jaws closed around her scruff and her eyes popped open in surprise. Deep grunts came from behind her as she felt herself being dragged. She raised her head weakly to see Romaus pulling her from the current. His teeth were hard against her scruff, but she gritted her teeth. Her eyes blazed and she pushed her paws to swim against the current, giving Romaus whatever assistance she could. Soon Versitha and Haska were by her side as well, each of them grabbing her and heaving with all their strength. She slowly pulled herself out of the current, the violent tugging on her fur ceased and her paws touched the solid riverbed. She panted and heaved herself onto the bank where she collapsed. The others collapsed around her, all drained by the effort. Haska pushed his nose into her sodden fur, whining softly. Versitha soon joined him, the fear and pain evident in her eyes. She looked around her to Romaus. He had pulled himself to a sitting position and was panting heavily. She watched him and struggled weakly to her paws, Versitha and Haska were flanking her in moments. She pressed against them for support. She opened her jaws to try and express her thanks, love, and disbelief that she was even alive, but Romaus stopped her.

"No member of this family dies when they can be saved, nor while I am strong." His eyes held determination and love and also a hint of pain and relief. She smiled weakly at him, but her smile disappeared when she remembered something vital. She spoke breathlessly, her voice a croak.

"Levada!" Romaus' eyes widened and his lips pulled back into a snarl reflexively. He was on his feet in a second. Instructions were wordless, motionless. With Versitha and Haska flanking her; the four wolves made their way back to the Den Site as quickly as they could. Progress was slow with her stumbling movements, unconsciousness threatening to overcome her at any moment. The clearing came painstakingly into sight. Romaus immediately raced across the grass to Derment who was still standing in guard position, completely unchanged and his growls still filling the silence. Derment nodded his head and stepped aside, his eyes flashing to her. He noticed her condition and his eyes widened with surprise, obvious questions penetrated his gaze. She too hurried to the den, followed by Versitha and Haska. The five wolves gathered together at the entrance, silently listening for signs from Levada. Romaus cleared his throat and ventured a call.

"Levada?" His voice was filled with worry and intense fear. They listened intently, leaning forward in search of her voice. A quiet exhausted bark answered them. Romaus sighed in relief and smiled as he opened his jaws to say more. He was stopped, however, by faint yelping and whining from inside the den. The wolves stood stock still and listened. They could hear small bodies moving against each other and quiet whines. Ameliora sank to the ground, no longer able to hold herself up.

TWELVE

It took the better part of three days for her to recover from her brush with a watery death. She spent most of her time sleeping and conserving her replenishing energy. It wasn't as if she was missing anything exciting, Romaus kept as close to the den as Levada would allow and the rest of the pack amused themselves in whatever ways they could. Spring weather was beginning to show as frail rays of sunlight penetrated the overhanging clouds and some of the hibernating mammals appeared out of their nests and burrows in the ground. There was an almost constant stream of quiet yelps and whines from the den as the pups grew and fed in the darkness. The pack was patient, waiting until the pups would finally be old enough to emerge from the den.

Days went by more slowly than they had previously for the pack anxiously awaiting its newest members. Romaus had more trouble than anyone else. He brought meat to Levada when she requested it, often attempting to steal a glance at his pups. Occasionally Levada would allow him to look at them, but soon drove him away. Romaus was at his happiest, his eyes dancing with pride at his new pups and his pack. He yearned for the day when the pups would leave the den and truly be introduced as part of the pack. For Romaus, three weeks passed by in a snail's silver tracks.

Soon, however, the day came. The younger members of the pack could feel it, the building excitement before something important happened. The sun had managed to escape from under its blanket of gray and shone down on the grassy clearing, its feeble warmth not truly enough to even dry the dew from the grass but welcome anyways. The pack gathered expectantly outside of the den. They sat in a small semicircle, their eyes glued to the dark hole. Romaus was standing beside the hole, poking his head in to talk to Levada as she prepared the pups. Haska's tail was thumping against the ground with excitement and his tongue lolled happily from his mouth. Versitha and Ameliora sat with their eyes shining expectantly and grins on their faces. Even Derment had cracked a smile for the special once a year event.

The clearing went silent as faint rustlings came from inside the den. Muted squeaks and yelps could be heard as the pups climbed over each other and Levada. Two sets of shining eyes appeared in the darkness, round and wide as they gazed at the older wolves. Another joined them and then two more. She leaned forward slightly, watching the sets of eyes. They started to back away, frightened, but soft growls from Levada pushed them forward again. The outline of their bodies was now visible, but still indistinguishable. She watched one pair of eyes in particular, they hardened with young determination and her smile grew.

One small pup marched himself out of the den. He held his tiny head high and his short tail erect. As far as young pups go, this little male was good sized. His coat was still the dark brown of newborn pups, but his unique pelt was becoming slightly visible. He had darker gray and brown splashes in places and gray paws. He stood in front of the den, staring defiantly at Ameliora, Derment, Versitha and Haska. She withheld the impulse to laugh at his young display of aggression. Romaus' deep chuckle sounded behind the pup and the youngster whirled around in surprise. He looked up at Romaus, his eyes wide. His eyebrows narrowed and a small growl came from his throat. Romaus laughed again and bent his head to pick up his son by the scruff.

"This one's a fighter that's for sure." He set his son down at his side and licked the top of the little pup's head. The weak growls died away as the pup evidently decided he liked his father. He smiled triumphantly, although she wasn't sure what he felt triumphant about. His tail thumped lightly on the ground. She turned her attention back to the four remaining sets of eyes. They were glancing at each other and their small bodies shifted as they watched their brother make his performance. Two seemed to nod at each other and slowly they moved forward. They crept to the entrance and paused before walking into the sunlight. They squinted their eyes but looked up at the five larger wolves.

One was a female and the other male. Both were about normal sized. The female had the first signs of a red black pelt while the male looked like he would be more of a brownish bracken color. The pups looked around wide eyed for a moment and then at their brother. They seemed to decide that the clearing appeared safe enough. The fearful expressions on their faces melted away and were replaced by excitement. They grinned up at their family. The female walked up to Versitha, her head tilted slightly and her ears perked. She grinned up at Versitha. Versitha smiled back at the little pup, dipping her head and flashing an apprehensive glance at Romaus.

Versitha need not have worried. The little pup nodded her head in reply but appeared to lose interest in Versitha. She wandered away from her and towards the others, looking them all over carefully. The male had been trailing his sister; he paused in front of Versitha and looked puzzled for a moment but said nothing. Eventually Romaus bent and picked them up as well, placing them next to their brother. The three siblings looked at each other excitedly and sat close together. She turned back to the den again, hearing Levada growl a bit more forcefully. Her bright eyes became visible behind the two remaining pups. She lowered her head and pushed them forward with her nose. The pups squeaked in surprise but came tumbling out of the den. They landed in a tangled heap, another female and male. The female picked herself up first, shaking the dirt from her fur and standing to look at her family. Her coat was much lighter than the others, the beginnings of the pure white ivory color that Levada had. She watched her carefully, the little female was much like Levada in the ways she held herself and the calm serenity in her eyes. She chuckled.

The male was small, much smaller than his siblings. His fur had tinges of light brown and chocolate and his small tail wagged. He looked up at Haska with bright excited eyes. Haska beamed back. The pup started towards Haska, but Romaus grabbed his scruff and picked him up to put him next to his four siblings. Levada emerged from the den finally, shaking clumps of dirt from her pelt and stretching. She smiled at her pack and sat by her pups, who immediately began to climb on her and yap happily. She shushed them, looking up at Romaus. Romaus tilted his head at his mate.

"Have you named them?" Levada shook her head in reply. Romaus grinned and looked down at the pups. Levada cleared her throat.

"I was hoping you would, I've never been good with names." Romaus nodded excitedly and looked down at his pups. His eyes settled on the fighter, the one who had come out first and growled at his father. He picked the pup up again by the scruff and set him down in from of the pack. Romaus was silent for a moment, pensive as the thought.

"Gyern." The newly named Gyern barked excitedly and turned to look haughtily at his siblings. He marched over to his father's other side and sat down, holding his little head high. Romaus stifled a laugh at his young son. He turned back to the remaining pups. He picked up the red and black tinted female and set her down as he had Gyern. He took less time thinking about her.

"Alentra." Alentra barked at her new name and grinned as she scampered over to join Gyern. She knocked into him and he yelped, startled. She giggled quietly, but Levada shushed them both with a glare. Romaus continued, picking up the male who had come out with Alentra.

"Socah." Socah smiled a small smile and padded over to join Gyern and Alentra. Romaus turned to pick up another pup, but the white female had already stood and padded to sit in front of her father expectantly. She looked up at him as if this was the most natural thing to do. Romaus seemed surprised for a moment, but recovered. He looked at her thoughtfully, his eyes looking her up and down. He bent down and nuzzled his daughter.

"Irradess." Irradess smiled up at her father and stood regally to join her three siblings. She walked with an unusual grace for a young pup, only adding to her mounting similarities to her mother. She watched Iradess closely, this pup would grow to be a rare beauty. Romaus turned to his final pup who was sitting quietly. His eyes kept straying to Haska, who would smile encouragingly at the tiny pup. Romaus was especially gentle as he picked up his last pup, the runt of his litter. The pup grinned and laughed, lifting a paw to bat at Romaus' muzzle as he was set down in the grass. Romaus chuckled.

"Bander, may size never be an obstruction to you." Bander buried his head in his father's leg fur, nuzzling him happily before turning and scampering to join his siblings. She watched the pups lovingly. She could already see that their personalities would be as varying as their pelts.

True to their nature, the pups were endless bundles of energy. She had difficulty even walking around the small clearing without one of them running beneath her paws or tackling her. They gave the pack life and a sense of renewal. She watched them all closely in the days following their introduction. Their personalities began to emerge in full strength. Irradess followed Levada everywhere, preferring to sit silently by her mother than engage in mock battles with her siblings. Alentra was a down and dirty type of pup, she loved to battle and roll in the dirt. She and Socah were almost inseparable. Socah intrigued Ameliora in particular, he was observant and noticed things that pups usually didn't. He was quick minded, but playful. When he wasn't shocking the pack with his inquiries, he was rolling around with Alentra. Bander glued himself to Haska's side. The little runt adored his older brother and even took to sleeping curled deep in Haska's fur. The two were very similar, both jokers and had a fiery love of life that could not be quenched.

Gyern was the only pup that slightly worried her at times. He wrestled with Alentra and Socah and acted much like any other young pup, but inside him was a brutal domineering quality that unsettled her. He was massive already and much stronger than any of his siblings. He was a fighter to be sure, but she wondered if he would take too strongly to more violent actions in favor of peaceful settling of disputes. Often she would push these thoughts from her mind, shaking her head and chastising herself for being suspicious of her pup brother.

Days passed in leisure with the pups as they explored the small clearing and attempted on more than one occasion to sneak off into the woods. She found herself padding over to eavesdrop on whispered conversations of escape plans and carry pups by their scruffs back to the den. They didn't understand the full danger of the world away from the adults of the pack. Haska was less of a help on this front because he was still young enough to have his immature moments. She didn't blame him, she had been absolutely useless when Haska was a pup; often finding herself wanting to go along on his misguided adventures. Caring for the pups was exhausting, and she found herself falling into a quick deep sleep every night. Her slumbers had been strangely lacking her almost nightly dreams from weeks past. In ways she yearned for Morenia's visits to her once more, wishing to inquire further on the riddled words that had plagued her since their last meeting. While the pups distracted her from her thoughts of Rangatha, they didn't banish them completely.

A particularly tiring day some weeks after the pups' introduction, she crossed the clearing to her favorite patch of soft grass. She lay down, curling her tail tightly around her nose and burying her face deep in her own welcoming warm fur. The sounds of the night creatures began to create a melody lulling her into sleep. She blinked her eyes open and flicked her gaze around the Den Site as she checked on her family. Derment and Versitha were sleeping under some trees not far from her; their still unbreakable friendship evident in their absolute comfort with each other. Haska was wrapped protectively around Bander near the den, the tiny bundle of light brown and chocolate fur nestled against Haska's side. Romaus and Levada slept near Haska and Bander, Gyern, Irradess, Alentra and Socah gathered around their parents and sleeping soundly in various positions.

She smiled and yawned. Her eyelids were heavy and she let them droop closed. Her flanks rose and fell steadily as her breathing evened and she lost herself to the familiar oblivion of sleep. She opened her eyes seconds later, knowing instinctively that when she did she would not see the grassy clearing or her slumbering family. The dark forest had returned and she felt a mixture of relief and terror fill her. She stood quickly and scanned the shadows of her black surroundings. She breathed in deeply trying to scent something, anything that would give her a clue as to who would visit her tonight. She perked her ears and searched desperately for any sound that would give away the presence of deadly enemy or shining savior. Her eyes narrowed as she peered around her, turning in circles as she grew more and more nervous. A deep breath was let out behind her and she whirled around. Her hackles were standing on edge and her lips pulled back into a snarl as she prepared to face Rangatha should he appear.

Mournful white eyes stared at her from the shadows and a second later Morenia stepped from the cover of the trees. Her pure white fur still shone brightly and Ameliora squinted momentarily against it. Morenia looked at her for a long time before speaking, her eyes conveying a sense of despair that she had never imagined the calm spirit capable of. The snow white jaws parted and Morenia's voice quietly slipped from between them.

"Ameliora, forgive me." Anguish shone in her eyes, but also the first glimmerings of weak hope. She gazed in confusion at Morenia.

"Forgive you for what Morenia? What has happened?" Morenia shook her head sadly and looked into her eyes. She began to speak quietly, almost like a distracted babbling.

"I didn't see; I didn't realize what he was doing. He was careful, too careful for me to detect. He has been working, planning in secret." Her insides grew cold and fear pounded in her chest. Her eyes grew wide and she barked out louder than she intended at Morenia.

"You didn't see what Morenia? What didn't you see!" Morenia was sufficiently startled by the rising in her voice for her quiet words to cease. She took a deep breath and her eyes hardened.

"Rangatha, he has a host." She felt herself break, as if every dream and good thought had been ripped and smashed onto the ground. She repeated Morenia's words in a state of whispered shock.

"A host...how Morenia? How did he find a host without you seeing it?" Morenia shook her head, the anguish had faded from her eyes and determination shone through. She looked up and stepped closer to her.

"I do not know, Ameliora, I do not know. Remember what I have told you, your memory shall be your greatest asset." She trailed off suddenly and she became stiff. Her eyes became glazed. She recognized the stance as the one Morenia had had just before delivering her former riddled message. The voice that was Morenia's and not Morenia's came once more and with it the quiet words that managed to thunder in her mind.

"When Rangatha breaks from his prison,
And no longer is kept bound.
Then shall one dead be risen
And then shall the lost again be found.
A loss that turned all gaity black
And drowned a brother in pain.
Returns to beckon the torturer back,

Enveloping all in sorrow's chain.
Hidden amongst the quiet obscure,
Are the four who will depart.
But what oh the trials they will endure,
Only three return with a story to impart.
One shall be the Unspoken.
Known to none but Four.
Two was always the Broken,
Able to laugh no more.
Three will be the Unknown,
Bear neither truth nor reason.
At the last minute it will be shown,
Always destined to end a season.
And Four is but the Messenger,
A high purpose all its own.
To be only ever the Messenger,
And to her the pathway shown.
Hope lives on to breathe anew,
Life into those with hearts unbound.
One survives who always knew,
Revealer of secrets however found.
Good and Evil a battle shall rage,
And two shall die as to portend.
Remember this through the coming age,
The wolves who watched Rangatha's end."

She sat in silence as Morenia slowly lost the glazed
look and shook herself of the stiffness. Her mind whirled

with questions and confusion. She looked anxiously to Morenia.

"What does that even mean? How can someone who died be raised? Morenia I am so confused, you have to help me." Morenia looked pityingly at her and shook her head.

"I have given you all that I can give Ameliora, but there will be others. You must leave. You must find Rangatha's host." Her voice lowered to a whisper. "I can't explain why, I know nothing but what I have given you. But for reasons beyond our power, you are the catalyst to it all. You must destroy him." She stepped back in shock, her eyes wide and disbelieving.

"Why me? I can't do it Morenia. You do it, you did it before!" Morenia shook her head sadly.

"You can and you must. If you turn your back on this, all will crumble and then – when you regret your cowardice, there will be nothing you can do." Though Morenia's voice was soft, there was a certain chill in her words.

"I don't understand why you can't defeat him like you have before, like you have in my dreams."

"I cannot Ameliora, I have lost all mortality I once had. You must do it, I cannot reveal how but you are connected to this. You have been destined to play this part. You must bring the Four together." Her voice began to fade as well as her shining form. "We have been waiting for you. Leave, find Rangatha. Leave…" Morenia's voice faded to silence and the last shadowy outlines of her body vanished from existence. Ameliora's heart was still racing and she called out for Morenia to return, to explain. Her calls went unanswered. She raised her muzzle, howling her confusion and distress. As her song faded into the silent blackness of the night, she was jolted from her sleep.

Derment was standing over her, his muzzle pressed deep in her fur and concern in his eyes. He growled slightly and he was tugging her ear gently. She raised her head and stared wildly around her for a moment before realizing she had awoken and Morenia was gone. She looked up into Derment's irritated face.

"You were crying out in your sleep and depriving us all of rest." She looked at her paws silently, her ears flicked slightly. Derment shook his head, rolling his eyes as he muttered something about selfishness and stalked away. She glared after him, but was only able to stay concentrated on Derment for a few moments. Her mind returned to what Morenia had told her. Now that she had woken, the terror from the night before had left her. She took a deep breath, she knew what Morenia had said was true. She had to leave, immediately. Sadness flooded her at the thought of leaving her family for the first time. She steeled herself, Zanlac and Wresh had done it so she could too.

But hadn't that been completely different? Zanlac and Wresh, their departure had been expected. Romaus and Levada had always known their sons would leave to make new lives for themselves. It had been discussed, open and acknowledged. It had become only a matter of time. She found herself wondering why she had never spoken, never gone to her mother and father for the help she so desperately felt she needed.

She knew the answer to that too, though. They would have never believed her. And even if they had, how could she have introduced a new fear into lives already fraught with peril? Morenia had never said a word about her pack, they were not a part of the great destiny that apparently awaited her.

She stood and shook her fur out. The pack was loosely gathered near the den. She closed her eyes and took a deep breath before padding over to them. She cleared her throat quietly and when the murmuring died down and all eyes were on her, she spoke.

"I'm leaving, today, immediately." There was stunned silence, although Romaus was the first to recover.

"Why? Where are you going?" She looked over at him, opening her jaws to explain about Rangatha, but closed them again. Somehow she knew she could never tell them, that Rangatha and Morenia would not be believed. She thought quickly and answered.

"I want to find my own pack. It is time for me to begin my own life." Her heart ached with the lies, but she prayed her family would believe her. Romaus seemed shocked and slightly angry. He opened his mouth to argue, but Levada interrupted.

"Go Ameliora, go where you must." She nodded at her mother gratefully. Romaus didn't argue further, but walked to his daughter and nuzzled her gently.

"Be safe." She could only dip her head, unable to speak. One by one her family approached her, wishing her safe travels. Versitha hung back, watching her with uncharacteristically unreadable eyes. She stepped forward, her gaze evenly trained on hers.

"I'm coming with you." The small pack now whirled to face Versitha, jaws gaping. Pain and surprise flooded all their eyes as they stared in disbelief at her. She forgot her own pain for a moment, overcome by shock. This time, there were no words. The stunned pack stepped forward, murmuring blessings and words of love. Their gazes flicked between Ameliora and Versitha with disbelief.

She wished fervently she could explain, but knew she could not. Derment hung back, his dark eyes following Versitha's movements. There was something in his gaze that she couldn't identify, something akin to resolve. She bade them all farewells one by one and extracted herself from the frenzied nuzzles, licks and sorrowful eyes. She bowed her head one last time before standing and walking across the clearing, Versitha silently at her heel. She looked over her shoulder once more at her still family; she hoped they would come to understand. She turned away and with a swift bound, disappeared into the trees. When her tail had swished and the very tip was gone, she broke into a run. She ran swiftly, dodging tree trunks and fallen logs. Versitha kept easy pace beside her, the older she-wolf's gaze still unreadable. She ran without thinking, knowing she could not afford to concentrate on her family. She wasn't sure where she needed to go, but something pulled her in a western direction. She traveled through her pack's territory, drinking in their fading scents.

They reached the edge and paused. But for entering Armourn's territory or going on hunting expeditions, she had never left her pack territory. She did not know what she would encounter outside of the safety of what she had always known. She looked out at the trees and grasses. She breathed in deeply, scenting no territory markings. She glanced behind her at her family's land spread out behind her and somewhere beyond that Armourn's as well. She turned away and stepped over the boundary line. She once more began to run, her paws flying over the land as she did. She kept her ears perked and her senses alert as she searched the unfamiliar landscape for threats. Days passed like miles under her paws, and still the silence between Ameliora and Versitha persisted. The sun rose and set, and still the she-wolves traveled. They hunted small mammals when they could and slept lightly in case of attack. The whole time She meditated on Morenia's words and what they could mean. None of the prophecy made any sense, if it even was a prophecy. She went through it line by line. She assumed the prison that Rangatha broke from referred to his finding a host, but that was the only part she could work out. She tried to keep thoughts of the prophecy from her mind when the lines concerning boiling pain and particularity "Two must die as to portend." This line made her insides go cold as she meditated on the death that was certain to come, the question that plagued her was *whose* death.

The seasons had gone from warm breezes, to crippling heat. The two travelers had spoken little, both absorbed in meditation and grief. She had found a small river that was shallow enough for them to cross. She had a headache from the boiling confusion in her mind and her throat was dryer than sand. She bent her head to drink from the river, gulping down the cool water. Versitha did the same at her side. She lifted her head and looked at the water. Summer was upon the land in full and the sun beat down on her. She padded further into the water, sighing as the icy river flowed around her legs and stomach. She stood peacefully and silently as her fur was tugged in the gentle current. She opened her eyes when she felt uncomfortable, just as a quiet growl rippled from Versitha's throat. Her neck fur began to rise and she quickly yanked up her head, searching in all directions. Her ears perked and she listened intently as her heart began to race. A loud snap behind her caused her to whirl around, Versitha doing the same. Her lips pulled back in a snarl and she lowered her head aggressively. She was surprised to see another wolf standing on the banks of the river, mere feet from Versitha.

He stood watching them with hardened eyes. He was a large male with medium gray fur. His pelt had lighter brown highlights and his underbelly was more of a cream color. He had a light brown muzzle stripe and bright chocolate brown eyes. His tail swished back and forth as he stood watching her. She felt fear rise in her as she took in his well-muscled form against hers. If it came to a fight, even against the two of them, he would win. She took a deep breath and her eyes widened in fear as he took a step towards her.

THIRTEEN

Ameliora wasn't aware of her growl until it rumbled somewhere deep in her throat and the male blinked in surprise. He stepped back slightly, lowering his head but keeping his eyes on her. Her hackles would not settle and her lips were still frozen in a snarl. Versitha looked much the same, her lean form was doubled by her raised fur. She kept her muscles tense, but the male had made no aggressive move towards them. Her still dripping tail swished back and forth against her legs and the water continued to tug at her belly fur. She raised and tilted her head. She cleared her throat slightly, just as Versitha spoke in a challenging voice.

"Who are you and what are your intentions in approaching us?" She looked to Versitha in surprise. In all their silence, even in their occasional words, she had nearly forgotten the older she-wolf was even there. The male made no response for a moment or two, his eyes looking them up and down while giving nothing away to what he was thinking. He stepped forward again and sat down a short distance from them. He looked at them evenly, while no aggression was obvious, neither was there any signs of good intentions. When he finally replied, his voice was light and even.

"Settle yourselves; I have no want to harm you. Your first question, however, is not one I can answer quite as simply. Who I am is who I have always been and who I have always been is the same as you yourself. I am a wolf and nothing more." She listened silently, her eyes warily glued to his. He spoke with subtle confidence tinged with traces of pompousness. It felt almost as if he was testing her in some way, yet asking her no questions. She pondered his words for a few moments, glancing at Versitha in an attempt to gage her reaction. Her fur began to lie flat and she let the snarl fade from her features. The growls died away in her throat. Her ears which had been laid back flat against her skull now came forward once more and perked with mild interest. She could see Versitha reacting in much the same way, though her gaze was still wary. He spoke again before she had gathered her own response.

"My name is Nadav." She blinked and smiled slightly. She dipped her head in greeting and spoke quietly across the water to him.

"I am called Ameliora, and my companion is Versitha." Nadav nodded in reply, his gaze still flicking between the two females. He finally tore his eyes away from them and looked away as if in embarrassment. He cleared his throat slightly.

"I apologize for my rudeness not moments ago. I spoke with a pretentiousness not fitting me in an attempt to conceal my own surprise and nervousness." Her eyes widened with unconcealed interest. She looked to Versitha to see barely concealed amusement on her friend's features. She looked at him intently, finally nodding her head firmly and speaking quietly in response.

"I too apologize; it is not in my normal character to act so hostile without need." She dipped her head to him. He smiled tentatively towards her and she returned his with a small upward twitching of her own mouth. She wasn't quite sure what it was, but something about Nadav put her at ease. Or perhaps it was the reassuring presence of Versitha. He stepped hesitantly closer and when she made no move to stop him, he approached her slowly. Versitha watched the two of them, her muscles slightly tensed. As he approached, she could make out some of his more subtle features. There were a few faint scars on his muzzle, indicating his past as a fighter or at least having been in quite a few fights. His eyes were soft and trusting, as though he knew her more than he let on or even possibly could. He sat down on the very tip of the bank and only then did she notice she was still standing in the water. She padded out of the shallows and onto the bank. She shook her fur dry and settled beside Versitha, keeping a few feet between herself and Nadav. She glanced at Versitha.

Her fur settled and as it did she sat down. Her tail curled reflexively around her paws and she looked at Nadav curiously. She could feel the slight tension Versitha held.

"Why are you here exactly? Is your pack near?" She felt slight nervousness creep up in her. She hoped his pack wasn't near. Perhaps they had crossed onto their territory without realizing it, if so they would have to make their escape quickly. She looked to Nadav for a reply, her muscles taught and ready for flight. He simply looked back at her with confusion for a moment and then understanding. He shook his head.

"I'm alone. My pack is a few days travel from here. As to why I am here, I'm embarrassed to say I couldn't tell you." She listened and her nervousness died away. He was a loner, just like them and so far no threat. Her ears perked at his last line. She looked at him quizzically, her ears twitching in silent question. Her head was tilted slightly to the side. Nadav sighed deeply, his eyes holding indecision. Versitha's eyes were narrowed, peering at Nadav with silent questions in her eyes. He looked over and began slowly.

"I just needed to leave my pack. I don't know why. It was like," he paused for a moment searching for the right words, "an inner pull deep within me. Something was tugging me, telling me to move. I've just been following it wherever it leads me." She stared at him in surprise. That was exactly what they were doing, except she had rare guidance from Morenia. She looked at Nadav mutely for some time before turning to Versitha. She motioned sideways with her head. The two rose wordlessly, moving a few feet towards the trees to converse in whispers.

"I think he's harmless." Versitha was the first to speak, her voice low but certain. She glanced occasionally towards Nadav who sat waiting, fidgeting with his paws.

"We're alone now. We can't just go with our gut. We don't have the pack to protect us." She cast Nadav uncertain glances, her gaze clearly wary.

"I don't think he's who we need to protect ourselves from." Versitha's words made her stiffen. She nodded her head curtly, trying to convince herself that the double meaning in Versitha's words was purely coincidental.

"We can't guarantee that we're going to the same place, but you are more than welcome to travel with us if you wished." Versitha's gaze was calm, a look reminiscent of Levada. Nadav's answer was not long in coming. His ears perked immediately. He looked to Versitha with gratitude, flicking his eyes towards Ameliora who now remained silent. He stepped towards the two hesitantly.

"Thank you." He was at a loss for words and so said no more. She nodded back silently, her lips a thin line. She was still slightly uncomfortable around Nadav, not completely trusting him. Something told her that having him around would be useful though, even if only for hunting. Versitha smiled, dipping her head towards the male. Both females turned away from the water, having drunk their fill. Nadav kept his eyes on them, though she could feel his eyes resting on her neck. She looked away, nodding again and padding back into the woods with Versitha at her side. She could hear Nadav's heavier paw steps behind them as they weaved through the trees. She peered intently up at the trees. For now the leaves were still green and lush, but quite soon they would be falling; littering the forest floor with hues of gentle browns, oranges and reds. She sighed quietly, so much time had passed. How old would the pups be now? She thought back quickly, surprised at the result. The pups had been born in mid-spring, amid the quieting rains and warming breezes. Summer was now creeping closer to a close. That put the pups nearing four months of age. Sorrow filled her, she desperately wished she could have been with her family to watch her brothers and sisters grow into yearlings. She was consumed with her thoughts and hadn't noticed Nadav come up alongside her as Versitha moved ahead. He was looking at her curiously, his eyes probing but jaws clamped shut. He cleared his throat quietly.

"What's troubling you?" She looked over at him with a startled expression. She shook her head, pushing the pups from her mind. She debated simply telling him nothing was wrong and moving on. She had Versitha to confide in, why trust another? Suspicion still tinged her gaze whenever she looked at Nadav.

"I was just thinking of my young siblings. We left them just after they were introduced to the pack." She trailed off quietly. Versitha would be pleased that she was at least making an attempt at trust. Nadav was nodding his head.

"I miss my family too. I often ask myself why I am even going, where I am going, why I don't go back. Then I realize that I don't have any answers." She looked at Nadav askance. She was surprised by his words and their depth. She found herself nodding her head, even feeling comforted. Wasn't she doing the same thing? At least she had Morenia to direct her. Nadav was alone. The two continued the day's traveling in silence, neither having much to say to the other. Versitha seemed content to lead the way alone. She found herself wondering if perhaps Versitha's musings ever wandered back to Derment. They let their paws carry them where their instincts pulled them, none surprised that their pathways were identical. The first night passed as did the second day. They became more comfortable with each other. She found herself opening up to Nadav in ways she hadn't expected, telling him of her family and even her stream. She only kept Morenia and her dreams from him, carefully edging around anything related to them. Versitha joined in these conversations, relating stories of their shared youth. In return, Nadav told her of his home and family.

She learned that Nadav had come from a pack many miles west of her pack's territory. Nadav and his sister had joined the pack shortly after dispersing and both had no other relation to the pack members. He spoke fondly of his sister, whom he had left behind. Her heart ached for

Nadav, it must have been nearly impossible to leave his sister. She had wondered if he had a mate or pups he had left, but he didn't mention them if he did and so she assumed he didn't. The two formed a tentative friendship, based if not on their similar journeys then on their deepening bond. Nadav put her at ease, distracted her from her worries. She made Nadav feel like he was home. Together the three found solace in each other.

The lush greens woven throughout the canopies above their heads as they traveled began to change to browns, reds and autumn oranges. Brittle leaves began to fall from their branches and blanket the forest floor. They crackled underneath their paws as they walked. Mice and small rodents scurried around and under the cover of the fallen piles as they searched out winter stores. She watched her surroundings closely. Together, she, Versitha and Nadav had passed over many miles of land. They crossed rivers, traversed valleys, mounted hillocks and raced through the waving grasses of gentle caressing meadows. They hunted what they could and ate when possible. Prey was becoming somewhat scarce as autumn came on in full, and still they traveled. The mountains which had seemed so far to begin with began to grow frighteningly close. She wondered if they would have to cross the mountains, and if they did – would they be able to survive. There were only three of them. The chances seemed grim.

Most of the time she pushed these thoughts from her mind, but at times they plagued her and robbed her of much needed sleep. It was on one of these nights that she was joined in disturbed slumber. She was laying curled near Nadav whose chest was rising and falling gently as he slept. Versitha was curled against her other side, creating a snug block of warmth. The three were sleeping in a small clearing they had found for the night and had fallen exhausted into soft piles of dead leaves. Nadav had been asleep almost instantly, his back pressed up against hers. She found herself unable to succumb to the numbness of sleep. She closed her eyes and reflected to herself. Mostly her thoughts dwelled either on her family or what she would find and occasionally Morenia's haunting words. Who was the host? Where was she going? She was so lost in thought that she didn't notice Nadav begin to toss and turn in his sleep. His paws began to twitch and then his tail began to lash. His eyes were screwed shut but his lips were pulled back in a silent growl aimed at those only he could see. When a low growl rumbled in his throat, she looked at him sharply. Her eyes were startled, but she calmed as she realized he was still sleeping. She watched him curiously, wondering what he could be dreaming of that would so set him off. She didn't have long to wonder because Nadav's eyes snapped open. In seconds he was standing a few feet away from her, his fur was bristling and growls ripped from his throat. His eyes were confused and he obviously didn't recognize her. She stood slowly and backed away from Nadav. She wasn't sure what was wrong with him or why he was acting so aggressive towards her.

He was breathing heavily. She spoke quietly and soothingly to him, casting terrified glances at the still slumbering form of Versitha.

"Nadav, calm down, it's just me, Ameliora. No one is going to hurt you. No one is threatening you." She repeated these words over and over in her quiet calm voice. Her legs shook, but she kept her voice even. She wasn't sure how she did it considering she was thoroughly terrified. Nadav's eyes began to clear and slowly the confusion melted from him. His lips relaxed and his fur settled. He shook his head as clarity descended on him. He padded back to her, his eyes puzzled and apologetic.

"I'm sorry Ameliora. I don't know what came over me. It seemed so real. I was sure you were him." He paused as he said the last word, his voice trailing off. Her ears perked and horror settled on her. She pleaded deep inside herself that the "him" Nadav had referred to wasn't who she thought it was. She ventured to ask.

"You thought I was who?" Nadav looked down at her with indecision in his eyes. He was sitting close to her again. She sat too, curling her tail around her paws. Her eyes were on him, studying his expressions and reactions. Nadav sighed heavily, obviously deciding to tell her. His voice was quiet and hesitant as he began to explain.

"Were you ever told the old legends?" She nodded silently and he continued. "Do you remember the stories about the two battling spirits, Morenia and Rangatha?" Her silent pleading grew louder in her mind, almost to a howl as she again nodded. "I dream Ameliora; I dream that *he* visits me." The pleading stopped, it was true. Rangatha had come to Nadav. Nadav didn't have to say who "he" was, She knew and it showed in her eyes. She cleared her throat quietly.

"I am visited too, Nadav. Morenia comes to me," She paused and continued, "I didn't know whether to tell you earlier, how you would react. I think the time has come for both of us to be honest, to explain." She waited and watched him. His eyes flicked shock, relief, curiosity and then acceptance. He nodded his head in agreement. She glanced behind him to where Versitha still lay curled in the oblivion of sleep. Nadav followed her gaze.

"Does she know?" She shook her head. It was incredible, really, that through all their travel the two she-wolves who had been like sisters had never questioned each other. Perhaps it had been a feeling, a lack of ability to invade in the other's personal reasoning. Whatever it was, Versitha knew nothing. She watched as Nadav stood and padded silently to Versitha. He bent his head, gently nudging her shoulder. She stirred, but made no further move. Nadav nudged her again, this time pawing at her. Versitha raised her head with a gaping yawn and a none-too-pleased glance in Nadav's direction. He returned to sit a few feet from her. Versitha joined them a moment later.

"Why am I awake? The sun is far from rising." Versitha was irritated, but not really angry. Her nature was far too gentle, too easy-going for true ill-temper. Nadav spoke first.

"I feel I should begin." She nodded her head and waited with anticipation to see what he would reveal to them. Versitha looked on in confusion, but kept her jaws closed as he began to speak, taking a deep breath. She readied herself for a long story. "It started maybe three seasons ago. I would fall asleep and find myself in a dark forest. I would be confused and turn and shout, trying to find someone, anyone in those dark woods to help me. No one would answer and I would run, simply searching." So began a tale so similar to her own that it chilled her inwardly. Nadav's story differed from hers greatly though. While Rangatha viciously killed her in her dreams, in Nadav's Rangatha was his savior. Rangatha would appear, saving him from the black loneliness and silence the forest represented. Rangatha would weave words in Nadav's mind, telling of strength and power to be his. Rangatha told of what Nadav could do to be powerful unlike any other. Nadav told her of his distrust of the black wolf with pits for eyes, of his fear of the wolf that made himself seem like a savior. They listened in silence. Her eyes shone with understanding, while Versitha grew more and more perplexed.

Nadav's story began to turn darker as he told of his dreams slowly transforming. They went from the dark woods and being saved by Rangatha to being met by Rangatha in the dark clearing. The male would simply sit and talk to Nadav, always speaking of power and a future they could have. Finally Nadav had asked Rangatha what he was doing, why he wanted Nadav.

"Rangatha answered simply, and it was his answer that so scared and angered me." She had been listening intently, saying not a word. Nadav's gaze had been flickering between the two females, his uncertainty clear. She ventured one last question quietly, although she feared the answer.

"Nadav, what did Rangatha say to you?" Nadav looked up at her, his eyes hard and determined, with touches of anger.

"He told me he would be returning, that he would soon reclaim his throne." Nadav paused, finally looking down at his paws. For the first time, he refused to meet either of their gazes. "And he told me that if I follow you, I will die."

FOURTEEN

Whatever fragile strings that had been holding her heart aloft and soaring snapped suddenly. Her heart plummeted down through her chest and straight down to her paws where it sank in to the hands of despair reaching up to snatch it and hide it away deep in its dark recesses. She stared in mute horror at the wolf she had come to think of as a friend. Was he what he seemed? The question burned inside of her mind. She couldn't bear to think of Nadav as one of Rangatha's despicable pawns, another muscled puppet in his murderous game. Versitha sat at her side, confusion written all over her features. Nadav's eyes held a deep feeling of panic mixed with tinges of anger, hope and honesty. She gazed at Nadav, her eyes bewildered. Her whispered words escaped her parted lips like a sudden cold winter breeze.

"Should we fear you?" She feared to hear the answer as much as she feared to ask the question. Phrases of the strange prophecy scrambled through her mind as she attempted to sort through the flying pieces of information that seemed to be being hurled at her from all directions.

Nadav took a step back from her, his eyes incredulous and hurt. His voice was disbelieving.

"No, I could never hurt you. All that lives in him is blackness, but I believe in the light." The black claws holding her heart in her paws loosened intangibly. Ameliora smiled slightly at Nadav, who stepped closer once more as the frazzled emotions melted from his eyes. He cleared his throat and spoke again since she hadn't. "What do you dream of?" In all of the excitement, she had quite forgotten about her own story. She paused for a moment to gather her thoughts. Nadav had trusted her enough to reveal his very soul to her, his dreams and fears. How could she not do the same? She took a hesitant breath, looking to Versitha. Her eyes begged for understanding, for patience.

"My dreams used to be much like yours..." And so she began her tale. She took him through the very beginning. She told him of her first dreams, being chased by the shadowy figure and murdered nightly; her howls for mercy going unanswered night by night. She told of Morenia's appearance, and the revelation of Rangatha. From there she slowly detailed the information Morenia had given her. Nadav listened silently, his eyes intent. They were pained when she talked of her repetitive deaths and shining as she described Morenia in her iridescent beauty. She came to her most recent dream, with Morenia telling her to leave and search out Rangatha's host. Fear crept to the corners of Nadav's countenance, but also a hint of piqued interest. When she had finished her tale, the last quiet words fading in the autumn clearing, he spoke again. Versitha, her gaze contemplative, said nothing.

"You mentioned a prophecy of sorts, a message Morenia gave to you while in a trance." She nodded her head, though her gaze now lingered on Versitha.

"I've been trying to puzzle it out since she gave it to me, but all has come to naught." Nadav looked curiously at her, his eyes pensive and hopeful.

"May I hear it?" Her eyes widened in surprise but she nodded her head enthusiastically. She smiled at him.

"I'm glad to share it with someone after all this time." She cleared her throat and closed her eyes. The words were burned into her memory. She parted her jaws and to recite the mystic words by heart, but found herself interrupted.

"All of this, it has all been dreams?" It was Versitha, finally speaking in a voice much like a cracking whisper. They looked to Versitha with identical flashes of surprise. In her silence, it had been easy to forget their third companion. She found herself nodding.

"They are less like dreams, more like visions in ways." She paused, searching for an explanation. "Do you remember when you found me one morning, I had a scratch to my muzzle?" Versitha's brows furrowed, but she nodded. "Rangatha struck me, and when I awoke his mark was there upon my face." Versitha's eyes widened with fear, she muttered quietly.

"These are no simple dreams." They nodded silently in unison. Versitha closed her eyes for a moment. "I wish you would have told me, would have told *someone*." She shifted her paws guiltily.

"I was afraid you would not believe me. There was so much going on, always something more important." Her ears flattened against the back of her head, a quiet whine in her throat.

"But you could have helped me understand." Ameliora and Nadav looked to Versitha with surprise. "I've felt this, this pull. I've felt it since before the pups were born. Whenever I would get too far away from you, it rose up inside of me. And when I followed it, it always led me right to you." Versitha paused, shaking her head. "And when you announced you were leaving, I knew I needed to go too. I think," she paused again, "I think that whatever this is, I'm supposed to be with you." She finished quietly, staring at her paws.

They were silent for a long moment. She had noticed Versitha's near constant company, had wondered why she had chosen to accompany her, but had never considered asking. Now to hear Versitha's explanation, it felt like a missing piece of the puzzle – one among thousands, but important in itself.

"I think you are one of the four." Before Nadav or Versitha could question her, she continued. "Morenia's prophecy," She cleared her throat and began to recite.

The words held mystery and haunting beauty. Her quiet voice gave the words a somber and chilling feeling.

"When Rangatha breaks from his prison,
And no longer is kept bound.
Then shall one dead be risen
And then shall the lost again be found.
A loss that turned all gaity black
And drowned a brother in pain.
Returns to beckon the torturer back,
Enveloping all in sorrow's chain.
Hidden amongst the quiet obscure,
Are the four who will depart.
But what oh the trials they will endure,
Only three return with a story to impart.
One shall be the Unspoken.
Known to none but Four.
Two was always the Broken,
Able to laugh no more.
Three will be the Unknown,
Bear neither truth nor reason.
At the last minute it will be shown,
Always destined to end a season.
And Four is but the Messenger,
A high purpose all its own.
To be only ever the Messenger,
And to her the pathway shown.
Hope lives on to breathe anew,

Life into those with hearts unbound.
One survives who always knew,
Revealer of secrets however found.
Good and Evil a battle shall rage,
And two shall die as to portend.
Remember this through the coming age,
The wolves who watched Rangatha's end."

Her voice cracked slightly near the end as she spoke of the ones who would die to see Rangatha's end. This portion of the prophecy troubled her greatly. Nadav listened intently, his eyes on his paws but unseeing and distant. His ears twitched and the tip of his tail flicked, occasionally stirring dead leaves from the cold hard ground. She was silent as she watched them, wondering what they would say. Versitha was pensive, her gaze too on a calculating look. Finally Nadav lifted his gaze to hers. He spoke quietly and haltingly as he unraveled his thoughts.

"How do we find that which is lost?" She looked at him hopelessly. She looked utterly lost.

"None of it makes sense." Nadav looked up at her in surprise and smiled slightly.

"Parts of it make sense, or at least don't exactly have to." Nadav and Ameliora looked to Versitha. Her brows were knitted together in concentration. "There are obviously four meant to partake in this prophecy, if it is a prophecy. If we assume that we are three of the four, we should be able to identify ourselves."

The three of them went through each line of the eerie message, attempting to decipher its cryptic words. No more secrets were to be found that day, nor very soon. The information that had been found kept running through her head. Together they, plus an unknown fourth, were the Unspoken, the Broken, the Unknown and the Messenger. And apparently they were destined to find that which was lost. The major problem was that none of them knew what was lost. They eventually gave up trying to understand the twisting words, each of them now plagued with headaches and thought trails leading to nowhere. None of them had slept well the night before, so after a quick respite which didn't do any of them much good, they were off again. The pull was only getting stronger in them.

None of them knew where they were going, nor what their purpose was. It was difficult traveling without either direction or purpose. They were guided solely by their instincts and the internal pull. It resembled the migratory instinct in great flocks of birds and grassland herds. There was a time to move and the time had come. Their travel was slowing as they encountered more obstacles. They were getting nearer to the towering Eastern Mountains and encountered a greater amount of hills and stony ground as well as a lessening of the great forests both wolves were accustomed to. She found that her toughened paw pads less often encountered soft bracken floors covered in fallen pine needles and damp moss. Instead the terrain was rough and uneven. The hard packed dirt beneath her paws often had sharp pebbles and rocks embedded in it. What foliage the three happened upon was often brittle and snagged at their lengthening fur. Summer had passed and fall was ending. Winter would be upon them sooner than they could wish. Even together, it was rare that they managed to bring down large game. She missed hunting with her pack and the thrill of a successful kill. Nadav, Versitha and Ameliora alone had little luck. They lived on smaller rodents and the occasional hare they were able to catch themselves.

Occasionally they would attempt to figure out more of the prophecy's strange riddles, but it all amounted to nothing. For each small tidbit they unraveled, new questions and confusions arose. The prophecy sank into the neglect of silence. The three wolves assumed that perhaps only time could reveal the questions they so sought. She longed to speak with Morenia, to have words of guidance from her spiritual protector. Her dreams were vacant and undisturbed though, and no help was forthcoming. While Nadav wished for her sake that Morenia would come, he dreaded and feared that perhaps Morenia's coming would also bring Rangatha. Versitha added what she could to their conversations, but never once found herself envying her companions. Descriptions of the dark spirit they faced sent shivers up her spine. Rangatha haunted Nadav's waking mind though his true presence never entered Nadav's slumbering dreams. Since the afternoon the three companions had discussed the prophecy, Rangatha had been absent. Ameliora, Versitha and Nadav avoided bringing Rangatha up, none wished to discuss the possibility of failure or what it could mean.

As continuous nights passed without disturbance, Nadav began to gain confidence in the assurance of an undisturbed rest. He grew comfortable and hopeful that perhaps his answer had finally been heeded; perhaps he had proved himself useless to Rangatha. He slowly began to lose the built up fear and Rangatha became less of a living enemy and more of a fading nightmare.

They reached the base of the Eastern Mountains as late autumn was fading from the land and the very beginnings of winter were blowing in on icy breezes. The sheer cliff faces rose sharply up in front of them like an insurmountable wall. A narrow winding path of hard stone showed the direction taken by those who deemed it necessary. It was difficult to see how hunting would even be possible. It was then that doubt began to rise in them. Were they truly meant to pass through these mountains? Not many had done it before and none knew what lay beyond the towering peaks. It was early evening and the fall sun was already beginning to set. The temperature was dropping quickly. A decision would have to be made in the morning.

It was nearly impossible to find soft places to sleep like the ones they had left behind in their forested homes. They settled for a sheltered spot under one of the few remaining trees. It was spindly and thin, its branches long deprived of its leaves which littered the ground below them.

Curling up against each other, they allowed themselves to drift into slumber. Ameliora and Versitha's chests rose and fell evenly and her mind was calm. Nadav though, felt himself fall deeper and deeper into a chasm of slumbering chaos he knew all too well.

FIFTEEN

Nadav blinked open his eyes and raised his head. He was under the same tree which he had fallen asleep under, but something was different. He swung his head in all directions, his ears perked. The fur along his neck and spine prickled. Something felt wrong. With a start, he realized what was missing. Ameliora and Versitha were no longer beside him. He sniffed along the space he knew she had occupied, but there weren't even faint traces of her scent. He stood quickly, a low growl building in his throat. His chocolate eyes shone as he scanned the area around him. Everything was black, the night having covered everything with its darkness. A small sliver of a moon provided miniscule light to the bleak trees and mountain face. A light mist covered most of the ground beneath Nadav's paws. As he stared down at the mist, swirling around his legs and blanketing the earth in its cold grasp, he realized something else. The mist was familiar in a way it should not have been. It rolled in through the trees in an unnatural way and its silence was thick in the air.

Nadav perked his ears again. He could hear nothing, the world was silent. It was quieter than was natural, than was normal. There was no soft rustling of sleeping animals tossing and turning, no crack of twigs as nocturnal mammals passed over them, no breeze stirred the fallen leaves. Nadav shivered and his eyes widened with fear as he understood where he truly was. He was in his dreams. The thought coursed through his mind, taking hold in every nook and cranny. The mist and the silence should have told him immediately. They warned of *his* presence. He should have known. He spun on his heels, looking in all directions wildly. He hated the fear, the uncertainty. He needed to know where Rangatha was hiding. The growls were building in his throat once more and his hackles were fully raised. His paws were planted wide apart and his tail lashed out. He couldn't see his dark stalker anywhere. He snarled out at the silence, breaking it as his voice echoed eerily.

"Where are you?" His voice was angry and deep, tinged with fear and desperation. In many ways, he hoped an answer wouldn't come. Was it better to spend his night in fear or be confronted? He couldn't say which he would have preferred. Unfortunately, it was not his choice to make and the decision had been made long ago. A malicious chuckle echoed through the trees, seeming to rebound off of the stone cliffs behind Nadav. Nadav spun again, searching for the owner. Nadav saw him then.

Rangatha was sitting at the base of the mountain, so close his pelt must have rubbed against the hard stone. He was in shadow, as always. His almost black fur was nearly invisible against his surroundings. His head was high and his tail was wrapped around his paws, much like Ameliora usually did. His eyes, the glint of which should have given his position away, were narrowed and filled with cruel joy. Nadav felt shivers go through him again and his spine tingled as he stared at the black pits that were eyes and not eyes. He shook his head, backing away unconsciously. Rangatha laughed again, louder this time, and spoke finally.

"You truly back away from me still after all the time we have known each other?" Nadav had turned his head to avoid looking at Rangatha, but now swung it to look the malignant spirit dead in the eye. He growled a response.

"I will never know you. Why do you come to me again?" Rangatha only chuckled again, shaking his head.

"I come to you for the only reason I ever have. I am here to protect you, to warn you of the danger you so obliviously march towards." Nadav's eyes narrowed and he snarled a response. Rangatha had done nothing to him and he was feeling braver.

"You were never my protector, only my torturer. The only threat here is to you." The deadly amusement in Rangatha's eyes broke suddenly and was replaced by burning fury. His words boomed, seeming to shatter the silence forever.

"You fight a losing battle foolish warrior. This is your last chance to flee, to save your miserable life, or to join me and see glory. If you continue on this path, death will come to you, to those you love." His eyes narrowed, his voice lowering while a small smile floated across his lips. "Would you risk *her*?" His voice grew soft and persuasive near the end. The fire in his eyes dimmed. Mist still rolled around his paws, eerily entangled in his shadowed fur. Nadav parted his jaws to reply, but Rangatha had risen and was padding silently towards him. He drew close, beginning to circle Nadav lazily. His black pits were fixed on Nadav, boring into him. "You feel drawn to me, by my power. It tugs at your inner being, pointing you in the right direction. Like an instinct, you feel a pull to come to me. You cannot resist it Nadav."

His words floated through Nadav's mind, winding around his thoughts. The pull, was it truly from Rangatha? Nadav shook his head to clear his mind. Rangatha's words were seductive poison. He growled, his tail lashing defiantly. His eyes glinted with triumph.

"And that is where you have failed Rangatha! Ameliora and I have felt your pull; indeed we have followed it to the base of the Eastern Mountains. We are coming for you and we shall bring you down." His voice lowered to a whisper, a smile played across his muzzle. "Or have you not heard the prophecy?" Nadav was confident now; sure that Rangatha had given away the only answer Nadav had truly needed. Words of the prophecy resurfaced in Nadav's memory, their words caressing his ears.

Remember this through the coming age, the wolves who watched Rangatha's end...

That spelled it all out clearly. Rangatha's end was near. Nadav returned his thoughts to Rangatha. The shadowed spirit had halted in front of him. His hackles were standing on end, his tail lashed against his hind legs. Dead leaves swirled up beneath the mist with the force. A wind howled suddenly through the trees, tearing at the fragile trees at the forest's edge. Nadav was reminded of who truly controlled his dream realm. He felt himself shrink back a little, but pressed forward again. Rangatha could do nothing to him. Rangatha's jaws parted, though his lips did not move. His angry words sounded through the clearing, coming from everywhere and nowhere simultaneously. His eyes burned and smoldered.

"Fool! I have indeed heard the prophecy you speak of. It is lies created by a desperate mind to engender hope in my defeat. How do you possibly expect to defeat me? You are mere mortals while I shall never die." His eyes narrowed as he turned away, beginning to pad towards the mountains once more. He paused, not bothering to turn his head. "Know this, the closer you come to my realm; the closer you bring Ameliora to her death." He chuckled darkly, sending shivers through Nadav as his last whispered words sounded through the rising mist. "Or have you not heard the prophecy?"

With that, Rangatha was gone. The mist had risen to envelop him and now all traces of the dark spirit had vanished. Nadav was left alone; once more Rangatha had had the final words. The whispered taunt had sent chilling claws slicing into Nadav's heart. How was it possible? It said nothing of the death of "fair beauty" in the prophecy. He recalled the words, replaying them in his mind.

Good and Evil a battle shall rage, and two must die as to portend...

Those words, they echoed through Nadav. And one must die. How had he missed that? How in all the times that he had poured over the prophecy with Ameliora, had he missed that? He sat, curling his tail around his paws. The mist was gathering, growing and expanding around him. It rose, covering his paws, then his tail. He closed his eyes, waiting for it all to end. The chilling off white clouds crept higher and higher, slowly enveloping him. The unearthly silence had descended once more. Rangatha was gone, and Nadav was alone. As the last tendrils of mist wound around his ear tips, Nadav opened his eyes once more.

His head was rested upon his paws and he could feel Ameliora's warm body pressed up against his own. She was still breathing evenly, deep within her own slumber. He raised his head slowly, casting a glance towards the sky. The sun was only beginning to rise. It sent stripes of orange, gold and pink across the baby blue sky. Wisps of clouds were scattered throughout the sky and twirled around the peaks of the Eastern Mountains. Nadav stared up at them. What had he come to encounter? Where was he going?

He knew he would be unable to go back to sleep. His mind was whirling with thoughts of the prophecy. Would it be better to simply quit? If it would save her, maybe it was. He couldn't bear the thought of bringing her to her death. Something in the back of his mind told him that he couldn't turn back. He had to go on. He rested his head back on his paws, gazing at her. He had to go on, no matter what it meant. This was something that had been foretold. He vowed to himself, he would protect her even if it meant his own life. He would not lead her to her demise. A thought occurred to him. What if it wasn't Ameliora meant to die? The prophecy could just as easily be speaking of him. This thought, in some way, comforted him.

She began to stir beside him, bringing him out of his own tangled thoughts. Her eyes scrunched up before flickering open. Versitha, on Ameliora's other side, still slept. She looked around bleary-eyed for a moment, before blinking the sleep from her eyes. She smiled at Nadav and yawned, standing and stretching leisurely. She looked towards the Eastern Mountains, oblivious for the moment of Nadav's obvious stress.

"Are you ready to climb that? I never thought I'd be climbing a mountain." She trailed off, her voice full of wonder and apprehension. Nadav was silent, watching her and going over how he would tell her. Did he have to mention Rangatha's threat? No. She never had to know. He smiled slightly, pushing the thoughts away. She turned back to Nadav, tilting her head quizzically. "Is everything alright Nadav?" Her eyes were concerned. Nadav smiled back reassuringly before telling her.

"I had another dream last night." Her eyes immediately widened with worry, fear and then curiosity. She lowered her voice.

"Rangatha again? We should wake Versitha, she's a part of this now too." Nadav nodded in reply. She was pensive for a moment, though moved towards Versitha. She nudged the other female awake, gesturing silently towards Nadav in reply to Versitha's quizzical glance. The two females moved back towards Nadav. "What did he say?" Nadav looked away, gathering himself. He had to convince her, but he had never lied to her before, to either of them. They trusted each other, yet he would outright lie to them now. He turned back to face them, his face smooth and calm.

"Nothing unusual, he threatened death and horror." He grinned at her, his eyes laughing. They laughed lightly. They had been worried, but Nadav put them at ease. They grinned matching grins at him. Versitha questioned Nadav, her voice light.

"Well, how did he like that?" Nadav laughed in reply, now that he was awake Rangatha seemed much less frightening, much less real.

"Not very much, he may have mentioned something about me being foolish and spurning a power unlike anything else." She laughed, shaking her head.

"We have nothing to worry about then. Let's get going, I want to get an early start on these mountains." Nadav nodded, though paused.

"Wait, he said something else. He says the pull we feel, that we follow, it comes from him." She whirled around to face him, her eyes filled with trepidation. Versitha had frozen, fear filling her usually impenetrably gentle eyes. He grimaced and continued. "He says we feel the pull of his growing power." The three fell into grim silence.

"Where could we possibly be going?" Her voice was quiet, uncertain in the revelation Nadav had revealed. Nadav said nothing more. Rangatha's words haunted him still. He would not tell her. Could she tell that he wasn't telling the whole truth? It didn't seem so.

"Quatar's Valley." Versitha spoke up suddenly, her voice hushed by seriousness. Ameliora and Nadav looked to her with surprise. "We're close to him, we all feel it. And Quatar's Valley is the only known oasis in the mountains." She nodded seriously.

Nadav nodded quietly, shoving thoughts of his own treachery from his mind. He padded up to stand beside her, nudging her gently and smiling. His eyes glittered, filled with determination.

"And somewhere, our fourth companion awaits us." He looked up at the towering peaks apprehensively. She nodded and padded to the base, scanning for the best place to begin. Versitha stood slightly behind. She glanced at the other she-wolf, noticing for the first time the deep worry lines that had aged her in the past months. She looked back to the mountain. There was a gentler sloped pathway leading up on a diagonal, though it was in obvious disuse. She shook her head slightly; there was no hiding that the going would be tough. She turned to look at Nadav, her eyes full of determination as she put the first paw upon the rocky earth. Nadav padded up behind her, Versitha taking the back.

They began to climb the impressive cliff face, padding slowly one paw after the other. They had gone but feet when a sudden bark from below, filled with surprise and confusion, stopped them. They turned their heads in unison to stare down at a sight Ameliora would never have thought to see. Her eyes widened, taking in the group of wolves that had called to them.

"Daughters of Romaus!"

ᖇᖇ
SIXTEEN

Standing at the base of the mountains Ameliora, Versitha and Nadav had only just begun to ascend, was a familiar ash gray male wolf. His name came like a whispered breath from Ameliora's gaping jaws. Her eyes were wide as she looked beyond him and to the wolves gathered behind him. She slowly turned from Nadav, descending the small distance they had begun to cover together. Versitha stayed behind, her eyes had taken on a mournful stricken appearance. Nadav was silent, staring at her with confusion. He followed more slowly behind her, slightly intimidated by so large a pack and uncomfortable with their unfamiliarity. She came to face the ashen male and Nadav stood just behind her, eying the other male suspiciously, slightly nervous at the prospect of a possible attack. She seemed comfortable, but Nadav was still a bit paranoid from his dream from the night before. She now spoke again; the name she had spoken earlier was more distinct yet still quiet with shock. Nadav strained his ears to make out what she had said.

"Armourn?" Nadav's eyes flicked to the ashen male, apparently named Armourn. A tan brown female wolf with darker highlights stood behind Armourn, Nadav guessed her to be Armourn's mate. The female's gaze had drifted to Versitha, who stood slightly concealed behind Nadav. Armourn nodded slowly, his eyes held the same shock as hers as well as a new joy. His tail swished against his back legs as he spoke again.

"Ameliora, Versitha, what are you doing here? And where is your pack?" His voice held tinges of worry as he queried after her pack. Nadav began slowly to relax, it seemed that they knew each other well from their past. If Ameliora trusted Armourn, Nadav figured he could as well. Versitha, on the other hand, shifted with growing anxiety. She, however, was oblivious of both Nadav and Versitha. All her attentions were trained on Armourn. Slowly, her own eyes ventured to each of the pack members behind Armourn. Slightly behind Armourn stood Clea, silent but her eyes shining with the same motherly gentleness she had loved. Ontris, Elera and Forella stood in a small group behind Armourn and Clea. Ontris was as impassible as ever, standing with muscles tensed as he eyed Nadav warily. Elera was watching Armourn, her eyes slightly distant. She had an aurora of sorrow about her that made her want to wince. Elera – at least for as long as she had known her – had seemed quiet in a sad sort of way, but it had gotten much worse since she had last seen her. She stood close to Forella, seeming to draw strength from her sister. Forella, true to her form, sat with her tail curled around her paws. She flashed her a grin and dipped her head in greeting. She drew her gaze back to Armourn, a smile growing on her lips.

"I could ask you the same thing, Armourn. As for my pack, I can only assume they are back where you last saw them. I have been traveling separately for quite some time now." She paused and glanced to Nadav. He had noticed Ontris' piercing gaze and was now staring the other male down. He was oblivious to the conversation. She cleared her throat, but he didn't respond. She nudged him and he finally turned his head, blinking at Armourn and dipping his head silently. "This," Ameliora continued, "is Nadav, and I'm sure you remember Versitha. We're on our way to Quatar's Valley." She looked to Versitha for the first time, noticing with belated surprise the overwhelming guilt and sorrow in the other female's eyes. She looked away, clearing her throat. Armourn nodded and looked Nadav up and down before nodding a greeting to Nadav. He turned his gaze back to her quizzically.

"Quatar's Valley you say? I've heard it mentioned in passing. It lies beyond the mountains does it not?" He shrugged and Clea chuckled quietly. She tilted her head in confusion.

"That it does. But what of you? Why are you so far from your territory?" Armourn shrugged again, now looking slightly confused himself as he began to explain the situation.

"We just couldn't stay any longer. Everywhere we went, dark memories haunted us." He cleared his voice, looking to Clea whose eyes flashed a deep sorrow. "Every instinct screamed the need to move. We weren't sure where we were going or why, but eventually we decided to follow it. We've simply been letting our paws lead the way. We found ourselves near the Eastern Mountains." He looked up at her, his eyes flashing multiple feelings. Somewhere hidden inside of him was doubt, concern, worry and faith. She said nothing for a moment, darting a glance at Nadav who met her eyes. His were unreadable. She turned back to Armourn hesitantly.

"I understand, Armourn." She, spoke quietly. She couldn't help but see the similarities between her own reasons for journeying. She wondered if any among Armourn's pack had been visited by Rangatha. The thought sent shivers down her spine. Her gaze darted to Elera, imagining Rangatha taking hold of the susceptible female's mind. She looked back to Armourn, placing her words carefully. "Nadav, Versitha and I are following this same pull you described. Have you seen others on your travels?" She glanced at Nadav who was now looking off into the distance with a masked expression. Versitha had moved slightly away, and stood now staring at the peaks. She returned her attention to Armourn.

"We've scented many other wolves on our ways, though never stopping to investigate. We wanted no trouble while passing through territories." She nodded, letting out an inward sigh of relief. Whatever she and Nadav were venturing towards, it Armourn's pack didn't appear to be involved.

"I would say that no one will know the meaning until the end, when all truth is revealed." She wasn't sure where her own words came from. They were hers, and yet not hers. She shook herself, beginning to turn away from Armourn with a renewed fervor in her paws. She sent Nadav a glance before turning an apologetic smile to Armourn. "I only regret that we cannot stay in each other's company longer, for Nadav and I must be on our way. We are tight pressed to reach Quatar's Valley within the rise of the new moon." She did not give a reason, knowing Armourn would not ask. With a dip of her head, and a smile to the rest of his pack, she turned away. Nadav's eyes flicked the slightest curiosity, but he followed her lead. He too dipped his head respectfully to Armourn, his eyes still flicking distrustfully to Ontris. The other male only narrowed his eyes and shifted closer to Elera.

"Farewell and safest travels to you." Armourn's voice was curious, though implied that they would meet again. She didn't doubt they would. She didn't turn as she called over her shoulder.

"And to you as well." She put a paw on the first stone and bunched her hind legs as she pulled herself up the first steps of the steep incline. Versitha followed closely behind, seeming eager to bound up the stones and away from the gathered gazes. Nadav came last, his tail swishing rapidly against his legs and his ears twitching back and forth. He was deep in thought, though about what, she could only guess. As the shapes of Armourn's puzzled pack began to dwindle, a last voice called out to her. The words burned themselves into her mind. Versitha, Ameliora and Nadav froze simultaneously.

"May Morenia watch over you." Forella's voice was almost too distant to hear, but only almost. Her faint words twisted around her thoughts, sending a jolt of fear through her. She couldn't turn back, couldn't let on the effect of Forella's words. Forella's voice was innocent enough, only invoking the protection of the spirit of old times. The truth behind Forella's words was eerily accurate, making her wonder if Forella knew anything she hadn't let on. Ameliora knew it was impossible, and yet the chance phrasing of words had rattled her. Nadav's ears had perked as well and he had frozen momentarily before continuing. They were far out of ear reach and had left Armourn's pack behind in the shadows of midday when Versitha ventured to speak.

"Before the new moon rises? I was not aware we had so little time." Her voice was quiet, yet held a hopeful hint of a lighthearted joke. She sighed, not looking back at her as she replied in a whisper.

"Neither did I. Think about it, Versitha. This is more than just the three of us now. Morenia and Rangatha have drawn the world we know into their struggle. This is no longer the tales of old leaking into the times of present. They have full on collided. We must reach Quatar's Valley before all is shaken to its roots and stability is unattainable." The enormity of what they had to accomplish grew in her mind, expanding to encompass all her fears and doubts. Phrases of the prophecy given to her replayed over and over in her dazed mind.

Then shall one dead be risen. Her first thought, of course, was Armourn's deceased son. The fear in Versitha's eyes mirrored this thought. She remembered the mangled body of the small pup, the crisscrossing lacerations in his pelt and the stench of death that had so thoroughly engulfed him. The thought of sightless eyes blinking open once more was enough to make her blood run cold. Though of course, why did the prophecy have to concern a death that she had known of? Couldn't the resurrected wolf be someone Nadav knew? Or Morenia? Or Rangatha? Or none of them? Her tail flicked slowly as she called back to Nadav. She wished they could walk side by side, but the narrow trail prevented it.

"Who have you known that has passed away, Nadav?" The question seemed to startle him, though he recovered quickly enough. He thought for a moment and she imagined she could hear him swallow a question of his own. His voice, when he did speak, was tinged with curiosity and puzzlement.

"No one, actually, or at least no one that I know of." She nodded, though of course he couldn't see her reaction. That left out Nadav, but still included a long list of possibilities. She growled slightly with annoyance. "Why do you ask?" Nadav's voice brought her back.

"One of the lines of the prophecy," She answered him, "it says 'then shall one dead be risen'. I've been trying to figure who exactly might be resurrected. I figured it might be someone known by you, me, Versitha, Morenia or Rangatha who had died. You don't know anyone, so that narrows down the list some. We have my uncle, Jandem, and one of Armourn's pups." She spoke collectively, including Versitha. Her voice caught slightly as she imagined the heart broken family being confronted with the ghastly resurrected corpse of their lost pup. She shivered. The trio had fallen silent, no doubt each picturing their fallen loved ones.

"I would say that no one will know the meaning until the end, when all truth is revealed." Nadav's voice was even as he quoted her words back at her, a smile hidden in his voice. It was wise, yet she found herself dissatisfied. How was she supposed to halt Rangatha's return if she would only know the truths she so desperately searched for when all had ended, for the good or bad?

SEVENTEEN

Hours passed into days, and days into weeks. The travel was grueling, though Ameliora, Versitha and Nadav found that their paw pads were soon hardened against the rough stones that dug into them as they climbed. The passage of time was both achingly slow and too quick to comprehend. She dreaded the day when they would reach Quatar's Valley, unsure of what awaited her there or beyond. Yet she also hurried towards it with a growing fervor as her feelings of fear and desperation mounted silently inside of her. As the three had continued to travel, evidence of seasonal changes were becoming obvious. A lingering scent, chilling winds and fallen leaves caught in hardened mud told the story of the time that had passed as they travelled.

Winter had come upon the mountains in earnest. She wouldn't hesitate to say it was the worst time possible for travelling in the mountains, but she couldn't afford to wait for spring and easier travel. The icy wind whipped at her fur, sending sharp needles into her skin. She was permanently chilled, though was thankful that snow had not yet fallen. Occasionally she would pause and look up at the peaks of the Eastern Mountains. They were capped in white that was slowly but surely extending down from the peaks as the temperatures dropped and winter extended its frozen grip over its dominion. The winds were forcing them to make frequent stops, slowing them down to a painful crawl.

The winds howled, buffeting them as they struggled up the steep slope. Their paws sank deep into the chilling snow, making progress agonizingly slow. She kept her eyes narrowed against the onslaught of wind and snow that pelted them. Her limbs were quickly becoming weak with exhaustion, and her muscles screamed with protest against the freezing wind. Nadav turned to Versitha who was a step behind him, and Ameliora a step behind her. The path had become too narrow for them to walk side by side. He had to shout to be heard over the wind.

"We have to find shelter for the night!" Ameliora and Versitha looked up, having kept their heads down to avoid the sharp frozen snow getting into his eyes. They nodded quickly, conserving their energy instead of making a vocal reply. Nadav turned back to the path ahead of them, scanning the mountainside for anything that could offer respite from the storm. A gaping black opening greeted him, it's dark depths both unsettling and relieving. Nadav looked back to Versitha, but the females had spotted the same opening and simply nodded again. They pushed their way to the cave, hurrying to get out of the fierce wind.

The comparative stillness of the air within the cave was astounding. The three collapsed on the cold stone immediately. Their flanks heaved with exhaustion, their legs shaking. Their progress had been slow, but each step felt like a hundred. They lay down near the mouth of the cave, uncomfortable going any further into the forbidding depths. No scents greeted them. There was no hope of finding prey in the cave and the idea of venturing out of the cave in search of a skinny rabbit was quickly dismissed. Ameliora and Nadav wordlessly curled around each other, sharing and preserving what little warmth they could muster. Versitha lay close to Ameliora, her back pressed against her. Ameliora laid her head on Nadav' paws while he rested his own head in the soft fur of her neck. Their breathing began to even as they started to succumb to the numbness of a much needed slumber. As Nadav' eyes drifted closed, murmured words came to her ears.

"We're going to make it." His words were simple, but they gave her strength. She pressed her face into Nadav' chest fur in way of reply. She had come to depend on him much more than she ever could have thought. Versitha had always been a sister to her, but Nadav had been something else, had given her something besides the comfort of family. Her lips twitched into a smile remembering how they had met. Each had greeted the other with suspicion and hostility, but even that had lasted only moments. They had become attached to each other, in a way that neither of them could or wanted to explain. She allowed her eyes to drift shut, concentrating on the even beating of Nadav' heart. She slowed her own breathing to match to quiet whistle of Nadav' breathing. Soon, the pair had drifted entirely to sleep.

She was filled with dread before she even opened her eyes. She had come to expect being greeted by the black forest. Yet against all her expectations, she had fervently hoped to see the blinding white of newly fallen snow outside the cave. She should have learned that her hopes would never be realized when she most needed them to be. She picked herself up slowly, wincing as her limbs protested. Even in her dreams, her body ached from the grueling journey through the mountains. She swung her head, looking in all directions. She knew better than to think Rangatha would be waiting for her. It had never been his style.

He was out there, somewhere, most likely waiting in the bushes. She could almost feel his pupil-less eyes on her. She shivered despite her best efforts to appear brave. She turned in a full circle, scanning the trees for any sign of the black pits that served as Rangatha's piercing gaze. The clearing was strangely silent. No wind stirred and not a single bird sung. She swallowed nervously, eyeing the trees. Without Rangatha, what stopped her from venturing out of the clearing that acted as her prison? She took a hesitant step towards the trees, waiting to see if anything would happen. When no response came, she moved forward. Even her paws padding against the dirt ground, stepping on fallen leaves, made no sound. The black trees towered above her, much larger and more intimidating than from afar. She closed her eyes, drawing on any courage she had remaining. She took a breath and stepped forward.

"I thought you would have come accustomed to our little routine, my fair beauty." She swore that her heart stopped beating. She was nose to nose with Rangatha, though he towered far over her. His lips were split in a grin, flashing all of his pointed ivory canines. The black swirling pits were concentrated on her. She imagined she could see them laughing. Her own jaw dropped in horror before she could stop it. She stumbled back in fear, reentering the clearing. Her paw caught and she landed heavily on the ground. She stared in terror as Rangatha calmly padded from the pitch blackness of the trees and entered the clearing. He took his time, relishing her fear. She swallowed, her heart beating rapidly in her chest.

"I'm nothing of yours." Her words were braver than she felt, though her voice shook as she spoke. Rangatha simply laughed, as she half knew he would. He had reached her and now was padding slow lazy circles around her. She felt like a fallen doe, simply waiting for the jaws of death to close around her throat. She shook, waiting for the torment that was sure to come.

"Why do you refuse to learn, my beauty?" He chuckled, not waiting for a reply. "You are mine through and through." He paused in front of her, leaning down and thrusting his face into hers. His voice dropped to a whisper and his eyes seemed to glow. "You are whatever I want you to be." She recoiled violently, wincing with disgust. Rangatha smiled, flicking his tail under her chin in a repulsively affectionate manner. She wrenched her face away, scrambling to her paws. She backed away from Rangatha, unable to tear her eyes from his face.

"I am the servant of Morenia." The confident smile on Rangatha's lips wavered, though not with fear. It wavered with the cold fury that flashed in his eyes. A deep rumbling growl permeated the clearing, seemed to reverberate through her rib cage.

"You serve a lost cause, only a fable of strength and power." He approached her, though she continued to back away from him. He was shaking his head, as if explaining to a pup the simplest of life's lessons. His tail flicked lazily against his back legs as he walked towards her. His eyes never left her face, sending chill after chill up her spine. She backed away until the backs of her legs hit the hard wood of a black cedar. She looked up, but by the time she lowered her gaze, she was once again face to face with Rangatha. He moved towards her, so close she could feel the fur on his cheeks brushing hers. Her legs shook uncontrollably. He parted his lips to accost her ears once more.

"Back away from her." Her jaw dropped as she recognized the deep bass voice of Nadav. The gray and brown muscular male stepped from the darkness, his eyes narrowed and his lips curled over his fangs in a fierce snarl.

A light behind him formed and began to grow. It shifted, a shining halo around his body to penetrate the darkness. The light began to shift and solidify. In moments, Morenia's shining form stood behind Nadav. Her white eyes were calm and trained on Rangatha. Rangatha's lips formed a sneer. He stepped back, standing at her side. She was still too petrified to move or make a sound.

"Truthfully, I expected better from you Nadav." He grinned as his eyes flicked to Morenia. He snorted with contempt. "And I expected nothing from *you* Morenia." His tail flicked back and forth, caressing her back with each swing. She shivered, turning pleading eyes to Nadav. Nadav' eyes smoldered with renewed fury each time Rangatha touched her. Nadav took a threatening step forward, barely able to keep the growls from rumbling in his throat.

"You will back away from her." Rangatha burst into laughter before Nadav had even finished his sentence. His chest shook and the clearing was filled with the booming sound of Rangatha's mirth. He shook his head, amused and not the least bit threatened. He tilted his head slightly, ignoring Morenia's presence entirely.

"I will do nothing but exactly what I wish. I would have thought you would understand this." Nadav didn't attempt to suppress his vicious snarls and growls as they broke free from his chest and lips. He stepped forward, Morenia just behind him. Her heart leapt in panic. She had experienced what Rangatha could do first hand. The faint scars on her muzzle were proof. Her eyes flicked between Nadav and Rangatha. Nadav was quickly advancing on Rangatha, urged by his fury. Rangatha's claws kneaded the dirt as he stood grinning and waiting for Nadav. She turned her gaze to Morenia. The glowing she-wolf gave the most subtle of head nods. Her muscles bunched and with every ounce of courage she had, she lunged at Rangatha.

Rangatha snarled in surprise as he crashed to the ground underneath her. She bent her head quickly, digging her teeth into his shoulder and tearing with all her might. Rangatha didn't even seem to notice. He shoved up roughly, sending her flying. She crashed into the ground with a heavy thud. Morenia's frantic voice reached her, urging her to her paws.

"Run!" Nadav was at Ameliora's side in an instant, helping her stand. She looked behind her to see Morenia and Rangatha grappling amidst snarls and flashing ivory teeth. Nadav nudged her and the two broke into a sprint. She held her breath as they passed through the trees. Nadav and Ameliora ran and ran until the sounds of the immortal battle faded into silence. They continued to run, unable to look at each other or stop for fear of being pursued. The black forest began to fade and become indistinct. A faint howl rose in the distance. As the dream faded from her eyes, words wound through her mind.

You'll always be mine...

She opened her eyes, jerking her head up with a start. Nadav did so at the same time. The two looked at each other for a long moment, not having to speak of the experience they had shared. Her heart still beat rapidly in her chest, the horror of the dream still fresh in her mind. Versitha lifted her head, blinking sleep from her eyes. Her gaze was wary as she looked to Ameliora and Nadav. She shifted, burying her face deep into the fur on Nadav' neck. He hushed her, nuzzling her face and neck with his muzzle in comforting reassurance. The two huddled together, seeking comfort in each other's warmth and physical presence. Neither closed their eyes again, afraid to return to their dreams, and the assurance of Rangatha's wrath.

⁓
EIGHTEEN

Despite their best attempts to delay their departure, eventually Ameliora, Versitha and Nadav were compelled to leave their stone sanctuary. The cave, though damp and dark, had become a safe haven for the wolves. Its warmth and security provided a welcome respite from the snow storm. But now the storm had stopped, or at least paused for the moment. The icy air had hardened the fallen snow providing a base, preventing their paws from sinking into the deep snow with each step. The ground was a mixture between ice and snow, neither fully one nor the other. It crunched loudly under their paws and Ameliora felt they should walk with care. She felt like everything would crack and shatter beneath her at the slightest misstep, causing her to plummet to a certain death and Rangatha's waiting jaws. She shivered.

They had only taken a few cautious steps outside their cave. Though the stone was hard and the cold of it had seeped into their bones as they slept, anything was preferable to fighting the storm. She glanced back over her shoulder longingly. She knew they had to leave, if not for their quest, than for food. She couldn't remember the last time her stomach was full. What scant prey they found was often thin – its meat stringy and sparing. She found her mind wandering to her pack, waiting far west of the great Eastern Mountains she was now crossing. She found herself lost in her memories, specifically those of a hunt. She could almost hear the bellowing of elk and Romaus' commanding growl. She could feel her heart pound with the thrill of the chase and then her own triumphant howl of victory as the scent of fresh blood permeated the plains. She whined softly under her breath, her eyes sorrowful.

"Which is it – family, food or warmth?" Nadav' voice broke through her thoughts. She had thought her whine too soft for him to hear, but she had misjudged the silence in which they currently travelled. She shifted her paws uncomfortably. The path they walked had temporarily widened, allowing the two to walk side by side through the crunching snow. Versitha was ahead. She had taken to separating herself from Ameliora and Nadav. Her words were few and far between. The remorseful depth in her eyes seemed to grow with each slow step. She sighed heavily, glancing towards Nadav and then away to the cliffs they walked beside.

"It's all three actually." Nadav nodded mutely, following her gaze to the cliffs. They were trapped on both sides. Nearest to Nadav, on their left, was a towering wall of granite and stone that made up just one of the Eastern Mountains. On Ameliora's side, to their right, their small pathway abruptly dropped into plummeting cliffs. She dared to look over the edge and swallowed. Far below them, jaggedly sharp stones rose. Should either of them overstep the edge, they would be greeted by a long fall and impalement, a bloody death to be sure, but at least a quick one.

"You never really told me about them." She tore her gaze from the cliffs, looking to Nadav pensively. Thinking back over their previous conversations, she realized he was right. She'd only spoken of her family in general terms and she wasn't entirely sure why. She had nothing to hide from Nadav. She shrugged lightly, shifting more towards Nadav and away from the steep cliff side. She looked again to Versitha, who showed no inclination towards joining the conversation.

"I guess you just never asked." Nadav rolled his eyes and sent her a grin. She smiled back, though her mind was now settled firmly on her family. Their faces flashed before her, memories from her life with her pack came flooding through her carefully constructed mental barriers. Her lips twitched and she spoke again, her voice thoughtful. "I don't think you would have liked them, for the most part." She turned to him. "Though perhaps you would have gotten along with my father, Romaus." She smiled fondly, "He has a warrior's spirit, a leader through and through." She chuckled and looked back to the horizon, searching for Quatar's distant valley. "He was what kept the pack moving, alive and motivated, much like you do for me." She lapsed into silence following her final comment, unsure of how exactly Nadav would choose to interpret her words.

"Perhaps you have more of your father in you than you give yourself credit for." Nadav had been silent for a long time, more pensive than she had seen him in a long time. He hadn't looked at her until he spoke. His eyes flicked as he watched her face. She wondered how he could make such a statement, since he had never met Romaus and knew only what she had told him. She parted her lips to disagree, but Nadav quickly interrupted. "You have bravery, as you seem to believe he has. Leadership and bravery go hand in hand; one is not found without the other." She had never considered herself brave. She had always done what she considered necessary, but nothing more. She looked to Nadav.

"I want to know you, like you know me." These were not the words she intended to say, but they were what came from her parted lips. She felt heat rush to her cheeks and looked swiftly away. A moment of surprise flashed on Nadav' face before his lips spread into a wide grin. He chuckled lightly. Without missing a beat, Nadav stepped towards her. He buried his muzzle swiftly in her soft neck fur, breathing in and nuzzling her lightly. He pulled away just as quickly, continuing to pad at her side.

"And I want you to know me better than I know myself." His voice was light and his smile confident, though his eyes were strangely serious. She was flustered, by both his actions and his words. She stumbled for an answer, finding she couldn't grasp the words to communicate her thoughts. She found she didn't even know what her thoughts were.

Their pathway widened further, leading to a clearing. Versitha had already entered the small space, pausing to stretch and roll in the snow. It was just a small circular space, one of the many unusual spaces found within the Eastern Mountains. Across the clearing, they could see the pathway as it continued its winding way through the mountains. They paused to stretch, making use of the space and shying away from the steep cliff side. She was still searching for some suitable reply. She turned to the cliffs, squinting at the horizon. She turned swiftly back around, her eyes bright and her words finally coming. Her face soon fell in horror as she cried out.

"Nadav, behind you!" Her eyes were wide and her jaws fell open as a burly light cream male wolf barreled into Nadav. Nadav landed on the ground with a heavy thud, rolling with the cream male in a bundle of snapping jaws and vicious snarls. Versitha was at her side in an instant, her hackles bristling. A second male, possibly larger than the first, stalked confidently towards the two females. His tail swished lazily back and forth against his legs. His dark ebony brown coat stood out starkly against the blindingly white snow. She cursed their foolishness. The wind had been blowing head on, keeping everything behind them downwind. Though these two males had undoubtedly been following them for miles, they had never noticed their presence.

She didn't have time to mull further on her thoughts. With a deep throated laugh, the massive ebony male rushed at them. She dodged to the side, but not quickly enough. He caught her hindquarters, sending her crashing to the ground hard on her right shoulder. Her paws scrabbled against the compacted snow as she scrambled to get to her paws. Versitha launched herself at the male, but he easily batted her aside. She cried out as hot breath touched her neck and the male sunk his teeth into the scruff of her neck. She felt her front paws being lifted bodily from the ground. She had always been small, unusually so. And this male was unusually massive. The combination was proving very unlucky for Ameliora. Versitha was struggling to her feet, preparing to rush again.

She cried out, struggling and craning her neck in an attempt to lock her teeth on something, anything that would cause the male to release her. Her paws scraped across the snowy ice, though her back legs were still firm on the ground. She lashed out with a back leg, kicking the male hard in the stomach. He let out a breath, parting his jaws. She slipped from his grasp, standing and darting out of his reach. Versitha sprinted, skidding to a stop panting beside her as the male began to recover. She caught her breath, her eyes flicking here and there until she spotted Nadav and the cream male still locked in combat. The snow they had rolled over was stained crimson and her heart plummeted. The two males were too tightly inter-locked for her to tell whose blood had been spilled.

Her paws flashed over the icy snow as she raced to the flurry that was Nadav and the cream male. Versitha sped past her, barreling into the fray with a snap of her jaws, A fu-rious snarl from the other side of the clearing told her that her own attacker would soon be upon them. She lunged, sinking her teeth deep into the leg of Nadav' attacker. She was rewarded with an agonized howl as the male paused. Nadav took advantage, reaching up his own jaws and fasten-ing them around the cream male's neck. He yanked, sink-ing his teeth in deep. Blood welled around his jaws and the male cried out in pain, stumbling away from Nadav. Nadav released him, standing. Versitha pulled away, having sunk her teeth wherever she could get a purchase. His chest heaved, his eyes were wide and half-crazed it appeared. His gaze was fastened on the cream male. The male shook him-self, bleeding heavily from his neck and leg. He too panted. He managed to choke out words between gasps.

"You...will all...face the wrath...of Rangatha!" Nadav snarled viciously, lunging at the cream male. The two had gotten dangerously close to the cliff's edge. Nadav hit the cream male like a ton of stones, he stumbled backwards uncontrollably. His paws scraped and flailed as he lost his footing and began to fall. He howled a long mourn-ful howl while she stared in horror as she saw the cream male's body strike the boulders landing sickeningly at the base of the cliffs. With aching slowness, Nadav too lost his balance. His paws scrabbled at the edge as he clung for something that would keep him steady. She watched horrified, moving towards him. Versitha was faster, snow spraying out from her paws as she fastened her teeth onto Nadav's scruff. She was distracted, forgetting her own assailant.

She was knocked to the ground again, her breath rushed from her. Her head slammed the hard packed snow and her vision blurred for a moment. The male stood over her, pinning her firmly to the ground. She struggled and writhed, but his grip was like iron. He smirked again, leaning down to whisper in her ear. Ameliora tried in vain to turn her head from his poisonous words.

"It's unfortunate my master has ordered us to terminate you." He grinned, a grin that sent chills down her spine as his eyes glinted cruelly. "I would have liked to spend more time with you." She growled, narrowing her eyes in disgust. The male simply chuckled again, adding on almost as an afterthought. "There's something about you that's just so similar to *her*." He looked like he was about to say more, but decided against it. He raised his head and as if from a distance, she heard Nadav calling her name in a horrified voice. Versitha echoing in a wordless cry. The ebony male peeled back his lips, displaying his pointed canines. He laughed a final time and his face rushed towards hers.

In a moment, she felt the weight of the ebony male lifted from her. A deep gray male with familiar red-brown highlights had tackled her assailant. They rolled and tumbled, a mixture of snarls and flashing ivory fangs. She struggled to her paws, shaking with fear as she searched for Nadav. Versitha had dug in her paws, hauling Nadav back over the edge. Her fur was plastered to her skin with blood and sweat. He panted, standing and moving away from the edge. The three stared at each other for a long moment before remembering her attacker and this new stranger. The new male stood over the ebony male, pinning him to the ground. Without warning or mercy, he sunk his fangs into the attacker's throat. He tore, spilling warm blood that sizzled as it hit the snow. The ebony male went limp and the gray and red-brown male stepped away from the body with a disgusted kick. He turned his head to her and she felt her heart both drop with surprise and leap for joy. Nadav spoke before either the male or Ameliora could, a growl in his throat. His muscles bunched as he prepared to attack, but Versitha darted in front of him, standing protectively in front of the stranger.

"Don't you dare touch him." Versitha's voice was more serious than Ameliora had ever heard her, a threat laced in her words. With his usual cold demeanor and seriousness, the gray male pressed against Versitha and approached the still speechless Ameliora and Nadav. Nadav bristled with suspicion and stepped protectively nearer to her. The male paused and raised a brow. He shook his head slightly and smiled, though it held no joy. His gaze was glued to Ameliora, Versitha still stood protectively at his side. Nadav's voice was hostile.

"Why have you done this?" The male looked back to Versitha, his gaze lingering on her skeletal weak form. They softened for a moment, before returning to Nadav with their former coldness.

"As if I would stand by and watch my sister die." Derment blinked and Ameliora, filled with shock, exhaustion and bleeding from her neck, collapsed on the ground.

NINETEEN

A familiar scent reached Ameliora's nostrils and she wrinkled her nose lightly. She scrunched her eyes tighter together, unwilling to open them just yet. She knew that when she did, she would be right back with Nadav in the mountains, forced to face reality once more. But for this moment, all she wanted was the keep her eyes closed and pretend she was home again. Her dreams had been so realistic. Derment's scent still lingered on her fur. It was this scent she most wished to preserve. She hadn't realized how much she missed her older brother until her subconscious had brought him to her attention.

Eventually, she knew she had to rise and greet the new day. Whether she wished it or not, she had a journey to complete. Thoughts of their journey brought images of Nadav and Versitha to her mind. She smiled and blinked open her eyes, raising her head to look to them. Her eyes bulged with disbelief as her gaze landed not on Nadav, but the bulky gray male sitting uneasily beside Nadav, Versitha close at his side. As if sensing her eyes, all three turned towards her. Nadav' eyes were filled with suspicion, a hard frown on his muzzle. Versitha couldn't seem to tear her eyes away from the bulky gray male. She slowly turned her eyes back to the red-brown highlighted male, Derment. His characteristically cold gaze was soft, tired but emotionally rather than physically. A small smile twitched at the edges of his lips as he met her gaze.

"What are you doing here?" The words burst forth from her lips before she could stop them. Her voice was incredulous, and tinged with suspicion. To have seen Romaus come to her rescue would have been one thing, but Derment was another. She felt a hint of regret as she saw the small smile on Derment's muzzle waver at her words, and the accompanying flash of outraged disbelief in Versitha's eyes. Nadav glanced at Derment before standing and walking to her.

"I've been asking him the same thing, but he refuses to speak with me." Distrust heavily laced Nadav' voice as he spoke to her. "He just whispers with Versitha." He took a seat at her side, his eyes moving to her neck with concern. The wound from their would-be assassins from the night before hadn't bled heavily, but the skin was torn and matted. She would address her injuries later. The appearance of her brother had distracted her from everything else. She looked to Nadav as he spoke, and then returned her gaze to Derment, waiting for his reply. Derment didn't even glance at Nadav, much less acknowledge his words. The tension between the two males was palpable. And it was evident Versitha had chosen to side with Derment. He kept his tired eyes glued to her, not wavering for an instant. He seemed to be searching her, at a total loss for words. She had never seen this side of her brother, this sort of emotional vulnerability that was now present in his eyes.

"I couldn't lose her, lose either of you." His words were a surprise to them all, Derment included. He turned his face to Versitha, who was smiling with soft encouragement. He had known, whether subconsciously or consciously, why he had followed Ameliora and Versitha. He had always known, but he had yet to say it aloud. He shifted his paws in the awkward silence that followed his words. She was flooded with fear. His voice was filled with grief, a loss that made her blood run cold. All she could think of was the family she left behind, and what might have happened during her absence. She stepped towards Derment, causing Nadav to stiffen at her side. Her eyes were filled with anguish and fear, her voice pleading.

"What happened Derment?" Her voiced cracked and she had to swallow. Images of Levada and the pups flooded her mind. She could almost see their bodies strewn about the clearing, their eyes glazed and unseeing. Her heartbeat was rapid in her chest, terror mounting. "Was it the pups?" Her voice was a whisper, breaking again despite her best efforts. Derment seemed to look at her in confusion for a moment, though his eyes suddenly cleared. He shook his head rapidly, his eyes wide with worry.

"No no! They're all fine, or they were when I left." Relief flooded Ameliora, making her knees feels weak.

She sat down to keep from falling, her shoulders slightly hunched. She took a few breaths, waiting for her heart to quit racing. When she lifted her head back up, her eyes were filled with questions. Versitha pressed against Derment, whispering something Ameliora couldn't hear. As she met Derment's gaze, she knew he had the answers.

"Tharamena?" It was a statement, but also a question. The responding surge of a mixture of raw grief and fury was more than enough to answer her question. Derment looked away, drawing in calming breaths, pressing back against Versitha for comfort. For a minute, he couldn't bring himself to meet her eyes.

"You're so much like her –" He choked, pausing again to draw in breaths. In the two years she had grown up with her family, with Derment, she had never once heard him mention Tharamena. He had never opened up. He had always been her older brother, her irritable angry older brother. She didn't say anything, afraid that if she did, Derment might shut himself away once more. She just sat in silence, wondering what similarities she could possibly have to her long dead sister. Derment looked back up, though he still couldn't look at her as he spoke.

"She used to visit the stream too, lie on its banks and press her ear to the pebbles. She liked to hear the rushing of the water as it passed." His eyes were wistful and the barest gleams of a smile touched at the tips of his lips. His voice was a murmur. Neither a bird nor a creature dared to break the silence that wreathed Derment's voice. He shook his head, obviously amused. "She used to say that if you pressed your ear close enough to the stones, you could hear the waves of the ocean." Her mind was alive with the image of Tharamena, lying where she herself had so often lain.

"She was adventurous, more so than me, but quiet too. I never knew quite what she was thinking, and always wondered where her mind took her." Derment shifted his paws. The touch of a smile faded from his lips and she knew instinctively what was coming. "I got tired of her adventures. I wanted to stay in the camp with Mother and Father." She was surprised to hear Derment use such terms of affection. They had always been simply Romaus and Levada. "So she went off on her own, snuck away like pups do." Derment heaved a sigh, straightening his shoulders he finally looked to her.

"And she died," he cut himself off, correcting his words. "She was killed and I wasn't there to protect her, to tell her that everything would be okay. She was all I had, and I let her die." She wanted to object, she wanted to move to her brother, but she knew Derment was vulnerable. There was no telling how he would react. Years of guilt and self-loathing could not be undone by simple words. Versitha's eyes filled with compassion as she rubbed her head against his shoulder. He seemed to draw strength from her.

"Then you came along." Her ears perked. She had expected the story to end, but apparently it had not. "You were so much like her. You looked like her, you talked like her." He chuckled, his eyes wrinkling though it looked almost unnatural. "You even got the same look in your eyes when you were thinking." She smiled, her eyes softening. She had never imagined Derment to look at her much more than he needed to. In a way, he had never been her brother. He had been a stranger to her, to them all. Only now did she realize that it was a mask he had worn, and the love he felt for her.

Derment continued to speak, speaking of his fear when she had come back from the river when Levada was attacked by the rabid male. He had felt so unwilling to show any emotion, to somehow keep himself from attaching to others. Then Ameliora and Versitha had left and though it had taken a few days of indecision, Derment had known he had to follow. He had tracked them, tracked them through the forests. He had been there, lurking in the background when they first met Nadav. He had been there when they reached the base of the mountains. He had been there through it all, a silent guardian.

She was left speechless, staring in awe at her brother. Yet something didn't fit, something he wasn't saying. He turned his head, no longer meeting her eyes. He stuck his muzzle into the soft fur of Versitha's neck, breathing deeply. The clearing was silent, the moment unbroken.

"I don't know where you're going, or why, but I can't leave you to it alone." His voice was quiet, and though it sounded as if Derment's words were directed at her – she was almost certain he referred to Versitha. She looked to Nadav. He shook his head. The decision was for Ameliora. She smiled, burying her face deep into Derment's broad chest. She finally withdrew, nodding.

"We have a lot to tell you." The rest of the morning was largely spent filling Derment in on the details of the prophecy. At first he was largely skeptical, though he did his best to hide it. He had sworn to protect Ameliora and Versitha, whatever their purpose may be. Whether he believed them or not, he would stand by their side. However, as she began to talk about Rangatha and the words of the dying assassins, a light came to Derment's eyes. No matter what he may have wanted to believe, he couldn't deny the coincidences.

Nadav had quietly slipped from the small snowy clearing, excusing himself to search for anything that could serve as a meal. He was giving the siblings time, but also arranging his own thoughts. Despite the outward good intentions, Nadav couldn't bring himself to trust Derment. He stayed on the outskirts, always within calling distance should she be thrust into danger once more.

"We have pieced out lines and words of the prophecy, but we're largely in the dark." Her voice had taken on a more scholarly tone. Derment occasionally cast skeptical glances towards Versitha, whose solemn nods reassured him. She was in full thinking mode, having grown more comfortable with Derment's presence. Derment himself was silent, lost in thought as he pondered the words of the prophecy which she had revealed. He had never been the intellectual that she, and for that matter Tharamena, had been.

"So this Rango –" She cut him off quickly, correcting him. It was second nature to her, her nemesis' name rolling off the end of her tongue.

"Rangatha." Derment shot her a slightly exasperated look, shaking his head. She shrugged slightly sheepishly, but Derment continued.

"Alright, so this Rangatha, why is he doing this?" She shook her head slightly, a sigh on her lips. She stood, pacing restlessly about the clearing. She was anxious for Nadav to return so they could be on their way once more. Versitha listened intently. Though Derment knew nothing, Versitha's own knowledge was pitiful. She had never been visited in her sleep, and much of her understanding came from conversations between Nadav and Ameliora.

"There isn't a why, Derment. Think of him as chaos. He's the embodiment of everything black in this world." She looked to him, her eyes flickering fear. "He doesn't need a reason, or a purpose or a drive. He just needs to win." Derment nodded, his lips a hard line.

"So why you? Why are you the chosen one in all of this?" Derment's voice held worry, not a hint of jealousy at his sister's position in the prophecy. She looked away, shrugging her shoulders and scanning the rocks for a glimpse of Nadav.

"I may not be. The prophecy talks about Four." Derment narrowed his eyes slightly, the look he always gave when he was frustrated with an answer.

"But you received these dreams, you and Nadav. Versitha and I," he paused, looking to Versitha and shrugging his shoulders. "We're just following your lead." She shifted uncomfortably, unable to quite meet his questioning gaze. The truth was, it was a question that put fear in her own heart. How could she tell him the conclusion that seemed inevitable? She was chosen to die. She lowered her voice.

"I'm too afraid to ask." Derment would have commented further, but Nadav bounded into the clearing. He glanced between Derment and Ameliora, suspicion clear in his eyes. He walked to her, regret now evident. He had come back with nothing, not a single piece of prey to share. She didn't comment. They had gone many nights hungry, this would be just one more. Few words were exchanged and the trio headed out. The afternoon was spent travelling in relative quiet. Occasionally, Derment and Ameliora would strike up some conversation. She asked all the questions one might expect. She was informed that the pups were well grown and healthy. Irradess took strongly after their mother. Haska and Bander had a close bond. She noticed that Derment avoided any mention of Gyern, but she didn't press the topic.

The sun had long set, shrouding the mountains in darkness, when they settled down for the night. She fell asleep nearly instantaneously. Derment and Nadav curled on either side of her, the three sharing necessary warmth. Nadav rested his head on his paws, while Derment still held his aloft.

"We should reach Quatar's Valley within the next day." His voice was a murmur, more to himself than Derment. The two males hadn't spoken much, at odds with each other. There was thick tension in the air around them.

"You don't trust me." Derment had never been one to beat around the bush. Nadav raised his head, turning to look at Derment. He waited a long moment before speaking. He gave the smallest of curt nods.

"I have no reason to trust you."

Derment was unsurprised by this answer and he looked away from Nadav, his eyes settling on Ameliora and Versitha, curled tightly around each other. They were small as they slept, curled up around themselves with their noses buried deep in bushy tails. Their chests rose and fell softly.

"Don't trust me then, trust them."

TWENTY

Ameliora's paws felt heavy, laden with ever-present exhaustion. Sleep did little to lift the weariness in her heart. The group travelled mostly in silence, though a light air of uneasy tension was still palpable between Nadav and Derment. The snow was slowly thinning, leaving sparse patches of hard stone and clumps of brittle grass. The wind still lashed unrelentingly, but was no longer accompanied by shards of ice. Signs of prey animals were becoming more common. Nadav had managed to catch a rabbit, serving as the largest meal any of them had had since entering the mountains.

Each was lost in their thoughts as they crested yet another of the many hills that made up the inner path of the mountains. Her eyes were downcast, her gaze distant as she repeated phrases of the prophecy in her mind. She didn't notice Derment suddenly halt at the very tip of the hill, Versitha at his side. She bumped into him, sending Derment stumbling forward. Both recovered their footing and were joined a moment later by Nadav. She peered around Derment's shoulder, curious at why he would have stopped. Derment was staring ahead, his eyes wide. She could just catch the barest glimpses of green. Her ears perked and she padded around to Derment's side. She felt Nadav' fur brush hers and knew that he too had come to see.

Spread out before them was a vast valley, an oasis amidst the snow and ice. Thick trees covered the western side, eventually thinning into a massive meadow. Cutting evenly through the meadow was a wide river. Towering walls of granite and cliffs surrounded the valley on all sides, leading back up to the elevations and the wintery climate. Her lips split into a grin, her voice was whispery.

"Quatar's Valley." Nadav nodded, tearing his eyes away from the valley below. He looked to her, burying his head in her shoulder fur. She could see the relief in his gaze, and the pure joy. Derment's gaze flicked to Ameliora and Nadav, though he remained silent. A satisfied smile twitched at his lips as he gazed down at Versitha, whose legs had begun to shake with anticipation. His tail flicked side to side as he eventually commented quietly.

"We made it." Nadav withdrew his face from her fur. The relief was still evident, though his eyes were serious as well. He looked to Derment, straightening his shoulders. Foreboding descended on Ameliora as Nadav spoke.

"But now we must face him." None needed ask who Nadav was referring to. They were all well aware that somewhere in the paradise stretched before them, Rangatha and his host were waiting. The four stood in silence for a minute, drawing on what remained of their inner strength. With purposeful steps, they began to descend the steep path into the valley.

The feeling of grass on her calloused paws elicited a sigh of pleasure. Though the skies were overcast and branches were laden with rain, the comparative warmth seeped into her fur. She had grown thin through their journey, her eyes sunken with hunger and sleep deprivation. The trees here were alive, birds chirped in high branches and leaves shook as squirrels leapt from tree to tree.

A quiet sound caused her ears to perk. She dropped into a crouch, breathing in the scent of mouse. She crept forward, springing and killing the small rodent quickly. She turned back to Derment, Versitha and Nadav, only to find that they too were stalking their own prey. She quickly ate her own morsel. These forests, uninhabited by predators, were teeming with prey. They stayed close to each other, hunting until they had eaten their fill. They regrouped once more, Derment still swiping his tongue across his lips.

"Why hasn't he come for us?" Nadav' ears perked and he turned to Ameliora. Her own pelt was prickling uneasily. In their time in the valley, they had caught no trace of Rangatha's foreboding presence. Only the small woodland creatures had revealed themselves. There were no signs of bears, any elk or deer, not even a badger. She shivered slightly. What had once seemed to teem with life now seemed unnaturally empty.

"Perhaps they don't know we are here." Derment's deep voice was comforting, but a voice at the back of her head knew he was wrong. With a prickling spine and apprehensive looks over her shoulder, she settled down for what she hoped would be a full night's sleep. Nadav curled near her, Derment and Versitha around each other. Soon their breathing deepened as weariness won out over fear. All four descended into sleep.

When Ameliora opened her eyes, she somehow knew better than to expect to see the still sleeping forms of Nadav, Versitha and Derment. She found herself curled in long grass, the edge of the forest nearby. She could only assume she was in the meadow they had seen from the hill. She stood slowly, looking over her shoulder with uncertainty. A rustle behind her caused her pelt to bristle and she whirled, preparing for Rangatha to make his grand appearance. Instead, Nadav stepped through the thinning trees, a sort of resigned look on his face. He paused slightly, seeing her, but approached her a moment later.

"He's going to make us wait for him again." Nadav' voice held annoyance, though it was a sure mask to cover his fear. She glanced around. When Rangatha summoned them, he did so in the black forest, where there was no sound. This wasn't his forest. But for the unnatural quiet, it was bright like any day. She slowly shook her head.

"I don't think he's coming." Nadav looked at her quizzically, tilting his head to one side. She glanced at him before tossing her head to indicate their surroundings. "Look how bright everything is. I don't feel threatened." She shook her head again, feeling reassured by her own convictions. "If Rangatha had summoned us we would be in his black forest, not here." Nadav slowly nodded, observing the bright silence around them. He sat down eventually, stretching out his front legs as his ears perked.

"Then why are we here?" She had a hunch. Her brows furrowed and she padded to Nadav' side. She settled herself down, wrapping her tail around her paws. She was about to voice her suspicions when the trees behind them began to rustle again. She turned her head, watching the branches quiver. They began to glow with a soft light. Ameliora was unsurprised to see Morenia step into their midst, as shining and beautiful as ever.

"I summoned you here." She nodded her head, having guessed as much. Morenia walked with a careful grace, circling to stand in front of them. She had almost forgotten how beautiful she was, the epitome of perfection. Morenia sat down, dipping her head to them in greeting. Her eyes held sadness, but also a touch of the same weariness that both Ameliora and Nadav felt.

"Where is he? Does he know we have arrived?" Nadav was the first to speak, to the point as he always was. She could see the tension in his shoulders. Any spirit, good or bad, put him on edge. Though Morenia wouldn't hurt him, she still wasn't natural in his mind. Morenia slowly nodded her head.

"He knows, as he has known every step of your journey. He never acts without a purpose." Her voice was heavy, laden with something she couldn't quite identify. She watched Morenia. Morenia had always seemed so strong, infallible. She would never fall, a perfect guardian. But to see her here, seemingly destroyed, made her heartbeat quicken with apprehension. She shuffled her paws, mulling over Morenia's words. She stared at her paws, thinking of the assassins Rangatha had sent. She lifted her gaze to Morenia again, her eyes questioning.

"Did you know about the attack, before it happened I mean?"

Morenia tensed suddenly, her eyes moving quickly away from Ameliora's. She was sure she saw guilt in Morenia's green depths. Her eyes hardened, it felt like a betrayal. "You knew, and you didn't even warn us. We could have been killed, the prophecy destroyed!" Morenia brought her gaze back, her eyes desperate and tinged with the smallest amount of fear. She shook her head quickly.

"He has grown stronger, stronger than I ever could have imagined he could be." Morenia straightened her shoulders, making an obvious attempt to swallow whatever misgivings she may have had. "My warning you would have done nothing. Fate is set to play out as it must. You were always meant to survive." She could feel Nadav breathing heavily beside her, his anger evident in his bristling fur. She drew a breath, seeing the wisdom in Morenia's words.

She pressed herself against Nadav reassuringly, looking to Morenia.

"If he takes his host, we are lost then." Morenia shook her head, her lips spreading into a small smile. Her shoulders seemed to sag a little with relief. She drew herself up again, looking for the first time since her arrival like the spirit She had always known. A hint of her old strength reentered her eyes.

"Rangatha is prideful, and in his vanity will become his downfall." She looked to Nadav with confusion, but Nadav was equally puzzled. She turned to question Morenia, but Morenia was already continuing. "Rangatha only exists now because at the time when we died, we were each half immortal, allowing us to continue to exist somewhere between death and life." She closed her mouth, listening intently. "Should Rangatha bond, his half immortality will mix with his host's full mortality. In gaining a host, he will sacrifice half of what he already has." Morenia's smile grew, though it was soft and hinted at triumph. "He will only be a quarter immortal, and his mortality will outweigh his immortality." Morenia paused, waiting for Ameliora and Nadav to comprehend what she was saying. It was Nadav who first caught on.

"So if he was killed after he bonded with his host, he would no longer have enough immortality to continue to exist in a way which would allow him to affect the mortal world." Ameliora sucked in a breath, looking to Morenia for confirmation. Morenia slowly nodded her head. Brief joy surged through her before a fearful thought occurred to her.

"We have to kill him in his mortal form." Morenia nodded slowly, her eyes solemn but her smile still showing hints of triumph. She looked to Nadav. Their new task seemed far more daunting than their mountain crossing. Nadav was serious, though his shoulders were set with determination. She looked back to Morenia.

"What will happen to you, should we succeed?" Morenia smiled a longing dreamy smile. She sighed, her eyes glazing with desire. Her gaze had a faraway look.

"I will exist, as I have always existed and will forever exist. But never will I return to you, to walk in dreams or among those of this earth." Her eyes returned to the present and she looked back to Ameliora. "My duty will never be done." She nodded slowly. She moved to speak more, but Morenia suddenly went rigid.

Her eyes gained a familiar glaze over them. It was the same as when she had first recited the prophecy. Everything about her was tensed. She turned her head in slow motion towards the far trees, staring straight at them though appearing to be unable to actually see them. She stared for a long moment before murmuring, almost under her breath.

"A loss that turned gaiety black..." Her voice trailed off and as it did, she heard footsteps. Her spine prickled with fear. She found herself almost too petrified to turn her gaze to where Morenia was staring. The shining light around Morenia began to dim. As she watched, Morenia slowly faded into mist. Her eyes were still staring at the spot in the trees as the footsteps grew louder. She vanished entirely just as a bulky dark form became visible in the trees. A moment later, Derment pushed his way through the thick branches, Versitha shaking at his side.

~
TWENTY-ONE

The quiet forest was no longer as peaceful and safe as it had once seemed. In the aftermath of Morenia's summons, Ameliora and Nadav were left to face the enormous task ahead of them. The four had awoken to early morning light filtering through the thick branches of the surrounding pines and cedars. Derment and Versitha wore the same look of confusion as he had during their shared dream. She wasn't sure what to tell her family, how to explain the phenomenon which she and Nadav had come to see as a normal occurrence. An awkward silence surrounded them as they settled into a new morning.

"Do I even want to know what happened last night?" Derment's voice broke through the maze of thoughts that Ameliora and Nadav had lost themselves in. They shared a glance, filled with uncertainty. Derment hadn't proved himself as good with accepting the unusual, the spiritual aspect of their journey. Derment wanted the outline, only the necessary facts. It was Nadav who ventured and answer.

"I'm not sure we could explain, even if you wanted to know." Derment stared at Nadav for a moment. She could still see the traces of suspicion in his gaze. Eventually he gave a slight nod. She agreed with Nadav' answer. What could they explain that hadn't already been said? They had already known they needed to defeat Rangatha, now they knew how.

After a few minutes of stretching and muffled yawns, the four set out again. They had covered most of the wooded land of the valley the day before. What had seemed so wonderfully expansive from the cliffs of the mountain pass was in reality much smaller than it had appeared. Walking through the cedars and pines, she was once again struck by how quiet everything was. Even the birds sang as if attempting to whisper. There had still been no sign of any creature larger than a raccoon. Even with Morenia's reassurances, she was beginning to doubt Rangatha's presence in the valley. Eventually, they reached the edge of the forested area. The meadow was laid out before them. In the far distance, a muted rumbling could be heard. She could only assume it was the river. She smiled faintly, thinking with fond memories of the small stream she had so often visited. Derment's gravelly voice interrupted her thoughts.

"We've scoured the woods, there's nothing there to find." Ameliora, Versitha and Nadav nodded silently in agreement. Derment motioned with his head towards the meadow. "Which leaves this the only place left to look." The four wolves stood at the edge, still within the cover of the trees. Farther out, there were sparse bushes, a few ferns, a lone standing tree or two. Then the meadow started in earnest, it's waving long grasses covering the earth as far as she could clearly see. She shivered slightly, her spine prickling uncomfortably. There should have been a scent, browsed grass, a pile of dung, something to indicate the presence of elk or deer. This was prime territory for them, nearly identical to the plains where Romaus had taken her pack to hunt. The emptiness made her nervous. She shifted her paws slightly, her eyes roaming the meadow.

"The meadow extends in all directions, there's no way we can cover this much ground together." Derment and Versitha nodded, but Nadav was already shaking his head. He could see where she was going with this, and he disagreed.

"If we split up and one of us does find him, we won't stand a chance. If we're really going to do this, we can't do it alone." Derment looked as if he might argue, or perhaps he was insulted at the insinuation of his own weakness against Rangatha. Whatever it was he intended to say, he never said it.

"I know where he is." The trio turned in surprise to Versitha, who had yet to say a word. Her head was bent, her small form seemed even smaller next to Derment's bulk. She continued, "I can," she paused, searching for the word, "feel him. Like the pull that brought us here." Her voice was hushed, her eyes confused as she tried to put her feelings into words. Her voice cracked slightly.

"He's growing impatient." She shivered at Versitha's last words. Versitha took a step forward. Ameliora, Derment and Nadav silently cleared a pathway for her. She walked through them, her eyes glassy. It was as if she walked blindly, following a path that didn't truly exist.

Derment was the first to move. He stayed on Versitha's heels, his stance protective as his eyes scanned the area around them. The tension in his body was palpable as he searched for the enemy that could be hidden behind every bush. Ameliora and Nadav followed more slowly. She watched Versitha with growing unease.

Their progression through the meadow was silent. She could do nothing but watch the grass wave as it brushed against her legs. The rumbling that had been distant before grew louder as they walked. Soon enough, the river had come into sight. It had seemed small, thin and lazy, from the cliffs above. Padding along its banks, she realized the enormity of the body of water that wound its way through the meadow. She swallowed as memories of her own near drowning surfaced in her mind. She shied away from the banks instinctively, nervously eying the rushing water. As she turned, a breeze ruffled her fur.

Simultaneously, Derment, Nadav and Ameliora froze. Their hackles rose in unison, though Versitha kept floating forward. There had been a scent on the breeze, distinctly canine, and unsettlingly strong. She kneaded the ground with her claws, her pelt prickling. Versitha called out in a hushed voice from ahead, she hadn't even paused.

"Don't bother, he knows we're here." She shook her head, again unsettled by Versitha's words. Her voice, her tone, everything about her was foreign. It was as if, gripped by this pull towards Rangatha, she had become a sleep-walker. She forced herself to move forward, Nadav at her heels. Derment bounded forward, returning to his position at Versitha's side.

A single blurred shape became visible through the grasses. It was small, hunched. It grew more distinct as the group neared. The shape didn't move, didn't make a sound nor twitch a muscle. Its head was downcast, its eyes invisible to the approaching group. She drew a fear-ful breath, fearing that perhaps they were too late – and Rangatha had already bonded with his host. But as they drew closer, she could see that the wolf was small, beaten and covered in scars. Her head hung low, her tail curled tightly around her paws. She was shaking slightly, despite her obvious attempts to control herself. She peered at the female. There was something familiar about her, some-thing she couldn't place. She felt Derment at her side suddenly rush forward. Her attention was jerked from the female to Derment. Derment's face was covered with a mixture of horror and disbelief as he cried out.

"Tharamena!" Derment was already bounding for-ward, but she was frozen with shock. Now she could see the similarities, the small body, the silver fur patterns, she was a ghostly image of Romaus and Levada. Derment was still moving forward, had nearly reached his lost sister.

Tharamena hadn't even raised her head to glance at her brother.

"There is nothing better than a family reunion, is there?" Derment froze in his tracks, his hackles raising at the stranger's voice. The voice was only unfamiliar to Derment. To Ameliora and Nadav, it was terrifyingly familiar. With a slow horror, their eyes were drawn to the faded shimmering shape on the outskirts of the group. All eyes were drawn to Rangatha, or the physical representation of him. His massive form towered easily over Derment and Nadav. His shimmering shape was pitch black, the pits that were his eyes were just barely visible enough to strike fear into her heart.

She could just stare as Rangatha stood, or his shimmering shape did. He walked, though his steps made no sounds. The grass did not bend under his weight. He had made himself visible, audible in the living world – though his abilities apparently didn't extend to physical touch. Ameliora wanted to shrink away as he approached Derment. He was grinning, a grin that made her want to scream. Rangatha approached, but he seemed solely concerned with Derment. He stood in front of Derment, between him and Tharamena. He grinned smugly, speaking in a slow low voice.

"It's funny, you know it's your fault, all your fault." No one breathed a sound, as Rangatha fully expected. He began to slowly circle Derment, as was a favorite tactic of his. "It was never meant to be her. It should have been you, all along. But you were a coward." Rangatha laughed, his black eyes seeming to glint with amusement. "You wouldn't go on the walk would you? You were too frightened, so she went alone. You doomed her." He paused, standing at Tharamena's side. He looked at her with something akin to fondness, though it was more fondness at what he had done to her. "She was a mistake, she became what you would have been." Rangatha motioned with his head to the numerous scars covering every inch of Tharamena's body. "Each of these is your fault." His words hung in the air, his small speech finished. Slowly, for the first time, Tharamena raised her head. Her eyes connected with Derment. They carried an immense sadness, hopelessness. She had been broken, physically and emotionally. The small adventurous puppy had been beaten out of her, day after day after day. What was left behind was the shell of a sister Derment had once and still loved. But amidst it all, there was still love in her gaze.

TWENTY-TWO

For a moment there was a blessed sort of silence, one that came along with shock and revelation. No one dared to even breathe. Rangatha's smile was gleeful. Rangatha had stopped his circling and seemed comfortable in his position at Tharamena's side. He moved closer to her, their pelts brushing, easily ignoring the furious growls that spilled from Derment's jaws. The growls faded away and Derment's shoulders sagged with defeat. He stared at the ground, unable to face the love that persisted in Tharamena's eyes. He spoke quietly, his voice softer than She had ever heard it.

"I'm so sorry."

Rangatha's ears perked immediately and his grin widened. Ameliora shivered, pressing closer to Nadav. She was shaking with fear. Versitha had frozen, her task seemingly complete. She now stared with empty eyes at Derment, watching with an anguish that tore at her heart. Rangatha turned his head deliberately pressing his misted face into Tharamena's fur. Tharamena froze, shrinking away with a muted yelp. This caused Derment to raise his head, his

253

eyes burning at the sight of Tharamena's cowering form. Though Rangatha was unable to touch her, the power he held was absolute. Derment's jaws parted, the beginnings of a snarl on his lips.

"What exactly are you sorry for?" Rangatha's voice was like an amused murmur. He looked away from Tharamena and back to Derment with narrowed eyes. He gestured to a diagonal scar that ran across Tharamena's chest. "Is it for this?" Rangatha turned to Tharamena, smiling again. His voice was slick and disgustingly sweet. "Why don't you tell him how that happened?" For a moment Tharamena looked like she would object, but Rangatha repeated with a hint of a growl in his voice, "Tell him." Tharamena swallowed, bringing her eyes back to her paws.

"I tried to run." Tharamena's voice broke and she ducked her head, as if she would curl into herself for protection. She had begun to shiver slightly. She swallowed again. "And He caught me." Rangatha feigned surprise, the benevolent protector, but the act was gone in an instant. Rangatha raised his head and laughed, his eyes bright.

"That was the very first time, wasn't it my dear?" Tharamena cringed away, but nodded obediently. Rangatha nearly purred, his delight clear. "Why don't you finish the story? What happened after that?" Tharamena looked to Derment, her eyes nearly empty.

"Every day there was something new, some atrocity I committed." Rangatha was nodding, seated with his tail around his paws as he listened to Tharamena.

"And what happened today, my dear?" He prompted her. Her muscles tensed and a flash of pain entered her eyes. "You must show them, you know you must." She nodded and stood, turning so her flank faced the small group. Her flank had previously been hidden by Rangatha's body and her seated form. Standing clearly now, deep puncture wounds were clear on her flank. The fur around them was matted with dried blood. Some of them still oozed slightly. She leaned forward, peering at them. They slowly formed a familiar outline, one of a jaw. She recoiled with horror. Tharamena spoke quietly.

"You came for me, so I was punished." She said it as if rehearsed. Rangatha was shaking his head, and rolled his shoulders as if suddenly bored.

"Yet through it all, she has yet to take a life." He shook his head, appearing somewhat amused. He stood and stretched lazily, turning to look at Derment. "Perhaps she hasn't the capacity. Perhaps she is truly perfect." He paused, padding forward to stand immediately in front of Derment. He tilted his head to the side, his lips splitting into a grin. "Or perhaps she was waiting for *you.*"

This was the last straw. With a fierce snarl, Derment swiped his paw at Rangatha, but passed straight through the shimmering spirit. He tumbled forward, unbalanced by his lack of contact and shocked. He landed with a thud and Rangatha stepped backwards, shaking his head. He laughed scornfully, unimpressed by Derment's display.

"This is really quite pathetic. You came all this way to protect her," he motioned towards Versitha, "but what do you think you can do? You already failed, years ago." He circled Derment as Derment began to pick himself up. "You never even believed my fair Ameliora, did you? You were always the skeptic." Rangatha chuckled. "And now you must admit that it's all true. I'm going to bond with our beautiful Tharamena, and you will watch. You will watch us wreak a new havoc upon this world," Rangatha drew a breath, lowering his head to Derment's ear, "and you will be able to do nothing." He paused, his eyes shifting now to Versitha. They flashed and he added in a quieter voice. "Perhaps, when all is said and done, the blame should truly fall on you." He breathed the last word, meeting Versitha's eyes.

Versitha met his gaze, though her own eyes were filled with paralyzing fear and confusion. Her voice shook as she spoke.

"I have done nothing." Rangatha was laughing before she even finished. His lips held a smug turn to them, recognition bright in his eyes.

"That's true to an extent. The only thing you ever did was live. A mistake on the part of a weak mind." He paused, peering at her intently. A long moment went by before he murmured. "You truly have no idea what I'm talking about." He was met with only stunned silent. Rangatha smirked and leaned forward. "If it wasn't for your feeble brother, Tharamena here would never have been chosen."

Rangatha stood slowly and stretched. All eyes were upon him, wide with shock. He reveled in the attention, in the absolute power.

"It appears I have a story to tell. You see, little one, originally I chose your older brother as my host. What was his name..Sa..sun...ah yes, Senach." He smiled as if the memories were fond to him. "He was such a rebellious soul. But that was all a charade, now wasn't it. It was no difficulty at all for me to influence your father's weak consciousness. All I had to do was make a subtle suggestion, really." The five wolves were speechless, listening with growing horror.

"All he had to do was take your brother and go, find himself a secluded place, and do as I commanded." His words had a wistful air to them. "But you had to go and make things difficult. You followed them, though your father had used such discretion. And what choice did he have, but to kill you?" A grin spread back across his face. "The only trouble is he didn't quite hit you hard enough. And here you are, unfortunately alive and well." He looked between Versitha and Derment now. Derment was stricken, disbelief written across his face.

His legs gave out beneath him and for the first time that she could ever remember, her brother stayed down, where he was, defeated. He lay there, utterly broken. The full horror of what they faced was rushing upon she as she gazed at her fallen brother. Bits and pieces of the legend Versitha had told them were floating back to her. What had once been would happen again, but this time they had no Morenia to save them. Versitha's voice floated back to her in fragments.

A power like mine cannot be gained from simple giving or granting. She stood frozen as the words floated back to her. The voice in her mind was slowly morphing, changing from Versitha's soft voice to a familiar calm intensity. Moments later, it was Morenia's voice floating through her thoughts. *A power like mine is found in the life of others.* It chilled her to hear Nithil's words in her voice, just as it had once chilled her to hear Versitha speak them. She forced herself to listen, knowing that for some reason the message was important. *You must be willing to sacrifice much to be one as me.* She was now blind and deaf to her surroundings, only Morenia's whispering voice existed – and Versitha's long ago words. She was stunned to realize that it had been nearly a year since Versitha had told the tale, so much time had passed. A final sentence floated through her mind. *To become like me, you must be able to take a life.* Her mind was silent once more, Morenia's voice had faded away. She slowly became aware of her surroundings once more.

Nadav was nudging her shoulder, her eyes filled with concern. Only their present situation kept quiet whines from escaping through his lips. Derment was still lying where he had fallen, though Rangatha still circled him – throwing taunts. Versitha stood frozen, her mind unable to grasp what had been revealed to her. Tharamena had taken a seat, her shoulders hunched as she trembled violently with fear, pain and grief. She was still stuck on the words, and what connection they could have. Her gaze darted between Rangatha, Derment and Tharamena desperately. As she stood staring, she understood.

She started forward, calling out to Derment. "Rangatha can't bond with Tharamena!" Rangatha's taunts fell silent and he hissed, taking a menacing step forward. Derment raised his head from the ground, turning his gaze slowly to her. All eyes were on her. Rangatha spat angrily.

"My fair, foolish, beauty, you know nothing!" Her eyes hardened and she stepped forward, adrenaline overriding her fear. Her legs shook, but her voice was strong.

"I know your secret!" Rangatha was shaking his head, growing more furious by the second.

"You know nothing." Rangatha's voice was quiet, his words repeated with insistence. His lips were beginning to curl into a snarl and a growl like thunder rumbled threateningly in his throat. She forced herself to turn away from him, to face her brother who was only just beginning to pick himself up from the dirt.

"Do you remember the legend, the one that Versitha told us?" Her voice was pleading. "Nithil could not bond with Sararo," she paused and looked to Rangatha triumphantly, "not until Sararo had taken a life willingly." Derment's paws lay flat on the ground as he pushed himself to a full standing position. He shook the dirt from his fur, snapping his head sharply to look at her. What she said had still not registered. She spoke quietly. "Tharamena has yet to take a life, she cannot bond with him." All around them was silence. She looked again to Rangatha, her voice hushed. "He has failed."

"How dare you!" Rangatha's voice was a broken howl and he stepped forward as if to pounce, though remembering his inability to touch her. She would not be deterred. She stepped forward defiantly, shouting to mask her fear.

"You failed! You brutalized her, you tortured and destroyed her – but you didn't break her! You couldn't! You couldn't get her to kill. Even now, as you grow in desperation, you cannot get her to raise a paw against another." Ameliora smiled, not sure in her triumph, if only for the moment. "You needed to corrupt her, as Nithil once did to Sararo. You needed to break her and destroy her. Others," She spat the word, " they were already corrupt when they came to you. But she was so innocent, so perfect. All you had to do was break her, and corrupt her. All you needed was for her to kill, and become your willing host. But she won't do it, she won't be your host willingly."

Understanding had dawned in Derment's eyes. He looked to Tharamena who had raised her head in confusion. She tilted her head to one side, apparently never having heard the legend. Nadav stepped forward, standing beside her. His tensed muscles reassured her. Rangatha was shaking with uncontrollable anger. His eyes burned, the black pits smoldering. She withheld the desire to scream and throw herself down for mercy from his wrath. She locked her legs, determined to hide their shaking. Quiet paw steps caused her to turn her head. Derment had approached Tharamena finally. They stood before each other silently. With a careful tenderness she had never seen, he buried his face in her scarred fur. He withdrew his muzzle, whispering words that Ameliora couldn't hear. All eyes but Rangatha's had shifted to Derment. With a slow strength, Derment turned to face Rangatha. His eyes had hardened, his muscles tensed and his jaw clenched.

His voice was a whisper as he took slow steps forward. His ears laid flat against his skull, his eyes narrowed and cold. Ameliora took a step back, out of the pathway of her brother. This was the side she had seen as a pup, the corrupted anger at the edges of his eyes. But now it was no longer held back. From the day of Tharamena's disappearance, Derment had been corrupted – indirectly by Rangatha. Now was their moment of confrontation. Derment paused, facing Rangatha with more courage than she could ever have mustered. He spoke quietly. "She may not willingly bond with you," he raised his eyes to Rangatha and slowly smiled, "but I will."

TWENTY-THREE

Derment stepped forward, his hackles bristling and his eyes crazed. Ameliora's legs were locked with shock. She stood, dumbfounded in silence. Derment was approaching Rangatha, his jaws parted and his chest heaving. Nothing existed in Derment's eyes but Rangatha. He passed her and paused, ever so slightly. A look flashed in his eyes, something tinged with regret – but it was gone in an instant. He took the final steps, confronting Rangatha's shimmering shape. Rangatha was spluttering with fury, protests hurled from his lips. He shook his head obstinately.

"Bond with me, Rangatha." She never thought she would have heard the words come from her brother's lips, but they had been uttered. She shrieked, recoiling from Derment with a sudden surge of loathing and the sharp pain of betrayal. Rangatha's outline faded slightly, though he howled his protests.

"You have taken no life! You have not known my corruption!" Derment laughed, a sound that chilled her. She couldn't tear her horror-filled gaze from her brother.

Derment continued to laugh, watching with satisfaction as Rangatha began to vanish.

"But I have, Rangatha, I have known it all. You corrupted me the minute you took her. Your touch has been an enduring presence, in every step of my life." Derment lowered his voice, victory sweet on his tongue. "And I killed your assassin, because I *wanted* to. I tore out his throat. I reveled in the warmth of his blood and the rip of skin." Derment's voice dropped even lower, though it could still be heard in the surrounding silence. "And I would do it again."

A rush of air blew her fur about her and she dug her paws into the ground to keep from stumbling. Derment, though, was knocked to the ground. In the same instant – the faded blurry outline that had been Rangatha vanished. For a long moment, Derment did not stir. She stepped forward, her voice soft and her eyes filled with fear.

"Derment?" As she called to him, her brother's limbs exploded into spasms. He jerked and writhed, his body twisting and turning unnaturally. His neck and back arched, his jaws opening and closing in piercing howls. He kicked and slashed at the air, his limbs twitching and flailing without any sort of control. His eyes were wide open, but unseeing. They seemed glazed open, as if blind. They rolled towards the back of his skull, then forwards again – continually searching for something they couldn't find. As she watched, darkness crept over his eyes. The white began to turn grey, then ashen, then the darkest of pitch black. The familiar expressive ebony irises began to darken, turning from a churning brown to black. The light left his gaze, until all that was left were empty soulless pits. She recoiled in fear. Behind her, Tharamena let out a shriek and dove for her brother. Nadav was there in an instant, physically blocking her. Tharamena struggled against his muscled form, protesting wordlessly. Nadav pushed her back. Tharamena stumbled back a few paces, her muscles tensed as she prepared to throw herself at Derment anew, but she froze.

Ameliora couldn't look away from Derment – or what had once been Derment. Something, a light in the corner of her eye, drew her gaze back to Versitha. She had yet to move, but a presence was visible at her side. The outline was faded and blurry, but familiar. Her eyes widened at the sight of Morenia. The protests and cries that had poured from Versitha's jaws quieted. But for Derment's howling, there was silence once more. All still watched the scene unfolding.

Slowly, Versitha seemed to be overcome by serenity. Her lips moved in whispered words and as she spoke, Morenia's ghostly form vanished just as Rangatha had. Versitha's locked muscles gave way and she collapsed – much in the same way Derment had. Her heart raced, but she knew better than to approach Versitha's fallen form. Unlike Derment, she did not writhe or howl. She was motionless, so still she could have been a corpse. But a moment later she began to move. She stood slowly, with a smooth grace that Versitha hadn't previously possessed. Her fur was glowing, as if surrounded by an ethereal halo. Her eyes were glowing white, staring straight ahead. Versitha's gaze unnerved her, it was lacking something. She couldn't place it, but she realized a moment later what it was. The fear was gone, the beaten down brokenness in her eyes, the grief and pain was gone. Her eyes were cool and calm; they were filled with Morenia's characteristic confidence.

Derment still writhed and howled. Versitha looked on him in silence for a moment before turning to her. She parted her lips, speaking in a commanding voice that seemed detached from Versitha's characteristic gentleness. It was firm, steady – Morenia.

"Do not look at me as a ghost of who you once loved." Her words were wise, so unlike Versitha. "The one you saw as sister is gone, as is Morenia." The figure that was no longer Versitha dipped her head. "I am Rhoswen."

"You are bonded." Rhoswen nodded. Ameliora had secretly suspected that if Rangatha were to have a host, Morenia would too. She had even begun to think that perhaps it was her role to play, her sacrifice to make, ultimately her destiny. Rhoswen's gaze had now moved from her. She was slowly approaching Derment. Derment's writhing was beginning to slow, his jerking now occasional instead of constant. His fur had changed for a dark gray, to pitch black. And as she watched, pure snowy white spread out over the russet fur that had been Versitha. Rhoswen stood before her, in all Morenia's righteous glory. Derment's violent movements ceased altogether. She looked on her brother with anguish in her eyes, her voice a whisper.

"What are you going to do?" Rhoswen's cool confidence wavered for a moment, revealing regret and sorrow. She heaved a sigh, her movements reluctant but resigned. She shook her head slightly, looking down on what had once been Derment. She murmured in a voice lower than a whisper.

"Two must die as to portend." She didn't think before hurling herself in Rhoswen's pathway with a strangled cry of protest. Nadav was suddenly in front of her, blocking her way. Ameliora struggled just as Tharamena had struggled. Rhoswen watched, her gaze was apologetic though she made no move to speak.

"Get out of my way Nadav! She's going to kill Derment!" Nadav barked sharply to get her attention. But she couldn't look away from Derment who was now still. Rhoswen was moving towards Derment again, her steps so regal they made her heart ache. Nadav' voice was gruff, desperately trying to get through to Ameliora.

"That isn't your brother, not anymore." Her chest was heaving, anguish in her eyes. Her struggles weakened, though she leaned heavily on Nadav' shoulder. Nadav lowered his muzzle, speaking softly in her ear. "He knew what he was doing. He sacrificed himself for you, for all of us. But that isn't Derment, your brother is gone." She pressed her face into Nadav' fur, her cries muffled against him. And as she did, Derment's body began to stir.

His paws laid flat against the ground, the quiet sound of scuffling paws permeated the area. She withdrew her face from Nadav, looking fearfully to her brother's rising body. Derment was now standing, but Nadav was right. The creature that had risen wasn't Derment. It was massive, as if Derment had suddenly expanded. Its eyes were black pools, as Rangatha's had once been. Its shoulders were broad and muscles rippled beneath the pelt. Most disturbing of all was the pointed grin, the look of triumph and anticipation. Like lightning, that gaze alighted on her and laughter filled the air.

"The prophecy is fulfilled, but not without you." He took a single menacing step forward, his eyes scornful. "Did you think you were important, a leader or a savior?" He chuckled darkly. "You were only ever the messenger, serving my creation." His lips stretched into a grin. "All will curse you for what you have done, the one who raised Kyran!" He broke into maniacal laughter and she shrank away. Whatever resemblances this creature, Kyran, might have had to Derment were gone. Kyran's head snapped to Rhoswen, looking her up and down and laughing. "And this is who you send to defeat me? This is the best Morenia could find?" He shook his head, amused at her perceived failure. "Not good enough."

A snarl ripped from Rhoswen's throat, though her jaws were barely parted. With a speed she had never seen,

Rhoswen lunged for Kyran. Kyran wasn't caught unprepared. He lunged forward at the same moment, the two clashing in a clawing mass of slashing canines and ripping snarls. She scrambled backwards, Nadav at her side. She found she could do nothing.

The pair would break apart for mere moments, time for Kyran to hurl insults and laugh maniacally before throwing himself back at Rhoswen. Ameliora and Nadav were forced to move, following the pair at a distance as the battle brought them farther and farther away from the center of the meadow. Her tail lashed against her back legs, panic surging through her veins as she watched the sister she never knew battle the monster she had inadvertently created. She whined with fear as Kyran darted forward, sinking his teeth into Rhoswen's shoulder. Rhoswen howled with Morenia's voice, ripping herself away and moving quickly out of reach. Crimson bloomed on her shoulder, dripping down into the soft grasses below. Rhoswen's jaw clenched and she threw herself at Kyran yet again, darting downwards and sinking her teeth into Kyran's foreleg. Kyran snarled in pain, kicking his leg and dislodging Rhoswen who stumbled backwards. Kyran glanced down at his own leg, bringing his eyes brimming in fury slowly back up to Rhoswen. A gooey black substance began to trickle down his leg. She felt her stomach heave at the sight of what flowed through the monster's veins.

"Are you feeling triumphant?" His voice was low, menacing with a sadistic madness. His chest heaved, though it seemed more with coursing adrenaline than weakness. "Are you rejoicing in a success that means nothing?" His voice grew louder as he spoke. Rhoswen only stood, her own chest heaving and her muscles tensed. Her calm gaze sat on Kyran, but Ameliora could detect traces of uncertainty in her gaze. Kyran began to laugh, picking up his injured leg. "Oh the beauty of immortality..." His murmur faded, his mocking eyes filled with laughter and trained on Rhoswen. Her own gaze was drawn to Kyran's foreleg. The trickle of blood was slowing, the lacerations made by Rhoswen's teeth seemed to knit back together until nothing was left but smooth unmarked skin. Kyran replaced his leg on the ground.

Kyran dug his paws into the ground, spurring himself towards Rhoswen. Rhoswen's eyes filled for the briefest moment with fear. She threw herself out of his path, stumbling slightly. She became slowly aware of a roaring in her ears. She lifted her head, her eyes darting in all directions until they landed on the source of the thundering. The river they had seen and heard from afar drew closer and closer, but the river was not what caused the roaring. The repeated blows had brought the pair – and their observers – to the borders of the water, and the falls they flowed into. Her heart was beating rapidly in her chest, her eyes widened.

Rhoswen was growing weak, her movements slowing and her head hanging. Her legs shook, but she still stood. Kyran held himself triumphantly, his back to the roaring waters and his paws planted on the banks. He tilted his head, victory in his eyes.

"Now you know hopelessness." He had to shout to be heard over the roaring of the falls. Ameliora felt her legs trembling, all their work had come to an end. Rhoswen wasn't strong enough, they would fall to Kyran. The words of the prophecy echoed in her ears *"And wrap the world in sorrow's chain"*. Her own shoulders sagged, but she forced herself to watch as Kyran prepared himself for a final assault.

But Rhoswen raised her head, a last surge of defiant strength. She hurled herself forward, barreling her body into Kyran with all the force she could muster. Kyran stumbled back into surprise, his paws scrabbling on the slick banks of the water. He snarled, covering his surprise even as his paws hit water and he felt himself knocked backwards. His paws flailed in the air above him, his eyes for the first time showed terror. Rhoswen fell with him, her muscles still. She caught a last look at Rhoswen's gaze, and was stunned by the pure resignation in her eyes. As Ameliora watched, Kyran and Rhoswen vanished underneath the water, only to reappear a moment later. She watched as they were swept over the edge of the waterfall, and Kyran's drowning howls echoed throughout the valley.

ꕥ
TWENTY-FOUR

Her paws pounded against the soft grass, flattening it beneath her as she sprinted to the river's edge. Kyran's body vanishing over the edge kept replaying in her mind. She could still hear his howl echoing around her. Despite the soulless gaze and the black blood that had flowed in his veins, he had still once been her brother. She heard Nadav call her name, then the heavy footfalls of his pursuit. She refused to stop, seeing nothing but the rushing water before her. She skidded to a stop on the banks, Tharamena appearing beside her as if from nowhere. Her chest heaved and her eyes desperately scanning the churning waters.

She was barely aware of Tharamena beside her and only turned her head when she felt fur brush her own. She glanced to her side, seeing Tharamena shaking her head desperately, her moves becoming frantic. She tilted her head in confusion, taking a slight step back to give Tharamena room. The female broke down, finally lifting her head in an ear-splitting cry of grief. She moved away as Tharamena collapsed in her grief. Her own eyes went towards the falls, a desperate hope flashing in them. She turned on her heels, racing towards the falls and the rocky cliff side. She plunged down, ignoring the sharp stones that cut at her paws and ankles. Her eyes scanned down the steep slope towards the bank of the pool the waterfall flowed into far below. Her eyes were drawn to a dark shape washed against the banks of the pool. Ameliora bit her lip, containing grief which was threatening to well up inside her and burst through her lips in an anguished cry.

She could hear Nadav as he descended behind her, but she couldn't pause to wait. A pure white form had washed up on the banks. She skidded to a stop beside the body. It was so small, diminished. The perfect purity of her fur had been marred by blood and dirt. Her eyes were closed, her body still. She felt a howl rise in her throat, but swallowed it as Rhoswen's eyes blinked open. Her voice, when she spoke, was weak, halting.

"It is finished." Ameliora took a step closer, shaking her head. Grief was raw in her eyes, confusion clear in her movements.

"You can't go. You took her from me." Her voice cracked as she searched for any sign of Versitha hidden somewhere in the depths of Rhoswen's glowing eyes.

"She did as she was destined to do." Rhoswen took a shaking breath. "Three will be the Unknown, bear neither truth nor reason. At the last minute it will be shown, always destined to end a season." Rhoswen quoted the prophecy, her voice growing weaker.

"I don't understand. I was three. I was destined to die!" Rhoswen's eyes fluttered closed. Her breathing becoming slower. Every breath was an effort as the life drained from her eyes. She forced final words from her lips.

"You were only ever the Messenger." As quickly as the voice had come, it was gone. Ameliora was left standing on the banks of the roaring river, Rhoswen's lifeless body at her paws. Nadav came up alongside her, staring down at what had once been Versitha, Morenia, and Rhoswen. He looked to each side, finally speaking.

"It wasn't your role to play." His voice was quiet, his words sinking deep into her. She raised her head, noticing for the first time that Tharamena had joined them. She stood much farther down, staring down at a second dark shape. She turned, not looking to Nadav as she spoke.

"And what was Tharamena's role? The sufferer?" She moved away from Nadav, not expecting an answer. Everything in her felt numbed, torn away by something she couldn't truly give a name to.

She drew abreast of Tharamena. Her elder sister's lips moved, through the roar of the water drowned out her voice. She leaned in, the words finally audible.

"I killed you." Her ears folded back against her head, and she bit her lip to contain herself. She moved hesitantly, questioning her actions even as she gently pressed her flank to Tharamena's.

"You didn't kill him. He was long gone before you found him." The two sisters couldn't bring themselves to even glance at each other. Both gazes were stuck on Kyran's body. Tharamena had to nearly shout to be heard, but she still managed to sound hushed.

"I could have saved him. In a way, I took Derment's life. Rangatha was right all along. He knew I would do it." Ameliora was shaking her head, sure of herself despite a lack of what to say.

"Rhoswen killed him." She was suddenly desperate to convince Tharamena of her innocence. It was somehow tied to her own innocence. Had she not brought Derment to his death?

"Even as I watched, I found myself hoping. I *wanted* her to do it, to kill him, to free me." Her nose wrinkled in disgust and her eyes burned with a passion she had yet to see in her elder sister. "I reveled in every injury inflicted on him. All I could see was a monster."

"He had become a monster, and nothing more." Tharamena was shaking her head obstinately, still unable to tear her gaze from the drenched corpse. She found that despite her desire to comfort her newfound sister, she had no more words to give. Instead she was awash in a wave of her own memories. Images of Derment's dark eyes flashed in her mind, tendrils of his snapping voice or pointed comments.

"Why did it take him so long to come for me?" For the first time, she could detect a hint of something other than bereft despair in Tharamena's voice. It was something akin to anger, perhaps frustration. She looked to Tharamena with confusion in her gaze. She waited for Tharamena to turn, repeat herself or at least meet her eyes, but she did not. She just kept staring at Kyran's body, her brows knitting together and her eyes sparking a growing light of anger.

"He thought you were dead, we all did." But Tharamena wasn't listening. Her jaw was clenched and her eyes fluttered closed as if she fought to control herself, but was failing. Her tail flicked back and forward, tension clear in her muscles. Her top lip twitched slightly, as if itching to curl into a snarl.

"Five years, it took him five years to come for me." At this she finally opened her eyes to look to her. She spat her words slightly. "And even then it wasn't him, it was *you*! He was my brother, my only sibling, and he didn't love me enough to find me." Her own anger flared at Tharamena's disrespect. She took a slight step forward, her eyes narrowing and her voice growing cold.

"He searched for you every day. I wasn't there, but I heard the stories often enough. The pack was forced to move away to prevent him from running into the forests in his mad quest to find you." Ameliora took another step forward, no longer concerned with preserving her elder sister's fragile emotions. "I saw it in his eyes. He never smiled. He never laughed. He died the day you vanished." Her chest rose and fell, her voice tout with emotion. "Every morning I went down to the spring, and every morning I came back to find him pacing and waiting for me. Every morning he would snap at me, about neglecting pack duties or sneaking off alone. And only now do I realize what it was! Every time I left, he feared that I might not come back – just like you." Her voice had risen in volume until she was shouting, her hackles raised and her head high and defiant. Tharamena responded with silence. The small light of anger, the knitting of her brows, had faded back to sorrow. She took a breath, calming herself. She stepped away, her fur lying flat again. She glanced quickly at Kyran, then upwards at the meadows. Her voice was a murmur just loud enough for Tharamena's ears. "All he ever wanted was to die for you."

"I never thought I'd see him again, any of my family again. And to finally be reunited, only to kill him-" Tharamena's voice choked off into silence. Tharamena turned her mournful eyes back to Kyran. "Sometimes I thought I hated him, I'd blame him for all of this. Have you ever hated someone you were supposed to love?" She looked to Tharamena and nodded quietly.

"Sometimes I hated you," her voice was hushed. "Because I blamed you for the blackness in Derment's eyes." Tharamena didn't seem surprised, didn't even react to her words.

"And how do you atone for something like that?" Ameliora looked at Kyran, her heart heavy but her words filled with assurance.

"You learn to forgive yourself. The only way Derment could forgive himself was to save you, even if that meant dying for you." She moved to Tharamena, nudging the elder she-wolf's shoulder gently. She slowly steered her sister away from Kyran's body, padding back towards the narrow path leading up to the meadow. The pounding of the waterfall faded slowly to a quiet roar.

"He died for her too, the russet female with you." Ameliora was silent, though gave a slight nod of her head. Tharamena continued. "I think he loved her, or would have loved her."

Tharamena lapsed into silence. Eventually she snuck a glance at her sister, but the elder female was only nodding her head. Her shoulders seemed to grow lighter and exhaustion came to replace the unbearable sorrow. Tharamena finally looked to Ameliora, smiling weakly. "Who was the male with you, another brother of ours?" She responded with a small smile of her own, affection pooling in her eyes as she shook her head.

"No, but you have a family to meet, a family that loves you, and mourned you, and will love you again." Her eyes gained a twinkle of anticipation, thinking of the family they would soon return to. The two wolves spoke quietly together as they climbed the steep cliff side, Tharamena inquiring endlessly about the family she had yet to know. As they crested the final boulders, stepping into the meadow, they were greeted with emptiness. Ameliora glanced around worriedly until her eyes alighted on Nadav, curled near the water. He raised his head upon seeing them, smiling with a tired relief. He stood and stretched, padding towards them. Few words were exchanged between the three as they simultaneously turned towards the mountains to begin yet another journey. However, there was a new lightness in their paws, and security in the knowledge that what was lost had again been found.

THE END

∽

ABOUT THE AUTHOR

Kylen Gartland studies anthropology at Washington University in St. Louis. Currently residing in Missouri, she works at the St. Louis Zoo studying gorilla behavior.

She started work on *The Messenger* at the age of fourteen and finished the novel before she turned eighteen. This is her first published work, born out of a lifetime of dedication to zoology and animal writing.

CPSIA information can be obtained at www.ICGtesting.com
Printed in the USA
BVOW06s0149200716

456209BV00009B/44/P